Also

TEXAS NAVY SEALS

A SEAL Never Quits

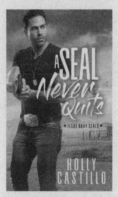

A SEAL Always Wins

HOLLY CASTILLO

sourcebooks
casablanca

Copyright © 2020 by Holly Castillo
Cover and internal design © 2020 by Sourcebooks
Cover design by Dawn Adams/Sourcebooks
Cover art by Craig White

Sourcebooks and the colophon are registered trademarks of Sourcebooks.

All rights reserved. No part of this book may be reproduced in any form
or by any electronic or mechanical means including information storage
and retrieval systems—except in the case of brief quotations embodied
in critical articles or reviews—without permission in writing from its
publisher, Sourcebooks.

The characters and events portrayed in this book are fictitious or are
used fictitiously. Any similarity to real persons, living or dead, is purely
coincidental and not intended by the author.

All brand names and product names used in this book are trademarks,
registered trademarks, or trade names of their respective holders.
Sourcebooks is not associated with any product or vendor in this book.

Published by Sourcebooks Casablanca, an imprint of Sourcebooks
P.O. Box 4410, Naperville, Illinois 60567-4410
(630) 961-3900
sourcebooks.com

Printed and bound in Canada.
MBP 10 9 8 7 6 5 4 3 2 1

Chapter 1

THE SOUND OF SHOTS FIRED IN THE DISTANCE STOPPED Phantom in his tracks. He listened carefully before dropping and rolling into the nearby shrubs. He paused, his body tense and ready to move the moment he heard a sound. The crunch of dry brush underfoot brought a smile to his face.

He pivoted toward the sound and aimed through the shrubs. His target let out a startled shout a split second after he fired. Chuckling, he stood, lifting his safety goggles.

"Shit, Phantom! You didn't have to hit me where it really hurts!" Hunter "Santo" Gonzalez groaned, glaring at Enrique "Phantom" Ramirez, his close friend and former BUD/S partner in crime.

Phantom's grin only broadened. "You should have been paying attention to your surroundings."

"As if anyone ever knows where you are," Santo fired back. "Your name is Phantom for a reason."

"Over here!" another voice called out. "Phantom brought him down."

"You know, just wait until it's your turn, pal. I'm going to hit you right in the cojones," Santo muttered as he glared at the paint-gun splatter from Phantom's shot on his upper thigh.

"That's if you can find me, punk."

"No, that's *when* I find you. Care to make a wager on how fast I make that happen?"

Phantom held up his hands and shrugged.

"Did I hear someone say 'wager'? If there's betting going on, I need a piece of the action." A large man walked into the small clearing where Phantom and Santo stood, the afternoon sun beating down on them.

"Buzz. Nice of you to join the party." Phantom clapped the big man on the back, earning a glower.

"Nobody said this was a race. You could have given the rest of the team a chance to catch up." As Joseph "Buzz" Gomez finished ribbing Phantom, several other men stepped into the clearing and began to laugh at Santo's frustrated expression.

"He took you down in less than eight minutes. That's a new record," Amador "Stryker" Salas, their SEAL team leader said, joining in the laughter.

Santo shook his head, though he, too, started to smile. "Glad you're all having a good laugh."

Together, the six men teased and joked their way back to their equipment shed to put up the paint-ball guns and goggles. Stryker held Phantom to the back of the group, giving them some distance from the rest, and Phantom's gut told him his team leader didn't plan to chat with him about his record-setting target practice for the day.

He sighed. After four hours of intense PT and a run through the hot Texas sun for their paint-ball training drill, he'd been looking forward to a hot shower and a cold beer. He shook his head at himself. He must be getting soft if such a light day made him ready to ring out before the afternoon was over.

If a new mission had come up, though… His gut clenched at the thought. They had wrapped up their last mission nearly a week ago. A surge of adrenaline pulsed through him at the thought they could be headed out again.

"How are things going in the horse industry?" Stryker asked, surprising Phantom. It was the last thing he had expected to hear.

"Good. I've got to say, working and training quarter horses is a lot different from handling the thoroughbreds I grew up with."

"When are you planning to get out into the community with them? You know that's a critical component of our assignment here."

Several months back, Admiral Frank Haslett had approached Stryker to put together a team of SEALs to go undercover in Hebbronville, Texas, a small town near the border with Mexico. Their cover was as a group of close friends who had gone in together to purchase massive Bent Horseshoe Ranch to raise cattle and horses, while covertly keeping their ears to the ground for information about illegal activities in Mexico and Central and South America that posed a threat to Americans. The more the team could do to eliminate crime south of the border, the safer it would be for immigrants, asylum seekers, and everyone else at the border itself.

Their last mission had involved a drug cartel that obviously had connections within the United States, but the SEALs hadn't yet identified the players on the American side. The team had succeeded in bringing down the cartel and the drug lord, Benicio Davila, but there clearly were larger stakes involved.

"To get out into the community with the horses means showing them. I'll need to understand quarter-horse shows a lot better before I take that step." Instantly, the image of a determined, energetic woman popped into his head. Elena Garcia had been the horse trainer for the ranch's prior owner—until two weeks ago when Phantom had told her they no longer needed her services. His intention had been to secure their undercover mission, but he was beginning to doubt his hasty decision.

Stryker paused and turned to face him, a knowing look on his face. "You need to talk to Elena."

Phantom scowled. "I can make it without her help. I just need a little more time." Even to his own ears his argument sounded weak.

Stryker shook his head. "Admit that she's your best chance at being able to network and get involved as quickly as possible. Activities in the criminal world aren't going to slow down while we get our shit in gear. We can't waste any time. Your job is to gather intel in the community. You can't do that working the horses out here on the ranch. We're SEALs. We're the experts in our field, but outside of it, we go to the experts in theirs, and Elena is the expert you need."

Phantom gripped his paint-ball gun tightly. He suddenly wished they had another drill to run so he could take out his frustration. "I'm not sure of the best tactic to approach her."

Stryker smirked. "Business is business. Anya talks about Elena all the time, and it sounds like the woman is smart as hell. If you come at it as a business proposition, I'm sure she'll take us back as a client."

When it came to business, Phantom often deferred to others who had a gift for it. He knew how to track an enemy for miles and sneak up on him in total silence.

He knew how to be a deadly force in nearly any situation. This experience outside an assigned mission was testing his nerves. He had to remind himself it all served their ultimate goal of defusing a hostile situation with minimal casualties. He'd have to take one for the team.

"I'll call her tonight," he said, relenting. Stryker's fiancée, Anya Gutierrez, and Elena were best friends, which meant he had to handle the situation even more delicately.

"It's best to conduct this type of transaction face-to-face. Calling her could put you at a disadvantage. Who knows? She may demand double the previous fees."

"That could still happen if I meet with her in person." Phantom doubted Elena would try to double the fees regardless. She didn't strike him as a person driven by money.

"Not as likely. Go out and meet with her tomorrow. Maybe you can even convince her to come back to the ranch to see that you haven't destroyed her years of hard work training those horses. I'm sure Anya would be thrilled to visit with her for a little while."

Phantom nodded. One way or another, he was going to convince Elena to take them back as a client. He cringed. He just hoped she didn't hate him for cutting her loose in the first place.

———

Elena barely lifted the reins and the horse jumped forward, moving swiftly and smoothly beneath her to cut the heifer from the small herd gathered in the arena. She balanced her weight in the saddle, shifting left to right to guide the horse, barely touching it with her heels. She had trained it to respond to her body's movements, not to the feel of spurs against its side or the bite of the bit in its mouth.

That wasn't the way some cowboys she knew worked the range. There were bad ones who were notorious for digging their spurs into a horse's flesh until its hide became tough from misuse, and a horse could become nearly unresponsive to a bit in its mouth that had been yanked around constantly. Those practices were out-dated, and with proper training for both horse and rider, a lighter hand could be used.

Fortunately, the ranch where she was working today employed her methods and style in the field, and none of the ranch hands wore spurs to guide their horses. She smiled as the horse began to move without a cue from her, having honed in on the heifer she wanted, and aggressively pursued moving it out. A few minutes later, the heifer had been separated from the herd and Elena chuckled, patting the horse's neck as a reward.

A couple hours later, the sun had climbed, and she decided it was past time to take a break. She dismounted smoothly and led the horse—the third she had worked with already that morning—over to the trough for a long drink of water. She began to scratch it between the ears, a favorite with horses as it was always a difficult spot for them to scratch on their own.

The horse cocked one leg in relaxation and leaned its head against her, and she chuckled. "That's a good girl. You did some hard work out there. I'd say you deserve an extra share of oats."

"Do you sweet-talk all of them like that? Is that how you get them to do what you want?" A deep male voice nearby startled her. It wasn't anyone she immediately recognized, and unease slid down her spine.

She turned and let out a small sigh of relief. "Do you always sneak up on people like that?"

"My name *is* Phantom, you know."

"Ah, yes. The name suits you. Are you friends with Henry?" she asked, referring to the owner of the ranch.

"I just met him. I came out here hoping to find you."

Elena led the horse away from the trough near the arena and started walking to the barn, Phantom falling in alongside her. She dug her phone out of her back pocket and waved it in the air. "Easiest way to find me." *Why is he here? What could he possibly want?* She couldn't say she was glad to see him. Just watching his granite features reminded her of the way he had tilted her world on its side with a decision that changed everything for her.

He shrugged. "Too impersonal. I prefer to look people in the face when I'm talking to them."

"You were born in the wrong times, then, I hate to tell you. Texts, email, social media… That's how everyone stays in touch. It's rare even to hear a voice these days, let alone see a face."

"Call me old-fashioned."

"Okay. I just might. Why are you looking for me anyway?" Her words came across a bit stronger than she had intended. She couldn't conceal her frustration at the way he had so quickly and casually told her he no longer needed her services with his horses. In a few brief sentences, he had cut her off from quarter horses she had been training for years and had practically come to think of as her own. With that same move, he had destroyed the main reason she had come to

Hebbronville—to work with some of the finest quarter horses she had ever seen.

The Bent Horseshoe Ranch had recruited her as soon as she graduated from A&M to train the quarter horses to be some of the best in the nation. She had jumped at the opportunity, and it had been her main source of income—up until two weeks ago. Once Phantom had fired her, she'd had to act fast to find new clients. She found a couple close to Falfurrias, but the cost of gas to drive out to them barely made it worthwhile.

"For someone who loves to brag about her tech world, you don't check your phone often."

Surprised, Elena clicked open her phone and found she had missed multiple text messages from Anya. "Is she okay? Did something happen?" she asked, quickly scrolling through the texts.

"Everything is fine. She'd like to see you, that's all. She wanted to know if you could come out to the ranch today. If we go soon, Snap will probably be making lunch."

Elena looked at him skeptically as she began to undo the cinch on the saddle. "Snap? Who else lives at your ranch? Crackle and Pop?"

For a moment she thought he was going to smile, but the face carved from granite stayed serious, though his tone seemed amused. "Good one. Never heard that before. We admit our nicknames are…interesting…"

"And yours? You specialize in sneaking up on people so you're called Phantom?"

"That, and I can make like a ghost and disappear."

"Right." She chuckled. "Good to know. So did you really come out here just because Anya wants me to come out to the ranch today?" She grabbed a soft brush from a bucket of cool water and began to wipe down the horse with long, smooth strokes. The horse looked half-asleep.

"That and I wanted to see my competition at work."

She hesitated midstroke, then resumed quickly. "Your competition? Does that mean you've decided to start showing the horses?"

"Yes."

Elena felt a dull ache in her heart. She should be the one showing his horses. She had trained them, guided them, prepared them to be their absolute best. *She* wanted to show them. "Good luck. I hope everything goes well for you."

"I've done a lot more research since I saw you. I appreciate the tip about the horses' feed, by the way. It made a world of difference when I did what you recommended and switched them from sweet feed back to coastal hay and oats."

Elena laughed as she remembered how hyper the horses had been on the sweet feed and his dismay when she told him what to do about it. "Glad I could help." She dropped the soft brush back in the bucket of water and led the horse into its stall, sliding the bridle off and turning the animal loose with a pat on the withers.

"There are still plenty of things I have to learn," Phantom said, stepping closer as she came out of the stall.

Hope blossomed in Elena's heart, making it thud hard in her chest. Could he be rehiring her? Was that why he had come out to the ranch to watch her work? Was this some sort of test?

"Always will be," she said with a bright smile. "The day you think you know everything about raising or showing horses is the day you find out you're wrong. I just got thrown by a two-year-old filly last week. I certainly learned a lesson that day." She nearly bit her tongue. She needed to tell him about all the things she was great at, not her misadventures.

He raised his eyebrows. "Are you okay? You didn't get hurt, did you?" She sensed genuine concern in his voice. Was there a human being beneath all that granite?

"I would think you'd be happy if your competition got sidelined for a few shows," she teased.

"Not my idea of fair competition. Seriously, are you okay?"

"I've got some bruises that are fading into lovely colors. Other than that, I'm fine. Thanks for your concern." She forced herself to look away from him. Something about him drew her in and made her curious to know more about him, especially this glimpse of a softer side she didn't think existed. "How soon are you going to start showing?" She hated talking about herself and wanted to hear more about her—his—horses.

"I'm not sure. That's another reason I'm here today. I wanted to pick your brain about the best horse shows to take them to. Given that it is your area of expertise and all."

Elena grinned at him. "So you *do* need me after all." *Yes! I'm going to get him back as a client!*

He gazed at her intently, then slowly nodded his head. "I could use some help."

She ran a hand through her thick, curly hair and fought back the cheer threatening to burst from her. She wanted to see the horses she loved so much. She had come to miss them greatly in the two weeks since he had dismissed her.

Did he really want her help, or was he simply on a mission for Anya and decided to take advantage of her expertise at the same time? The hope inside faded slightly, but she clung to it tightly. She wasn't going to give up on pursuing even the smallest crack in his shell.

"You know, my prices are generally pretty steep." She grinned, teasing him once again. "*But*, if you're throwing in a free lunch, I might be able to help you a little."

"Good. Anya's missed you since she's been out at the ranch."

"I've missed her too. Since she closed the veterinary clinic temporarily, things haven't been the same."

"She'll be back soon. She's itching to get back to work."

"I know it may not seem like a long time to you, but for the two of us to go a couple of weeks without seeing each other seems like an eternity." Elena studied the ground as they walked toward their trucks.

"Good. Then it's settled. You'll join us for lunch?"

She looked over at him and gave her brightest smile. "Wouldn't miss it." Elena was on a mission. She was going to win back her client.

Chapter 2

THE DRIVE OUT TO BENT HORSESHOE RANCH WAS SCENIC, though bumpy. The road had suffered from the late-spring rains, and county maintenance had yet to repair it. Phantom watched Elena's truck bobbing along behind his and smiled to himself. So far, his plan seemed to be working.

Watching her ride the horse earlier had been like watching a choreographed dance routine. He realized more than ever how critical she would be to his success with the horses and furthering his work out in the field as Stryker had mentioned.

He knew she had a real passion for his quarter horses and had put her heart and soul into developing them into well-trained competitors. He could tell she still held some resentment toward him for cutting ties with her, and he couldn't say he blamed her.

He admitted to himself he had made the decision to dismiss her too hastily. Having grown up and spent most of his life working and training horses, he found asking for help a hard pill to swallow. It was the right thing to do, though. He had watched a few quarter-horse show videos online and realized he was in over his head.

They arrived at the ranch house close to one in the afternoon, with the Texas heat in full force. The humidity made it feel ten degrees hotter. Phantom parked quickly and headed over to Elena's truck, surprising her at her door. She looked up at him with a smile, and saw flecks of gold and tan in her brown eyes. There was something about the way her smile lit up her face that made him want to see it as often as possible.

They had barely stepped onto the small covered patio when the large wooden door to the home flew open and Anya rushed out, grinning from ear to ear. "You found her! Phantom, you're the best!"

Elena brushed past him, and he caught her unique scent of Texas wildflowers. He had noticed it when he first met her, and it had lingered in his memory. Phantom watched her embrace Anya as if it had been years since they had seen each other instead of just a couple of weeks. "You know, those first couple of days when I didn't hear from you, you had me worried sick!" Elena scolded Anya. "I had to hear from the gossipmongers in town that your place had a break-in, and you know how my imagination gets carried away."

"I know, I know. I'm sorry. I should have called you as soon as it happened. I was so rattled, I didn't know up from down. If it hadn't been for Stryker, I probably would have fallen to pieces."

Elena shook her head. "I should have known you'd be with him. The way you've been mooning over him the last two months, I'm not surprised."

"I have not been 'mooning' over him." Anya shook her head back at Elena. "Who even says such things anymore? I swear, you and Phantom should compare notes. You both are old souls."

Elena looked up at Phantom, her eyes assessing him. "Is that what you are? An old soul?"

"So I've been told. Anya has been educating me. I did tell you I'm old-fashioned."

Anya laughed. "Yes, you are. Sometimes that can be a good thing, though."

"And other times?" Elena asked, an eyebrow raised.

"Other times can bore you to tears."

Phantom rolled his eyes and headed toward the front door. "Let's get out of this heat and see if Snap is working his magic in the kitchen."

He held the door open as the two women walked past him, lost in conversation. He watched Elena and plotted his next steps to get her out to the barn and back with the horses she loved.

"You're going to *live* here?" Elena wasn't sure she had heard right. Anya wasn't making any sense.

"Yes. I can't wait for you to meet the rest of the guys. They're such an amazing group. But Stryker… He owns my heart. I can't imagine life without him. I'm in love, Elena."

"You're joking with me, right? Love? I thought we agreed we'd be certified bachelorettes the rest of our lives. You're changing the rules on me."

"I'm just living with him, El. We're not making any wedding plans…" Anya's voice trailed off.

"…Yet. You practically said it. It's on the tip of your tongue! No way—Anya, has he *asked* you?" Elena stared at Anya, holding her breath.

"No, not exactly." Anya smiled slyly.

"Either he has or he hasn't," Elena insisted. She sipped her coffee, the delicious brew warming her from the inside out.

"He's hinted the question isn't far away."

Elena nearly choked on her coffee. "Okay, now I know you're messing with me. Anya! You've known him for two months! How can you possibly consider marriage? I mean, moving in with the guy alone is a huge step."

Anya shrugged and smiled. "If I were in your seat right now, I'd say the same thing." She leaned forward in her chair and grasped Elena's hands in hers. "I don't know how to explain it. Somehow when it's right, you just know. He's the one, El."

Elena stared at Anya for a moment of stunned silence. "Okay, who are you, and what have you done with my best friend?"

Anya laughed just as Isaiah "Snap" Flores arrived with a tray of bite-sized sandwiches: turkey and cheese, ham and cheese, and cucumber salad. On top of that, he had made a dreamy creamy tomato bisque soup. Elena tasted the bisque, and her eyes nearly rolled back in her head. "Snap, where did you learn to cook like this?"

Snap beamed proudly. Of the men she'd met so far, he appeared to be the youngest. There had to be others around, given the interesting nicknames Anya had been using, but so far she'd seen only Phantom and Snap. Apparently the rest were out working on the ranch. Snap disappeared back into the kitchen, giving her and Anya their privacy.

The sound of boots on the hardwood floor drew their attention, and Anya's eyes lit up as Stryker came striding into the room. At first he had eyes only for Anya, but

Elena saw his gaze flick over to her briefly. He leaned down and pressed a tender kiss to Anya's lips and she leaned up into the touch, her hand resting on his chest for a moment.

"Stryker, I want you to meet my best friend, Elena Garcia." Anya gestured toward Elena, and she smiled brightly. So this was the man who had claimed her best friend's heart. Elena had interacted with him months ago when he and his friends first bought the ranch and began remodeling the outdated ranch house into the beautiful home it had become. Their conversations had been limited to her work with the horses.

Elena stood and extended her hand. He smiled at her. "I seem to remember you lurking around when we were remodeling this place."

"'Lurking' isn't the term I would use," she replied with a smile. "I was working quite hard."

"That was around the time you won the Grand Champion trophy in Corpus, wasn't it?"

Phantom's voice came out of nowhere, gentle, and could that be with appreciation? He hadn't made any noise to alert her he had come into the room. She turned and found him leaning against the dining room wall. How long had he been there?

"Yes, it was," she said, watching his face for a reaction. If she wanted him back as a client, she needed him to fully understand how good she was with his horses. Knowing that he had seen the trophies she had won was a step in the right direction.

He watched her for a long moment, finally breaking eye contact to glance over at Anya and Stryker, who seemed to be in their own world. "When you have a moment," he said, returning his gaze to her, "I'd like to take you out to the barn. It won't take very long."

Had he finally decided he needed her on the ranch after all? Was she about to get her client back? Elena's heart pounded with hope. She glanced over at Anya, but she seemed fixated on Stryker. "I'm going to step out to the barn for just a bit," she said, though she doubted Anya heard her. Spying the sugar cubes still on the table for their coffee, she grabbed a few and stuffed them in her pockets as she stood.

She smiled to herself. Anya had fallen in love, something she'd never thought would happen. From the looks of it, she was beyond happy, which made Elena happy. She only wanted the best for her friend, and if Stryker brought that look of joy to Anya's face, Elena would support her no matter how crazy it seemed.

Elena looked up to find Phantom watching her intently, measuring every expression on her face. Nerves kicked into high gear in the pit of her stomach. Hope could be a dangerous thing. He turned and led her out of the house and toward the barn.

"You seem to be very close to Anya."

Was he trying to have a conversation with her? The day had been full of surprises already, and he seemed to be the lead instigator of most of them. She crossed her fingers that the surprises continued to be positive ones. "We've been best friends since we met in college. We've been through a lot together."

"I can understand that bond."

"Do you have a best friend?" she asked, then realized how lame that must sound. "I mean… Well, surely you must have a best friend. What I meant was—"

He glanced sideways at her and flashed her a smile—a real smile—and it took her breath away. The warmth in that smile turned his tanned skin a deep, molten bronze. The short haircut couldn't hide the slight wave in his hair, which made his face look less severe and intense. His dark-gray eyes—a color she'd never seen before—lit up and softened, the steel becoming magnetic and drawing her in. The corners of his eyes crinkled when he smiled, adding an extra layer of humanity she had thought he lacked. The man made of stone suddenly seemed more approachable than she would have imagined.

"What are you saying? You think I can't make friends? I know we didn't get off on the best foot, but do I strike you as *that* unpleasant?"

"No! I mean, of course not. Just because you don't like me or, um, didn't need me…um…" Hell, she was making a total mess of the conversation. She became annoyed with herself—and with him. He had put her in the predicament to begin with.

"I never said I didn't like you."

"You didn't have to," she replied, then nearly bit her own tongue. If her goal had been to win him back as a client, she was doing an exceptional job of mucking it up.

"I have a handful of friends I consider my brothers," he said, returning to the original topic. "I would die for them if I had to." His smile had vanished, and his serious demeanor had returned.

"Are they your business partners? Are Stryker and Snap your do-or-die friends?"

He didn't answer her as they walked into the barn.

The scents she loved washed over her as a welcoming balm—fresh hay, oats, leather, and horses. She walked quickly up to the first stall and a tall, red sorrel mare strolled up, knowing Elena was bound to have a treat for her. She pulled a sugar cube from her pocket and chuckled as the mare's lips moved along her flattened palm, finding the cube and licking it off her hand.

"So is that your trick to get them to like you?"

Phantom's voice was close behind her, very close, and Elena froze. In that moment she was back in time a handful of years, in the same exact place, but with a different man standing behind her. Disaster had struck, in the form of a ranch hand who had developed a strong desire for her. She hadn't returned the sentiment and had paid dearly for that.

A shiver ran down her spine, the memory of the pain so vivid. She didn't turn around to see how close Phantom was but moved quickly to the next stall before facing him, her heart racing. She had thought herself over the trauma of the disaster years ago, but it still had the power to sneak up on her when she least expected it. *You have to stop living in fear. The man who hurt you is gone. Pay attention to what is in front of you right now.*

"Wh-what did you want to talk to me about out here?" She hated her voice for trembling slightly, revealing her anxiety.

He tilted his head and observed her, his gray eyes always measuring, appraising. "Have I done something wrong?"

"What? No! Well, other than deciding not to be my client anymore." She flashed him a smile, pulling herself back together. "I'm just excited to see the horses again. I've missed them."

"I think they've missed you. But I haven't ruined them—yet."

Her smile broadened. "I never said you would. It's just a very different world to train and show quarter horses like these rather than your thoroughbred race-horses." She moved down to the next stall, making clicking sounds to get the attention of the horse inside. "So you wanted me to see that the horses are all right? Is that why you brought me out here?"

"And to pick your brain, remember? I need some guidance on horse shows."

Elena nodded. "I suppose it all depends on what your goals are with the horses." She glanced around the barn, trying to think of what she could say to convince him to see her logic and why she was the best person to show his horses. "Thank you for bringing me out here. It's good to see them."

"I think I may have made a hasty decision when we first met."

Elena's heart thumped hard in her chest. "Why do you say that?"

"Stryker filled me in a little on your experience work-ing this ranch."

"He and I barely talked. How did he know anything?"

Phantom walked closer to her. "He asked around when he met you out here. He and I have a lot in common. We both like our privacy."

"I can see that," she replied dryly, and he stopped directly in front of her.

"I want my horses to be successful. To do that, I

need help. From everything I've heard, you're the best around. I'd like to ask you to take us on as your client again."

Elena thought her heart was going to leap from her chest with joy. Certain things had to fall into place, though, in order for this to work. "I'll need the same role I had previously, with the same autonomy when it comes to training and developing the seasonal horse-show plans. We'll still need to work together closely, since we'll need to collaborate on big decisions regarding the program you want to implement, and I'll need your approval on any show schedules, especially since I'll be traveling with your horses. But I need you to trust and support my leadership ability."

A look of surprise crossed his features. "They're my horses. I'll be the one functioning in a leadership capacity."

Elena searched his face for several seconds. They had to work out an arrangement they'd both be comfortable with so he didn't cut her loose again if their styles clashed. She shoved her hands in her pockets and drew a deep breath. Time to take a chance. "I have a proposition for you instead. You need my expertise in order to get the most out of your horses. I need you to understand that I know how to run an operation like this and what we can make happen if you bring me back as your trainer."

He lifted his eyebrows in surprise. "I'm listening."

"There's a quarter-horse show in Edinburg this weekend. I'm entering a client's horse in the cutting and reining classes at the end. You'll get a chance to see how I work, and I think it will show you just how much you need me. Plus, we'll get some time together to figure out if coming back as your trainer is the best idea for me too. Consider it a trial run."

She chewed on the inside of her cheek as he watched her with a raised eyebrow. Would he agree? Normally she would have been ecstatic that he wanted her to take him back as a client. She couldn't take any chances he was just having a knee-jerk reaction to discovering how different quarter horses were from what he'd grown up training.

"That almost sounds like a challenge." He smiled at her again, and she felt the heat of a blush starting in her cheeks.

She shrugged. "I think it may show you a few things you didn't know about the quarter-horse industry."

"You continue to surprise me, Elena. I tell you I want you to take me back as a client, and you respond with a challenge. Yes, I'll go with you. I look forward to seeing everything you have to prove to me."

"There are certain rules you'll have to follow." Elena's heart pounded with excitement and a touch of nervousness. He seemed so incredibly close. She had to keep reminding herself that the man she feared was gone, and the one standing in front of her seemed to offer strength and protection instead of terror and pain.

She enjoyed the company of a strong man as much as any woman. It had taken her time to recover from the attack, but her passionate nature couldn't be held in check for long. She hadn't allowed the one awful experience to sour her to the pleasure she could experience with a man. Her relationships didn't last very long, though. Her busy schedule and desire to actively pursue her career didn't support the traditional role the men she had dated wanted her to play.

"Rules too?"

"They're very simple. Promise me that you'll go into this with an open mind and that you'll ask any questions you have, no matter how crazy they may seem."

"That could prove dangerous," he said softly, reaching out a hand toward her.

Unexpectedly, the fear she thought she conquered reared its ugly head, and she flinched. She wanted to growl in frustration. She knew her stress made her hypersensitive to everything around her, which had prompted her reaction. His smile slowly faded, his expression back to inscrutable. What was he thinking? "And if I agree to those rules, will you agree to mine?"

Elena chewed on her lower lip. What could his rules possibly be? "Within reason, of course."

"Only one. You must promise to answer all my questions honestly."

Elena gave him a relieved smile. "That will be easy enough. I'll pick you up at seven Saturday morning. Be ready for a long day."

His smile returned. "I look forward to it."

Chapter 3

"SHERMAN IS MORE THAN READY FOR THIS SHOW, TRUST me." Elena patted the horse on the neck as she dismounted. She had just finished running through a complex reining pattern, and Sherman had flown through the maneuvers effortlessly.

Jonas Franklin smiled at her. "There is no one I trust more, Elena. I just wish I could be there to watch you compete."

She forced a smile to her face and swallowed back her unease. Jonas always hovered, and more often than not, he invaded her personal space. Though he always seemed surprised when she tried to reestablish boundaries between them, she was fairly certain he was intentionally getting too close for her comfort.

Jonas's ranch was one of her regulars, one she had picked up not long after moving to Hebbronville. While the contract with the Bent Horseshoe Ranch had been good, she couldn't survive with just one client. She had five that she had cultivated over the years, but if she could, she would drop Jonas in a heartbeat.

"What classes are you entering again?" Jonas asked, following her to the barn. She could feel his eyes on her as she walked, and she had to repress her shiver of disgust. He was old enough to be her father, and yet he made no attempt to hide his interest in her. On more than one occasion she had turned down his request for

a date, letting him know as gently as possible she didn't
think they had enough in common and she didn't want
to make things awkward between them as she continued
to work with him. Obviously, he argued, but she held
her ground.

"Cutting and reining. Those are the two classes I've
been working on the most with Sherman."

"Excellent. It will be nice to add some new trophies
to the showcase." Jonas took a few quick strides until he
walked alongside her. "You haven't seen the showcase
I built for the trophies. You ought to come inside and
take a look."

Elena shook her head. "I appreciate the invite, Jonas,
but I have a lot of work to get done to be ready for the
show." She stopped just outside the barn, where she
transitioned Sherman from a bridle to a halter and tied
him up in the stanchion so she could begin bathing him.
She turned her back on Jonas as she began to undo the
cinch on the saddle.

His hands landed on her shoulders, lightly massaging. "You work too hard, Elena. Take a few minutes for
a break with me."

Elena swallowed the bile that rose in her throat and
fought the fear that clawed down her spine. She couldn't
help but compare the situation to the one that had gone
so horribly wrong a few years ago. The attack had
started similarly, with the ranch hand lightly caressing
her shoulders and arms as he tried to make a move on
her. When she'd tried to put a stop to it, the ranch hand's
anger had exploded. She hadn't ever witnessed Jonas
angry, but she had no doubt he could easily hurt her if
he wanted. She couldn't stop the trembles that started

in the pit of her stomach and worked their way out into her extremities.

She turned slowly and gently pushed his hands away from her shoulders, bracing herself for any negative reaction. "I appreciate your concern for my well-being, Jonas, but I don't need a break. I'm fine. I have a lot to get done before it gets too late in the day. Some other time I'll have to take you up on your offer to see the showcase."

Jonas's smile became tight for several moments before he stepped back from her and shrugged. "Suit yourself. You're welcome at the house anytime. You know that. I'll leave you to your work and wish you the best of success at the show. If I wasn't so busy with my work, I would enjoy going with you."

Elena said a silent prayer of thanks that he wasn't available. She doubted she could handle spending a day with him. "I'll bring you the winnings when I get back," she said, forcing a cheerfulness into her voice that she didn't feel.

"I look forward to it, Elena." His eyes traveled over her from head to toe, a smile still on his face. Then he turned and took off toward the house, whistling loudly.

Elena turned back to face the horse and rested her forehead against the saddle, letting out a long, shaky breath. With trembling hands, she began to take the saddle off Sherman and forced her mind to the list of things she needed to get done to be ready for the show. One thought remained strong, though. As soon as she could, she would drop Jonas Franklin as a client.

—⁓—

Early Saturday morning, the tiny Mexican restaurant in Falfurrias was busy for such a small town. Since they were hauling a horse trailer behind them, the drive-through hadn't been an option, but fortunately things moved quickly inside. Elena found a spot to wait for their to-go order where she could keep an eye on the horse trailer, and Phantom leaned against the wall, watching her.

They hadn't talked much on the drive so far, and he had enjoyed the opportunity to study her while he pretended to watch the countryside flying past them. He could tell driving a horse trailer was second nature to her as she maneuvered with ease and skill. He knew she had been up for hours already, heading out to the owner's ranch to pick up the horse and load the tack, then driving out to the Bent Horseshoe Ranch to pick him up. Even so, she seemed to be full of energy, her bright smile greeting him at exactly zero seven hundred hours that morning.

'Beautiful' seemed too simple a word to describe her. He couldn't remember the last time he had paused long enough to really appreciate a woman's beauty. He had always prided himself on being mission-first. Women were nothing but a distraction—or so he had thought.

When he had first become a SEAL, he had enjoyed the attention of women in between missions. After years of a living such a lifestyle, he had grown tired of women who seemed more interested in claiming they had been with a SEAL than in actually getting to know him. He began to long for a woman who wanted to spend time with him for reasons other than great sex.

The cashier called them back to the front to grab their

order. Elena cast a sideways glance at him with a smile that made him nearly stumble off the curb. Her smile took her beauty to another level.

"One of my favorite things about going to a horse show early in the morning is treating myself to good tacos. I'm addicted to the tacos from this little place and get them whenever I'm outside Hebbronville. There's nothing better with a good cup of coffee."

They climbed into the truck, and she got them back out onto the highway. "Is that the way to get into your good graces? Bring you a good breakfast taco?" He watched the small smile lingering on her lips.

Elena laughed, a beautiful, soft sound that seemed to punch him in the gut. She was unlike any woman he had ever met before. Her confidence and determination continued to impress him, and he liked the way she was ready to fight for what she wanted. He struggled to understand her reaction to him the other day, though. The way she had flinched away from him had taken him by surprise.

He had been reaching for a loose curl that hovered over her cheekbone when she'd jerked away from him so fast he'd thought she was going to turn and run. Her hair had looked so silky, falling in curls about her face, and he couldn't resist the urge to touch the strand to see if it really felt as soft as it looked. Her reaction had told him so much more about her than he'd expected.

His hands curled into fists in his lap. Someone had hurt her in the past. The idea sickened him. He hated the thought of her flinching from him again.

"The fastest way to get into my good graces would be do as you promised and go into this horse show with an open mind. You're going to see lots of things you'll have questions about, and you promised you'd ask." Her eyes were twinkling as she cast another sideways glance at him, and he struggled to swallow his bite of a carne asada taco.

"Why are you so fixated on my horses? I thought you supported other ranches around here as well."

Elena gave a half-hearted shrug. "I do. None of them can match the quality of your horses, though. The previous owner of your ranch saw me competing with one of my friend's horses at a state quarter-horse show. I placed Reserve Grand Champion, and he hired me based on that. The first competition he and I went to, we took home the blue ribbons in every class we entered."

"You're well known in the industry by now, I take it."

A rueful smile touched her lips. "Not as much as I'd like to be. Daniel—the previous owner—started out with grand plans to take the horses all the way to the national level. Honestly, the more time that went by, the more I could see just how overwhelmed he was by the amount of work ranching requires. He had gotten into the business with lofty dreams. Don't get me wrong—he was making money. But he was all over the board."

"I take it you never went to the national level, then."

She shook her head, her dark curls bouncing around her face. "No. He had far too much on his plate for such a lofty goal. I put together the schedule and paperwork and everything he would need to make it happen, but he couldn't do it."

"That explains why he sold the place," Phantom said with a nod, putting the pieces together.

Elena nodded as well. "It broke his heart. But he

had to. The good thing is that he walked away with a profit in his pocket. When I heard he'd sold the ranch, I thought he'd take all the horses with him. But he's decided to ease back slowly and is focused on figuring out cattle, first. He went on to buy a smaller ranch out near Corpus, and I hear he's doing really well for himself."

"So you'd like to be better known in the industry. What does that mean to you?"

Her lovely dark-tanned cheeks turned a shade of pink as she gnawed on her lower lip. It was a nice, full lower lip, one that he imagined would feel amazing in a kiss. He tore his thoughts off her lips and focused on her eyes. In the bright morning sunlight, the golden flecks shimmered, and he realized looking at her eyes was no safer than looking at her lips.

"I've had a dream ever since I was a little girl. I want to take horses to the National Championships. I want to be known far and wide as the best trainer possible for show horses."

"Is Hebbronville really the best place to get known for such a thing?"

Elena shook her head. "No. But it was a place to get started. I've been able to compete in a lot of shows with your horses, and I've picked up a lot of business that way. I even have clients in Laredo and Corpus. I suppose I'll have to move closer to them now. But I've fallen in love with Hebbronville. The people, the town… everything about it. So, for the moment, if I have to do a little bit of traveling, that's okay with me."

Phantom was just beginning to get to know her, and she had already brought a certain amount of excitement and energy to his life he hadn't felt in a long time. The idea of her moving away brought disappointment he didn't want to examine too closely. He liked the thought of her being nearby.

"What about you? What have you been doing since you left the world of racehorses?"

He had been a sixteen-year-old kid when he had made the decision to become a Navy SEAL. Uncle Jon had been one and sacrificed his life in the line of duty. Phantom had looked up to Uncle Jon for guidance and direction in his younger years because his father had been so consumed by the day-to-day operations of their multimillion-dollar racehorse facility.

It would have been easy for Phantom to sit back and enjoy the money his parents had set aside for him, slide into the job waiting for him and continue the family traditions. He didn't want to live the life his parents designed for him. When Uncle Jon passed serving his country, Phantom immediately knew what he wanted to do with his life.

"I suppose you could say I work as a consultant. Some people say I have a knack for strategy and placement. Until now. Returning to a life working with horses is as close to a dream as I could ask for." As a tactical member of the SEALs, strategy was his specialty. He had to remember his cover, though, and emphasize his new role.

Elena glanced over at him, a slightly shocked look on her face. "You gave up working with racehorses to become a consultant?"

"Don't get me wrong. There's nothing more exhilarating than the feel of a powerful steed racing around the track, carrying you at a speed you can only begin to imagine. It just wasn't the life for me back then."

"I can see you as a consultant. You're so calm and level-headed."

"Are you saying I'm boring?"

Elena sputtered for several moments. She swallowed hard and looked over at him, and he couldn't contain his teasing smile any longer. She laughed, the beautiful laugh he had started to crave. "Well, if the shoe fits…"

His smile broadened. "For that, I won't be getting you tasty tacos anytime soon."

They carried on an easy conversation about his life working with racehorses and her life growing up showing quarter horses, and it surprised him how much they had in common. He discovered they had experienced many of the same challenges and thrills while training those incredible animals, as well as the heartbreak of losing one to old age or disease. Soon they were pulling up to the arena in Edinburg, and the sound of horses calling to one another from different stalls and horse trailers filled the air.

Phantom helped Elena unload the horse she had brought, and they tied it to the trailer with a net of coastal hay to feed on while it got used to the new noises and smells. "That's a nice-looking horse," Phantom said, glancing back as they walked toward the front offices of the arena to begin registration.

"He belongs to Jonas Franklin, who has a ranch about forty-five minutes outside Hebbronville. I've been training his horses almost as long as I've trained yours. He would have joined us today if business hadn't kept him occupied."

Phantom silently thanked the rancher's business for that. He didn't want to share Elena with anyone else today.

Chapter 4

"ELENA!" A WOMAN STANDING NEAR THE REGISTRATION office called and hurried over. As they drew closer to the offices, Phantom realized with a jolt that his time alone with Elena was about to come to an abrupt end.

The woman embraced Elena in a swift hug. "I had hoped I would see you here today." The older woman's gaze turned toward Phantom, and she looked at him with speculation.

"Dolores, this is Phantom. He's one of the new owners out at the Bent Horseshoe Ranch."

The older woman raised her eyebrows. "How exciting! And such an interesting name too."

Elena turned to him, her eyes dancing. "I'll leave you to get acquainted. I've got to get registered."

Phantom nearly groaned out loud. Dolores reminded him of the gossipmongers he'd had to deal with when he worked with the racehorses many years ago. He smiled instead. He had to get out and network. It was part of the role he had accepted when he agreed to the assignment in Hebbronville.

He briefly turned his attention on Dolores. "It's a nickname. I earned it in high school." The name *had* come in high school, but only really took hold when he became a SEAL.

"Sounds like a fascinating story. Care to share?"

"I'll have to some other time, Dolores. I'm here to learn as much from Elena as possible."

"You couldn't be in better hands. She's one of the best in the industry. She's got real talent and can take your horses all the way to Nationals, if you give her a chance."

Phantom appraised Dolores with new appreciation. She obviously had Elena's best interests at heart. "That's what we're hoping for. Maybe I'll see you at the next horse show?"

"Absolutely. My David and I travel to these all year long. We bring several horses with us. We have the large hauler parked at the end of the lot. You'll recognize us every time."

His first attempt at networking had proved successful. He nodded to her and excused himself and headed for the offices. Laughter and chatter greeted his ears, though it all fell silent when he stepped into the room. Elena had been the center of attention as she filled out the registration forms, a mixed crowd standing around her. Upon Phantom's entrance, all attention focused on him.

Elena glanced up from her paperwork and smiled at him, and his stomach did a flip-flop. Exquisite. He latched onto the word that accurately described her. How had he missed so much about her when he first met her? *Because your mind was wrapped up in the mission. You were focused on what needed to be done.* He had been just days from leaving on a mission to take down a Mexican drug cartel when he had found her with the horses in the barn. In hindsight, he could have handled their first meeting far better.

"My friends, this is one of the new owners of the Bent Horseshoe Ranch in Hebbronville. He likes to go by the nickname Phantom, and I'm sure he'd get a thrill out of telling you why he has such a moniker."

Phantom hated being the center of attention. That was one of the reasons he preferred to stay in the shadows, stay hidden. He didn't exist to the world, and that was how he liked it. Now, however, several pairs of eyes were watching him with interest.

He watched Elena as he waded through polite introductions. When she had finished the paperwork, he made a generic excuse and left the office with her. "Thanks for throwing me to the wolves," he said, looking down at her as they walked toward the arena.

She looked up at him, a mischievous twinkle in her eyes. "I thought a man who goes by 'Phantom' must enjoy a lot of attention."

"Anyone ever warned you that you're too smart for your own good?"

She tilted her head to the side as if she had to think about it. "No, I think that's a first. I've been told I'm obnoxious, stubborn, difficult… Smart isn't anything I've been accused of before."

A chuckle rumbled in his chest. He had never imagined his time with her could be so enjoyable and entertaining. He wanted to put his arm around her, but at the last minute he remembered the flinch. He crammed his hands into his pockets as they walked along the side of the arena.

They came upon the stalls and he stopped walking, staring down the aisle where a handful of exhibitors were preparing their horses for the showmanship class.

"What *are* they doing?" he asked, staring at a couple of women as they wiped baby oil over the horses' noses and into their ears. Another woman toward the end of the aisle was carefully applying black polish to her bay mare's hooves.

Elena looked up at him with one eyebrow cocked. "You mean you didn't do this with your racehorses?"

"I've never seen anything like it in my life. Seriously, what *are* they doing?"

Elena placed a hand at his elbow and turned him toward the aisle. He took the touch as a promising sign and wondered if her reaction the other night had been from surprise. In his mind's eye, he recalled the flash of fear across her face and knew it had been more than just surprise.

They headed down between the stalls as she began to talk. "A few days before you go to show, you want to prep the horse by shaving the hair from its ears, muzzle, eyebrows, and fetlocks. You want to present as polished an appearance as possible. I've done some of the prep work on Jonas's horse already, but you'll get to see the final touches right before our competition."

"We shaved our horses, though not quite to this extent," he said as he looked at the horse being groomed meticulously.

"Prior to going into the show ring, you'll want to highlight their features with a light coating of baby oil. If any of your horses have white markings on their feet, which two of yours do, you'll usually trim the hair down on those areas, then touch them up with baby powder on the day of the show. Hoof polish is one of the final touches you'll give to the horse before entering the show ring."

"I think that halter has more silver on it than all of my watches combined…and that's saying something."

Elena chewed on her lower lip, and he could tell she was trying not to laugh. "You *have* been in the tack room, haven't you? Did you see the halters and saddles?"

"I didn't do a thorough inspection. I've just been using the general work saddles for daily exercise."

"Hmm." She didn't seem that impressed with his answer. Hell, *he* wasn't impressed. If he had really wanted to show her that he wanted to take on the quarter-horse industry, he had done a piss-poor job of it so far. Then again, he had been busy taking down a cartel and rescuing Anya from its bloodthirsty leader. He had good excuses. He just couldn't tell her any of them.

"Why don't we go to the stands? I'd like to see how this showmanship class works."

Elena gave him another of her stunning smiles and nodded. She didn't seem afraid of him today. Maybe the public setting eased any anxiety she had. Or maybe she had never really been afraid and had been comfortable with him already. He wanted to believe the latter, but felt certain something had frightened her the other night and wanted to know what he had done to trigger her reaction.

Sitting in the first row of the stands, Phantom watched the showmanship class with wonder. The exhibitors went through several different stages—walking toward the judge, jogging past, backing the horse up, and setting it up to stand with its feet aligned. The horses' coats shone. Their manes were all trimmed short and sectioned into thin strips held by tiny rubber bands. Their tails were combed to look as smooth and soft as Elena's hair, though straight as a pin and draping to within a few inches off the ground. Their hooves were polished, their features shining under the smooth wiping of baby oil. He had never expected it to be so incredible—or so complicated.

The entire time he had tons of questions, and Elena answered every one with enthusiasm. Frequently, her smile distracted him from the arena and he had to remind himself to focus on the activities of the show. Ultimately, he had an objective to connect and network, and the first step in the process involved getting Elena back as his trainer. He had to show her he could be counted on as a consistent client.

"And you do all of this?" He pulled his eyes off the competition and looked at Elena with admiration.

She gave him a half smile. "I used to."

"What do you mean?" Phantom schooled his features as he always did, expressing nothing, though inside he felt his frustration mount. "You mean that you only competed in this class with my horses?"

"Yours were the only ones talented enough. And they are incredibly good, Phantom. If you could only see them—"

Phantom raised his hand and she stopped talking, her gaze fixed on his face. "I believe you," he said.

They were silent through the remainder of the class, and he watched with rapt attention the subtle difference in movement that he knew would be enough to separate a winner from a loser. He had already picked who the winner should be and wasn't surprised when the exhibitor walked out of the arena with the blue ribbon.

For the remainder of the day, Elena served as his personal guide, explaining the intricacies of each class to him and making introductions to people she had worked with for years. With every passing moment, he wanted more time with her, though without as many people around.

The day passed quickly, and she had to get ready for her first competition. He helped her saddle her client's horse and noticed that the saddle she used was just as ornate as the ones used by the other competitors. The horse had also been groomed to perfection. The biggest difference was that the mane wasn't trimmed. Instead it was long and flowing.

She guided him with helping her apply the final touches to the horse before she vanished into the women's room to change into her show attire. He swallowed hard when she walked out. Her dark-brown slacks clung to her figure. With them, she wore a navy-blue jacket decorated with sequins, the shade of blue making the color of her eyes pop even more than before. Her long, curly black hair had been pulled back into a low bun at the nape of her neck, and her dark-brown cowboy hat was set low on her forehead. She looked absolutely stunning, but to top it off, she smiled at him, and his heart skipped a beat.

He couldn't fight the temptation and leaned down to her when she reached for the reins that he held. His lips brushed across her ear, his cheek lightly touching hers. "Good luck out there," he whispered.

An audible gasp escaped her lips, and she slowly pulled back. Awareness of his body so close to hers, then pleasure flashed in her eyes, and he got the sense she wanted to feel more of his touch. Quickly, though, confusion and a touch of apprehension crept into her eyes. The horse began to prance nervously, picking up on her emotions.

"Elena…" he began hesitantly, unsure exactly what he wanted to say to her. She had liked the feel of his skin against hers—that had been obvious. What had happened in her past to make her nervous with him?

"Thank you," she said, nodding to him curtly. She mounted the horse, not looking his way.

Phantom watched her ride into the arena, then took his seat in the stands. He observed, enthralled, as she carried out an intricate pattern that had her taking the horse through figure eights where it would switch its lead leg in midlope. Referred to as a flying lead change, the maneuver took a lot of training and skill to execute, but he could hardly even notice the transition.

When she raced her horse down the length of the arena and set back in the saddle, the horse slid nearly twenty feet, leaving him breathless with awe. She took it into a spin, where he finally understood the need for the long mane. It fanned out, creating an image he knew he would never forget.

He wasn't surprised when she came in first, though he stayed in the stands, waiting for her to go back in and compete in the cutting competition. She clearly had the advantage over her competitors. They worked to make their motions seem effortless, but hers were smooth as she guided her horse and selected a calf to cut from the herd. Again, she won first.

He carried the tack out to the trailer as Elena changed out of her show attire. He noticed the large trailer

Dolores had mentioned to him and smiled. It had been a day full of experiences, and all had been good.

"You'd be surprised at the money. Easiest cash I've ever earned."

Phantom hesitated as the stranger's voice drifted to him from the front of the sizable rig. He shook his head at himself. It had to be the driver of the trailer bragging to another driver about his job.

"Aren't you worried about the law?"

Phantom froze and stood behind the rig, listening intently. The other driver's response set off massive warning bells. He edged toward the corner of the trailer, attempting to see around it and catch a good glimpse of the two men talking.

"They've got it all worked out. The system is foolproof. The last batch I took all the way to Austin without a single hiccup." The first driver spoke again.

"You don't feel a little—I don't know the right word—crappy, maybe, for taking them?"

"Shit, man, someone's going to, one way or another. I might as well be the one cashing in from it." The first driver paused and lowered his voice, and Phantom strained to hear what he said next. "There's plenty of work to go around, I'll tell you that. They take several trailer loads at a time. I can put in a word for you, if you're interested."

"I don't know if I can stomach getting involved in hauling humans for sale."

Phantom nearly dropped the saddle. *What the hell?*

"Get over yourself," the first driver said. "So what if they're for sale? Most of the time it's because no one else wants them. More than likely they'd be dead in a ditch if it wasn't for the buyers. If you ask me, we're helping them out."

"I never thought of it that way," the second driver said. "Keep me in mind the next time an opportunity comes up."

Phantom began to whistle softly as if he came from a distance and gradually increased the volume as he walked past the large rig. He looked to the side, but the men had disappeared. He walked quickly to Elena's trailer and fished out his cell phone.

"Stryker, we've got an issue." He spoke softly, watching everything happening around him as he loaded the saddle into the tack compartment.

"Things not going well at the show?" Stryker asked.

"We need to set up a call with Haslett tonight."

"Can you share anything more than that?" Stryker asked, his voice intense.

"Not here, not now."

"Got it. I'll make the arrangements and text you the time. Are you and Elena safe?"

"Yes. I'll fill you in when I get back to the ranch tonight."

They signed off their call as Elena came walking out, leading the horse alongside. Phantom pocketed the cell phone and watched her, forcing a smile to his face. His mind whirled with the conversation he had just overheard. He needed to force it from his mind for a little while and concentrate on convincing Elena he wanted to be her client again and they would work well together.

"I'll drive us home," Phantom offered, opening his hand for her to toss him the keys. She shrugged and did.

He had just received a text from Stryker that the call had been scheduled later at night than he had expected. In a moment when he felt like things were out of his control, Phantom needed the feel of the steering wheel in his hands.

"What did you think of the show?" Elena asked as he guided them onto the highway.

"It was eye-opening, that's for sure. You certainly convinced me. Now, did I convince you?"

She pivoted in her seat so that she faced him. He glanced over at her and saw her bright smile. "You followed through with your promise, or at least you seemed to. Were there any questions you never got around to asking me?"

He returned the smile. "Yes. Would you like to go to dinner with me?"

Elena looked as if she had nearly swallowed her tongue. "Excuse me?"

"I'd like to take you to dinner. To celebrate your wins today."

He looked back at the road, but from the corner of his eye he noticed she started twisting her hands into knots. She must have seen him watching and clenched her fists in her lap instead. "I-I don't know."

"Are you hungry?" Her stomach answered for her by growling loudly. He gave her a half smile. "I'll take that as a yes."

"Yes, but the horse…"

"Will be safe in the trailer. I'll park close enough to the restaurant that we can keep an eye on it. Don't worry. Can you hold out until Falfurrias? Or are you going to start chewing your arm off?"

"You were the one that suggested dinner, remember? I can go for a long time without any food."

Phantom shook his head. "Not acceptable. With all the work you do, you need your strength."

She hesitated, then gave him a lopsided grin. "A chicken-fried steak does seem like a good idea."

He couldn't resist grinning back. "I know just the place."

A little over thirty minutes later, they were pulling into a small restaurant in Falfurrias. There were only a few other diners in the restaurant, which allowed them to be seated at a table near a set of large windows that looked out directly at the trailer.

"See? And you doubted me."

Elena gawked at him. "I did not *doubt* you! I merely questioned your sanity," she finished with a smirk.

A silky lock of hair had worked loose from her bun and fallen over her forehead, and Phantom wanted nothing more than to touch it. But he didn't want to ruin the moment and have her look at him with fear again. He needed to know why she had, so he could reassure her that she never had to be afraid of him.

They ordered their food, munching on the chips and salsa that had been brought to the table when they sat down. They debated for a moment whether the salsa could really be called hot enough by south Texas standards, before Elena gave him another of those smiles that made his heart pound. "Are you going to tell me what you really thought about the competition?"

"I've never seen anything like it. I had planned to go to a few shows to get my feet wet, but I would have been totally lost without your explanations. It wouldn't have been a good reflection on the ranch."

Elena shrugged. "Everyone would have thought you were a greenhorn."

"And everyone would have asked where you were."

A blush tinged her cheeks. The waitress delivered their food, and Elena's eyes rolled back in her head as she chewed her first bite. "This is heaven. Thank you for stopping for me."

"I was hungry too," he said after swallowing. "But I had another reason for wanting to have dinner with you."

She looked up from her plate quickly, and suspicion entered her eyes. "What?" She watched him with a combination of curiosity and wariness.

"I want to get to know you better. If we're going to work together, we should be comfortable with each other, don't you think?"

"Oh." She chuckled, looking back at her plate. "Well, other than what we talked about this morning, there isn't much more to me. I went to A&M to study, and that's where I had the chance to compete with my friend's horse. Daniel saw me and recruited me on the spot. I've been in Hebbronville ever since. I tend to five other ranches… Well, I've taken on a couple more now that you've decided you no longer need me."

"There's one question that's been gnawing at me for a while that you haven't answered."

"Oh?" She raised an eyebrow. "And what is that?"

"Who hurt you, Elena?"

Chapter 5

SHE SWALLOWED HARD AND DROPPED HER EYES TO HER half-eaten meal. "What do you mean?"

"You think I haven't noticed? You flinched from my touch the other night. Today when I touched you, I saw the unease in your eyes. Something happened to you."

"Have you ever thought it might be because you're as big as an ox and anybody in their right mind should be wary of you?" She pushed her plate away, and Phantom frowned.

"Is that what it is? You promised you were going to answer my questions honestly today. I've held up my end of the bargain. Now it's your turn."

"Phantom, I never asked you to do anything other than—"

"Don't, Elena. I know what we both promised. Tell me the truth. Why are you afraid of me?"

She was silent for several long moments, staring out the window at the dusk-colored world outside. She couldn't tell him what haunted her. She couldn't reveal the terrible experience. Only those closest to her knew about it, and Daniel. He had been the one to find her after…after… *Damn him! Damn him for making me think about it! Keeping it buried keeps me sane.*

She drew a deep breath as her gaze returned to her plate. She couldn't look at Phantom. She didn't want to see his reaction to what she was going to tell him. "I made you a promise, and I want you to know that I will always be honest with you. It's an important building block for a working relationship." She rubbed the back of her neck, wondering exactly where to begin. Somehow, the words began to tumble out. "It happened a few years ago. Only a couple of people close to me know the truth of what really happened."

She saw his hands tighten briefly on the table, then relax. He exuded control over his words and motions. Everything about him was controlled. When he had offered to drive the truck earlier, she hadn't even thought about it when she tossed him the keys. Yes, he had triggered memories of the painful night years ago. But that didn't mean she feared him. Quite the opposite. She found herself beginning to trust him.

"It… I was young and foolish. There was a ranch hand on Daniel's ranch—your ranch—who had developed feelings for me. More accurately, I should say, he lusted after me. I didn't recognize it. I thought it was just harmless flirting between friends. He didn't take it that way."

She looked back out the window, staring at the truck and trailer. Tears burned her eyes and she blinked rapidly, forcing them away. "He caught me alone in the barn one evening. I-I didn't know how to react to his advances. So I slapped him. It was the wrong move, and I paid for it."

Phantom was silent for a long time, so long that Elena thought he was done with the questions she didn't want to answer. Then, "How badly did he hurt you?"

Elena wrapped her arms around herself in a defensive

gesture, something she had started not long after the attack. She forced her arms to relax at her sides. "It was intense. I don't remember a whole lot."

"You remember more than you'd like." It wasn't posed as a question; it was a statement of fact.

"Yes." A tear slid down her face, and she hastily wiped it away. "When I woke up in the hospital, the nurses told me it was a miracle I had survived such a terrible accident. Daniel had told them that one of the horses had been spooked and had trampled me."

"Trampled you? Elena, just how badly did he hurt you?"

She didn't want to get into the details. She didn't want to talk about the event that had created her worst nightmares. She had only recently been able to get through a night here and there without them waking her in a cold sweat. She had made a promise, though, and she would honor it.

"I must have blacked out, because I don't even remember how Daniel got me to the hospital in Laredo. The concussion is probably why my memory is foggy. But when I came around, I had two broken ribs. A broken nose. A broken clavicle. A bunch of bruises and cuts that took weeks to heal."

"I hope Daniel got the law involved."

Elena nodded absently, her mind drifting back to the ordeal. "He tried. By the time they made it to the ranch, though, Billy had disappeared. The sheriff searched for him, but he was gone. He must have left as soon as he finished attacking me, knowing I would press charges against him. I wanted to confront him. I wasn't going to be his victim. But I never got a chance." She curled her hands into fists. What would she say to him if she saw him now?

"Elena, what happened to you—"

"I've tried to put it behind me. I've been able to move on with my life, and I'm no longer afraid of men."

"Then why do you react to me the way you do?"

"It's only when you catch me by surprise. Billy is a large man. Like you. He's tall and strong and hurt me so easily. I thought I had erased him from my mind. When you've done something unexpectedly, though, the memories come rushing back."

"I'm nothing like him, Elena. I would never hurt you. I couldn't. You're an incredibly brave woman, and you've been through a horrific experience," Phantom said, his voice projecting the same calm she remembered from the first day she'd met him. "It never should have happened. But if you carry that pain around with you, the weight of it will drown you. It will destroy you more effectively than Billy ever could. Burying the pain and the memories will make you vulnerable anytime a man as large as Billy gets close to you."

His words stung. *How does he know I've buried the pain? How can he presume to know what I feel?* "You don't know anything about what I've been through." The tears began to fall freely and she wiped at them angrily, hating that her emotions were getting the best of her. She had never cried like this when talking about what had happened, not even when sharing it with Anya. *Why am I letting this get to me? Billy has no power over me any longer. Neither does Phantom.* Still, a part of her had been taken the night Billy beat her. A part of the wild, free spirit she had always been.

"You don't understand." Even as she said the words, she wondered how he had been able to tap into the pain she'd thought buried and gone. She rose to her feet and grabbed for her purse. She wanted to go home.

"No," he said, and there was the hint of regret in his voice. "No, I don't understand everything about what you've been through. But I've known people who've gone through traumatic events, and I'm willing to bet this is the first time you've grieved for the loss of what you had."

How could he possibly know…? Elena grappled with her feelings. She knew the pain was all over her face—written in her tears. She'd had no idea she would react so intensely to his questions.

He stood and slowly—very, very slowly—reached down for her face. She didn't flinch from him this time. She realized distantly that her heart wasn't racing out of fear, but out of hope for something she couldn't identify. He touched her cheek and swiped the tears off one cheek, then the other.

The skin on his fingers was rough, but his touch was so gentle that she found herself wanting to lean into his hand. She had enjoyed a man's caress in the past, but the feeling of Phantom's skin on hers stirred her desire like no man's ever had before.

"I'd never hurt you, Elena."

Elena's heart pounded hard, and she was certain he could hear it. His fingers felt so good that she gave in to the temptation and leaned into his hand, laying her cheek against his palm. Then, her resolve returning, she pulled back. "I know." His eyes widened slightly at her statement. "You're nothing like him. I thought I had erased everything about him, but obviously I hadn't. I'm sorry I reacted to you that way."

"Elena, I'm not trying to make you uncomfortable, and you have nothing to apologize for. I could tell something was bothering you. No man should ever hurt a woman. You deserve to be treasured."

Elena looked back out the window, the day slipping into twilight. He hadn't pulled his hand away as she continued leaning into it, a thrill sliding down her spine as his long fingers caressed the back of her neck while his thumb rubbed gentle circles on her cheek. How long had it been since she had felt pleasure from a man's fingers? Six months? A year? She had been so busy trying to build her career that she had put everything else at the bottom of her list.

She and Phantom were working to build a business relationship together. She thought she had moved on from the pain, but he had shown her she still had a broken piece that needed to heal. Could Phantom help her put it all behind her for good? No man had ever challenged her the way he had. No man had ever tried to understand her beyond whatever it took to just have a good time together.

Elena turned away from the window and looked at Phantom. "It may not seem like it, but I'm grateful you asked me to talk about it. I hadn't realized it still had such power over me. But not anymore. You have my trust. What does that mean to you?"

"I hope it means you'll take me back as your client."

Stryker and Phantom met with the rest of the team in the conference room they had specifically built when the home had been remodeled. It sat to the side of their communications hub, an area that Buzz oversaw with multiple computer monitors, satellite feed, and every gadget a technology geek like Buzz could ever ask for. Installing and getting everything up to specifications had taken a lot of time, but the effort had been well worth it.

"Something unusual came up today at the horse show," Phantom began, and the team listened intently. A meeting wouldn't have been called if something serious hadn't happened. "I overheard a conversation about human trafficking."

Stryker sat up straighter. "What did you hear?"

"I'll break into the details on the call with Haslett. I have a serious concern that something is going down right under our noses."

At that moment, the conference phone began to ring and Phantom hit the button on the speaker. "Sir, the entire team is here."

"Good. Stryker didn't give me any information, other than it was urgent that we talk tonight." Admiral Haslett's voice came across tense and tired, but still attentive.

Phantom relayed in detail the conversation he had overheard. "Do we have any intel about a human trafficking ring operating in this area?"

"Hell, human trafficking has been going on for a long time, and there's a dedicated task force in Mexico that oversees such problems. That doesn't mean the traffickers aren't still getting across the border somehow."

"I intend to investigate it further on my end," Phantom said. "Anything you can learn through your network may help us put an end to a potentially dangerous ring."

"I will let you know," Haslett said. "Phantom, I want you to take point on this. I'll be back in touch soon."

They ended the call, and Stryker nodded to Phantom to continue. "Buzz, I'd like you to start searching on the dark web for anything regarding human trafficking or sex slaves. More often than not, women and children are sold into prostitution once they make it across the border."

"Not a problem. I'll begin running a search tonight." Buzz nodded firmly.

"I need all of you to start researching the human trafficking industry," Phantom added. "Try to network with local truck drivers to see if you pick up any details. It is obvious the victims are being shipped by large haulers, so that could be our biggest source of information."

"I'll tap into my connections within the federal government of Mexico to see if they've heard anything about a human trafficking ring operating close to south Texas," Santo volunteered.

"Good," Phantom said. "Also, check in with the judge you're friends with here in the county. She seems to always have her finger on the pulse of things."

Santo nodded, and Phantom looked around the room at the grim faces. They all knew the evil that lurked behind human trafficking rings. The thought that one was operating in their own backyard was disturbing and left them all on edge.

"This is what we are here for," Stryker said to the team. "Our main objective when we took this assignment was to keep our ears to the ground and get out among the people. We know bad things are happening, and we're seeing just as many people south of the border get hurt as here in the United States. More, even, if you consider the political upheaval so many countries are facing. Our job is to protect the border—both sides of it. Phantom has brought us the opportunity to do just that. Is everyone clear on their next steps?"

"Hooyah!"

~~~

Elena rubbed her hands on her jeans as she approached the front door of the large ranch house. Just yesterday, she had taken Phantom to the horse show and revealed her most painful memory. His reaction had not been what she had expected. Instead of showing pity, he had challenged her not to let the episode define her and weigh her down any longer.

Anya had called when Elena got home after dropping off the horse. She had been grateful that Jonas wasn't around, and she'd been able to get in and out quickly. Elena figured Anya wanted to know how the horse show had gone, but instead she'd invited her to breakfast with the entire Bent Horseshoe group the next morning.

Elena wanted to make a good impression on these men that Anya obviously cared about. She drew a deep breath and raised her hand to knock on the heavy door, but it was yanked open before she could. Anya stood in the doorway, grinning at her.

"About time you got here. What happened? You hit the snooze button too many times?"

Elena gave a startled laugh as Anya grabbed her by the arm and pulled her into the house. "It's seven in the morning! What time did you expect me to get here?"

"This *is* a ranch, remember?" Anya winked at her. "They get up before the sun."

"Yeah," said Stryker, the first man they encountered as they entered the dining room. "Not all of us get to work the easy hours like you and Phantom."

"I'll have you know there's nothing easy about our work," Phantom said, walking forward, and Elena's heart beat a little faster at the sight of him. "Good morning," he said, his gaze for her alone. "Did everything go smoothly with getting the horse back last night?"

She nodded. "Yes. No problems." He smiled at her, and she thought she might melt into the floor. His smile was dangerous. It made her crave things she shouldn't. They had barely started working together, but her thoughts kept drifting to the feeling of his skin against hers, his lips brushing her ear, his gentle compassion as he'd wiped away her tears. She thought it would be a good idea to stay focused on her job as his horse trainer.

Then again, they weren't *technically* working at the moment. And whenever they weren't working together, she gave her mind the freedom to fantasize about him as much as possible. She didn't see any harm in it as long as she stayed professional while training his horses.

"You'll get to enjoy more of Snap's good cooking," Anya said, having released her arm to lean in toward Stryker instead.

Elena forced her eyes past Phantom and struggled to

hide her surprise. The kitchen overflowed with some of the largest cowboys she had ever seen. They were all at least Phantom's size, and at least one was certainly bigger since he towered over everyone.

"Gang, look alive! We've got a guest in the house." Stryker's voice cut across the noise of all the men talking, and they turned to face her.

Anya pushed her from behind, nudging her farther into the dining room. "Good morning," Elena said, wondering if her eyes were bugging from her head.

"Of course, you met Snap already," Phantom said, "but there are also Santo, Buzz, and Brusco."

The men nodded to her cordially, and each stepped forward offering their hands to shake. She did her best to get all their names right as she greeted each of them individually. "I didn't know so many of you lived here," she finally said, unable to control her surprise any longer. "Are all of you partners in the operations of the ranch? *All* of you?"

"Yes," Stryker answered. "We've all become close friends over the years, and when the opportunity presented itself, we decided to go in together on the ranch. Plus, we've got enough elbow grease here that we don't have to hire twenty ranch hands to take care of this giant spread."

Elena nodded slowly, absorbing the information. "I don't think I've ever known such an arrangement before. Usually only a couple of people partner to run a ranch, and they still bicker and fight over minor details. You must all get along really well."

Snap laughed. "Oh, no. We bicker and fight plenty. But we've got it set up so that each of us is responsible for a certain aspect of the ranch. That way, we aren't dancing on each other's toes. It works well for us."

"Ah." Elena looked back at Phantom. "That explains why you run the horses."

He nodded, then moved toward her until he stood toe to toe with her. He leaned down and whispered loudly in her ear, "You better hurry and get some food before Snap or Buzz eats it all."

"I heard that," Snap and Buzz grumbled at the same time, and Elena laughed, turning toward the kitchen with Phantom following her.

Soon they all had loaded up on Snap's cooking and were seated around the large dining-room table. Elena had Anya on her right and Phantom on her left, and was surprised when they held out their hands to say grace over the food. She smiled as she bowed her head and listened to the short but sweet prayer of thanks. Then there was a short period of silence as everyone began to dig into the food.

"So, do you have any ranches to go out to today?" Phantom asked.

"No. That's one of the perks of being my own boss—I get most weekends off. Except, of course, on show weekends."

"How did the show go yesterday?" Anya asked from her other side.

"Terrific," Phantom answered for her. "She won in both of the classes she entered. And she taught me that I'm in desperate need of some help."

"I wouldn't say 'desperate,'" Elena offered, trying to reassure him.

"No? What would you say?"

Elena thought for several seconds, then said, "You are in *critical* need of some help," and laughed at the expression on his face.

"That's even worse than saying I'm desperate."

"Does that mean you've asked her to take your sorry ass back as a client?" Stryker asked from the head of the table.

"I've asked. She hasn't given me a solid answer yet."

Elena looked over at Phantom and saw the question in his eyes. He needed to know if she had accepted his request from the previous night. If she trusted him, she'd take him back as her client. Her heart pounded hard in her chest with fear of the unknown and excitement at the same time. "Yes. I'll take you back as my client."

He smiled brightly at her, and she smiled at him in return. They stared at each other for several seconds before one of the men asked Phantom a question, breaking the spell. His gray eyes had held her mesmerized.

Everyone ate as if they hadn't had food in years. Elena and Anya both praised Snap's cooking, which brought groans from the rest of the men about making Snap's head bigger than it already was. Elena enjoyed the banter between the men as they teased each other, and laughed and joined in when she could. She enjoyed elbowing Anya every time she started to make moon eyes at Stryker.

All too soon, breakfast ended and they began to clean up. Elena insisted she'd help and wouldn't take no for an answer. She and Phantom were assigned to clear the table, while Anya and Stryker began to do dishes. Buzz and Santo worked on storing the leftovers, which were few.

As they worked, Buzz began singing a Christmas song, making Elena hesitate as she reached for a plate. She glanced over at Phantom, one eyebrow raised. "He *does* know that it is several months until Christmas, right?"

Phantom smirked. "Try explaining that to him. He believes Christmas should be celebrated year-round."

Elena shook her head and continued her work before finally stopping and turning to face Buzz. "Are you doing that on purpose?" she asked him.

He paused in his singing. "Doing what?"

"Singing off-key and off-beat? I just wondered if you were trying to make up your own version of the song."

Phantom's deep laugh behind her took her by surprise and she turned to see him, his face full of joy as he laughed. So far, in the limited time she'd had with him, she had never heard him laugh. The sound was so delightful and happy, it made her begin to laugh too.

"Ha-ha. Very funny. You two chuckleheads enjoy your joke. Just because you can't appreciate my Christmas spirit... You're jealous, that's all."

Phantom laughed even harder, and Elena decided in that moment that she would do everything possible to hear his laugh as often as she could.

Chapter 6

PHANTOM HAD ALWAYS BEEN AN EARLY RISER, AND MONDAY proved the same. He took advantage of the time before everyone else woke up to get in his exercise in the gym they had built at the back of the house. He ran ten miles on the treadmill, then hit the weights. The entire time, his mind swirled with thoughts of Elena.

She had enchanted and enthralled the team during breakfast the previous morning. Hell, he was more captivated by her than anyone else. He felt things for her he had never felt for any other woman. He wanted to show her that a man could be kind and gentle and caring. He wanted to take away all her worries and fears. He wanted to hear her laugh and be the recipient of her incredible smiles.

He couldn't give her any of those things, though. At a moment's notice, he could be called in for a new mission that would leave her alone, wondering if he would come back alive. She deserved security and a man who could give her anything her heart desired.

His parents were madly in love. They had been married for thirty-five years and were still going strong. Their entire world revolved around each other, to the point that they neglected their children. Phantom had grown up practically raising his little sister on his own, and there seemed to be an endless string of nannies who looked after him and his sister when they were young.

Elena had him wondering if he could give her the kind of attention and adoration she deserved, considering the demands of his job. On top of that, he didn't want to become so obsessed with his partner that he failed as a parent like his own. His life revolved around the SEALs—how could he possibly be there for Elena the way she deserved?

He shook his head at himself. To even consider a relationship with her was beyond foolish. While he no longer wanted the short, meaningless flings with women he had experienced in his younger years, he didn't know how to be in a serious relationship with a woman. He didn't even know how to begin such a thing. And he didn't know why he entertained the idea of something different with Elena.

Because she's different. She is strong and independent and could be the partner to welcome you home from missions. She makes you smile—and laugh—and is giving you her trust after going through a terrible experience. You do have something to offer her. You can offer her a partner to lean on, someone who could care for her…

Gritting his teeth, he picked up a heavier set of weights. He needed to work her out of his mind. He had to stop thinking about her as anyone other than someone who could help him move his assignment forward.

He had just finished with one exercise when his cell phone rang. He grabbed a towel and wiped at his sweaty forehead before glancing at his phone, surprised to see the admiral's ID on the screen. "Yes, sir?" he answered.

"You stumbled upon some important information,"

Admiral Haslett said. "Are you in a place where you're able to talk?"

"Yes, sir. To get a phone call from you this early in the morning, I know the information isn't good."

"I wish it was. I made a few phone calls yesterday and discovered there is a human trafficking ring operating somewhere near the Texas–Mexico border, but they constantly move, making it hard to pin them down. The authorities in Mexico have been working the case for months and haven't been successful in stopping the traffickers yet."

"I assume the agencies on our side are involved as well, if it's been going on for so long."

"They are. But they, too, keep hitting a brick wall. Last week, a shipment of at least thirty victims made it all the way to Austin. They were gone by the time U.S. agencies had enough intel to move in. This group works with deadly precision and speed."

"I suppose since there are already agencies working on it, we can't touch it." Phantom sighed.

"No. We've been asked to go into a black op on this one. It's going to be blind. We're not going to know who we're working with in Mexico until we get there. But we're running point on the American side."

"Good. Do we know where we need to target in Mexico?"

"No. We're going to have to wait for the traffickers to gather up victims for another shipment. It's a crappy way to do it, but we have to catch these bastards trafficking people. Otherwise they could get off on a technicality."

Phantom frowned at the phone. "We'll continue doing our research on our end."

"Speaking of that, have Buzz start combing the dark web. Specifically have him look for anything that looks like the communication he saw from the drug deal."

Unease slipped down Phantom's spine. "I already have Buzz checking for any discussions about human trafficking. Is there something else you've come across?"

"The files were sent to me electronically late last night. There were several pages of coded communication. I hate to tell you this, Phantom, but the code looks identical to the code the drug ring was using."

Phantom's mind raced with possibilities. "Do you think the two cases are tied? Do you think this could be someone who also worked with the drug lord?"

"I think there are too many similarities for us to ignore. I've sent the files over to you for review. Show Buzz the coded pages and see what he thinks. We could be going up against a much bigger organization than we originally thought."

Phantom ended the call and headed back to his room to take a shower. The team would be up soon. He needed to be ready to sit down with them and have a difficult conversation. The nightmare they thought had ended when the drug lord had been killed could just be beginning.

Thirty minutes later, he joined the team in the dining room, grabbing a large mug of coffee. He had struggled to sleep, and after his early-morning phone call, he needed anything to help him stay alert for the long day ahead.

"What's the matter, bro?" Santo smirked at him. "Some curly-headed beauty haunt your dreams all night?"

Phantom narrowed his eyes at his friend. "I slept just fine, thanks."

"Sure. It's written all over your face. Why don't you just admit that you like her? Hell, I know I do."

"What's that supposed to mean?" Phantom nearly growled.

Santo raised an eyebrow. "It means I think she's a great gal and I enjoyed having her around. Jealous much?"

Phantom schooled his features and forced his emotions to go into hiding. "There's nothing to be jealous about. I'm glad you like her. The two of you seemed to really hit it off yesterday." It had irritated him how easily Elena interacted with Santo, and how animated and engaged Santo had been with her. It didn't make sense for him to feel such things if he didn't have feelings for Elena, and he had already convinced himself that was a bad idea for both Elena and himself.

"So you wouldn't mind if I asked her out?" Santo asked, a teasing quality to his voice. Phantom knew his friend wanted to get a rise out of him.

He shrugged. "Do what you want."

"You aren't fooling any of us, you know." Snap joined in. "We can all tell the two of you have chemistry off the charts."

"Don't go ruining things for me," Santo said, elbowing Snap hard in the side. "I might have a chance with her."

"Yeah, right." Snap laughed. "There was only one person she was interested in yesterday morning. Phantom."

Phantom wanted to smile at the comment, but knew

he couldn't—shouldn't—feel good about such a thing. He cleared his throat. "There's something I need to talk to all of you about." The seriousness of his tone drew everyone's attention, and they moved to join him at the dining room table. "I got a call from Haslett this morning. Things have gotten considerably more interesting since Saturday night."

⸺⫯⫯⸻

The tack room desperately needed an overhaul. Elena couldn't believe how much dust had accumulated in the month she had been gone from the ranch. She put the horses out on the different lunge lines to get them started with their exercise while she devoted her attention to the dirty halters, bridles, and saddles.

Soon she scrubbed vigorously with saddle soap, working hard to remove the grime, and knew she had made the right decision to wear her sturdiest work clothes. Dirt and the buildup of dust from the past few weeks covered her shirt and jeans. The heat of the day gathered rapidly, and drops of sweat slid down her back and between her breasts. Using her forearm, she rubbed away the trickles that threatened to roll down into her eyes.

By the time she had finished cleaning all the saddles and prepping all the tack for buffing and polishing, Elena desperately needed a break for some water. She stepped out into the breezeway of the barn and guzzled water from her large, insulated mug, then poured some over her head, enjoying the feeling of the cool fluid trickling down her skin.

"You look like you could use a break."

Elena jumped at the sound of Phantom's voice, then

forced herself to take a deep breath. She had never known a man capable of moving so silently. She felt the tingle of heat in her cheeks, telling her she blushed from the embarrassment of being found dumping water on herself. Especially in front of him.

She hastily wiped her face and smiled up at him. "This *is* my break."

"Have I let things fall into such a serious state of affairs that this is all you can afford for a break?"

Elena chuckled, smoothing her wayward curls back from her face. "I knew you were going to be a difficult client. I had no idea it would be this taxing," she teased. She could see the tension in his face and knew something was gnawing at him. She wanted to see him smile, and more than anything she wanted to hear his laugh again.

For a moment, it seemed he would smile. "At least you're honest about it. I know I've neglected the tack room a bit."

"Oh, just a bit." She glanced pointedly down at her grimy hands and delighted in the half smile that he gave her in return. "But don't worry. I think I finally have it all straightened out. You're more than welcome to take a look if you'd like."

"I trust you," he said, the half smile gone, his eyes assessing her. "Did you enjoy getting to meet everyone yesterday?"

"Yes. I can see how close you are to all of them. Now I understand what you meant when you said you had some friends you considered brothers. I'm an only child and never got to experience the good-natured ribbing and joking around I saw yesterday."

"What makes you think we were joking? We were being serious with every insult."

Elena laughed and shook her head. "I was about to take the horses off the lunge lines. Care to go for a ride? They could use a change of scenery."

A smile lit up his face, transforming it. "Absolutely."

Several minutes later, they were headed away from the barn on two of the best horses on the ranch. "Is this part of your usual training routine?" he asked.

"No. But you looked like you needed to get away from it all."

Phantom looked over at her. "What made you think that?"

"The corners of your eyes get tight when something's bothering you. You did that when I was telling you... When we were driving back from the horse show." She didn't want to bring up her story again. Once had been enough.

Phantom's eyebrow lifted. "You're far too perceptive for your own good, you know that?"

"Oh, really?" Elena smiled at him. "Just because I finally figured out your most basic tell? I've barely gotten used to your smiles."

His lips twitched. "I don't smile."

Elena shook her head. "Do you know how to reach the back forty acres?" she asked, her voice light and teasing.

"I *am* part owner of this ranch." He arched an eyebrow at her.

The late-afternoon hum of bugs surrounded them in the hot Texas sun, and she flashed him one of her brightest smiles. "Good. Last one to get there is a rotten egg." She laughed at his shout of surprise, leaning over her horse's neck and urging it forward. The wind whipped across her sweat-dampened face, carrying the scent of dust and mesquite. She moved farther forward over the horse's withers, the coarse mane brushing against her skin.

Weaving in and out of the trees, Elena guided her horse toward the back forty, leaning low over its neck and encouraging it to run faster. She was startled when she noticed Phantom from the corner of her eye, riding up fast on her left side. He was shooting in and out of the shrubbery, also leaning low and effortlessly encouraging his horse to move at a speed she hadn't thought possible with Phantom's tall, muscular weight added to its load.

She encouraged her mare to move even faster, standing up in the stirrups and leaning forward, tangling her hands in the equine's mane. When she rounded the next tree, though, she was shocked to see Phantom edging ahead of her. She nudged her horse with her heels, but it wasn't enough.

Phantom pulled up at the fence and waited there, a large smile across his face. It was the happiest she had ever seen him, and the competitive streak in her took a back seat to the joy she felt from the ride. He was laughing again, and excitement zinged through her. She, too, was laughing by the time she stopped her horse alongside his, turning so she could face him directly.

"I would like to be extremely ticked that you just beat me, but I forgot I was going up against a man who used to train racehorses." She smiled up at him.

"You did that on purpose." He was still smiling broadly at her.

"If you are trying to imply that I let you win, you are sorely mistaken. I fought as hard as I possibly could to beat you. Now, if you're referring to the fact that I could tell you needed to let off a little steam…" She shrugged. "Guilty as charged." They were close to each other, their horses breathing heavily, and she couldn't get enough of his smile.

"Elena…you are an amazing woman. You realize that, don't you?"

Elena's breath caught in her throat. The way he looked at her made her long for the feeling of his skin touching hers again, even though she knew her thoughts were far from professional. But, oh, how she wanted it. If only he did too…

And suddenly they were kissing, his mouth pressed to hers, and she was kissing him back. The feel of his firm lips brought her warmth that had nothing to do with the late-afternoon sun.

The movement of their horses caused them to break apart, and they both stared at each other. Elena knew she was breathing as heavily as her horse, and her lips felt tender. Her eyes searched Phantom's face. *Which one of us started that?* All she could think about was tasting him, inhaling his unique scent that reminded her of the leather saddle soap she had just been using and his own warm musk.

He watched her as closely as she watched him. Slowly he licked his lips, and she felt the breath shudder out of her. "You taste like cherries." His tone wasn't the same easy coolness that she had grown accustomed to. The husky sound wrapped around her and made every nerve ending in her body spring to life.

"Do you like cherries?"

"On you I do," he replied softly. "Elena…"

Her heart pounded in her chest. She didn't know what his next words were going to be, and she didn't know if she wanted to hear them, whether they were to ask for another kiss or apologize for the one they had just shared. She shook her head. "Let's not make any excuses for what just happened. It was amazing. Let's leave it at that."

He shook his head in return. "I just got to kiss a beautiful woman, and she kissed me back. I don't see the need for any excuses."

She felt a blush burning up her neck to her cheeks. "Good. I like your smile. Your laugh is something I'm growing particularly fond of, though I've only heard it a couple of times. You should do it more often."

"I get the feeling that isn't going to be hard to do with you around. Now, what do I get if I beat you back to the barn?"

Chapter 7

As a Congressman, his schedule never stayed the same. One day he would meet with constituents, the next he would be arguing the merits of the next bill up for vote with his fellow party members. He rarely had a moment to himself, and it seemed everywhere he turned, there was a reporter hoping to either catch him saying something that could make him look bad, or wanting an exclusive statement from him about current legislation.

To make a private phone call on an untraceable phone seemed impossible. Fortunately, he had connections in the right places that got a clean burner cell to him, and he took a leisurely stroll in the Botanic Garden. The line was picked up after two rings, and he cringed at the sound of the voice of an older woman who had obviously smoked her entire life. "I'm calling for Barbados," he said, using the code name he had given his contact. "Please let him know the Puppet Master is calling."

There was the sound of the phone being handed over to someone else, and he could hear the woman coughing grotesquely as she walked away. He shuddered and had the inclination to touch his face to make sure no spittle had landed on him through the phone. At least *she* wasn't the one he needed to talk to. He didn't know if he'd be able to get through the conversation without gagging.

"This is Barbados." The voice of a middle-aged man came over the line.

"I was beginning to wonder if something had happened to you," the Congressman said, forcing cheerfulness into his voice that he didn't feel. If anything, he had bypassed pissed and teetered on the edge of enraged.

"Yes, sir. I'm sorry. I know I'm supposed to check in with you frequently. It's just that—"

"Do I strike you as the type of person who wants to hear excuses right now?" the Congressman asked, forcing his voice to remain light.

"No. No, of course not, sir. It's just…I think we're being watched."

The Congressman nearly stumbled in his slow, leisurely walk, but quickly regained his composure. "What makes you think so?"

"The men have been getting increasingly uneasy. We've been in the same spot for days, and usually we're on the move by now. I know you're trying to get a larger shipment this time…" The man let his voice trail off, obviously hoping he was about to receive some answers.

"Have you seen anyone? Has anyone been acting odd? Are you keeping people stationed at all the key locations I told you about?"

"Sí, I mean, yes. Yes, we've done everything as you instructed. As far as I can tell, there aren't any new faces hovering around, but you know how large the city is. People come and go so quickly."

"You're being paranoid. The location I found for you provides more than adequate coverage unless you've done something to warrant attention."

"No! No, we've stayed inside unless there are others we need to get."

"You are supposed to call me every other day with a

status report. It's why I gave you a burner phone, and why I text you a new message every few days with a new number for me. When I don't hear from you, what am I supposed to think?"

"I'm sorry, sir. It won't happen again."

The Congressman sighed heavily and pinched the bridge of his nose in frustration. He needed to find more competent workers. Too often lately he was disappointed by the men and women working for him. Only weeks ago, his major breadwinner, a drug cartel in Mexico, had been mysteriously gunned down, and its leader—someone he had at one time considered an ally, perhaps even a friend—had been killed on U.S. soil.

Even with all his connections, the Congressman couldn't get much information on what had really happened to the drug lord, Benicio Davila. All he could find were documents indicating that a drug deal had gone terribly wrong. He knew Benicio didn't involve himself with the day-to-day operations of selling the drugs. For some reason, an elaborate cover-up had been concocted, and he had yet to solve the mystery of why.

"What is the status, Barbados? Where do we stand in achieving our goals?"

"We have twenty women so far, fifteen young girls and a handful of boys, and about ten men that will do well for manual labor."

The Congressman sighed heavily into the phone. "You still need to get me at least ten more women. The demand this time is high, and we're going to capitalize on it."

"Just give me some time, sir. I just need a little more time."

"How much is a little more, Barbados? Do you need to broaden your search area?"

"I already have, and we're having a lot more success. There are a lot of women refugees from Venezuela who are perfect to take. And they're already so tired from fleeing their country, they put up very little fight."

"Good. Keep getting them together, and I'll let you know when we are ready to move them. It probably won't be for another couple of weeks."

"A couple of weeks? Sir, with all the respect in the world, we can't afford to stay in hiding in the same location for so long. Someone is bound to find us."

"Can the women or children be heard yelling or screaming outside the building?"

"No."

"Are you or your men doing anything that draws attention to you?"

"No."

"Then you have nothing to worry about. There's a reason I chose this location. You aren't directly in the city like you have been the last few times. It keeps your exposure minimized. If your men stick to the plan, all will be fine."

"Yes, sir."

"And Barbados?"

"Sir?"

"If I have to be the one to reach out to you for a status report again, it will be the last phone call you ever get."

Elena had an incredibly hectic schedule. Too hectic, in Phantom's opinion. She came out to the Bent Horseshoe

Ranch three days a week—Mondays, Wednesdays, and Fridays. The other two days she set aside for the other ranches she supported. He knew she had two in Laredo, an hour away from the Bent Horseshoe, two more on ranches within thirty to forty-five minutes of Hebbronville, and one client in Corpus. He had no idea how she juggled it all.

Still, she seemed full of energy and enthusiasm whenever he saw her. And from the look in her eyes this time, she had plans for mischief today too. It was Friday and she had come out to the ranch early, grooming the horses, mucking their stalls, and then putting them on the lunge lines for warm-up.

"You want to do what now?" Phantom asked, trying to make sense of what she had said.

"I want to teach you how to ride for a western performance class."

He shook his head. "I know how to ride. I think we already established that, didn't we?"

It was the first time either of them had brought up their wild ride from a couple of days ago, and he could tell from the faint blush on her cheeks that she was remembering their kiss. Hell, he hadn't been able to get it out of his mind. All he could seem to think about was the sweet flavor of fresh cherries. He wanted more.

"You may know how to ride fast, but riding for a western performance class is far different."

"Why do I need to learn this? Don't you do all the competitions?" He wasn't opposed to learning something new. Elena tempted him like no other woman ever had, which put him in a difficult position. He wanted to keep their newly built professional relationship, but he also wanted to kiss her again. And from the way she acted around him, her eyes always on him and her smile warm, he felt fairly certain she wanted the same thing.

So then, what's the problem? *If she wants your touch, your kiss, then by word, who are you to keep it from her?*

"Let me ask you this… What is your vision for your quarter horses? What do you want to do with this part of the business?"

No one had asked him that. When Stryker had asked him to join the special ops team, Phantom had agreed without hearing the perks. When he learned he would be in charge of the operations of their quarter-horse business, he had realized he could be living his dream. Working with horses again—while still serving his country—had been something he thought would be impossible.

"I want to make it a very lucrative business. We have an incredible black stallion and five brood mares that aren't being used. I want to build up the breeding side of the business and make it so that people start coming to us to get their high-quality show animals." As the person in charge of the horse program of a thriving ranch, what he had listed were exactly the things people would expect him to want. As an undercover SEAL, he wanted whatever involvement was necessary to get him access to more intel. He couldn't tell Elena those details, though.

"What's your plan to bring in these customers?"

"I'll advertise, I suppose. It was easy to get customers when we were racing."

She arched an eyebrow. "Really? Why is that?"

"Because thousands of people saw our horses

winning the races, and…" Light bulb. *Damn*. Her presence had a profound impact on him, sending his brain on temporary vacation whenever he heard her voice or caught the intoxicating scent of her skin. "I get where you're going with this. But I still don't see what that has to do with me learning a different way to ride."

"As it is right now, I can only show one horse at a time. You have four incredible horses. Two of them came from those brood mares and that black stallion. If I had you showing the horses with me, we could at least double what we're doing now. And if any of your friends here wanted to help, we could show all four. Think about the impact we could make!"

Her enthusiasm brought a smile to his face. "You think you can get me to show the horses? I'll flub the whole thing."

"Not if you let me train you."

He took a step closer to her and she licked her lips, her cherry-flavored lips. He ached to taste her again, which told him he was treading in dangerous waters. "You're going to train me as well as my horses? Is this going to cost me extra?"

Something flashed in her eyes as she looked at him, and she bit her lower lip, tilting her head to the side. "It might. Are you going to be a difficult student?"

She was teasing him. She was flirting with him. He moved even closer to her, so close that if she drew in a deep breath, her body would brush against his. He really wanted her to try it. "I'm always difficult."

He saw the muscles in her delicate neck work as she swallowed. "Perhaps we can work out some type of arrangement."

"Elena," he whispered before his head dropped. He lightly brushed his lips over hers, barely tasting her sweetness. Her hands lifted to press against his chest, and for a moment he feared she would push him away. But she leaned against him instead, tilting her chin so that he could deepen the kiss, and he groaned with pleasure.

His arm slid around her narrow waist and he pulled her against him, his other hand sliding into her soft curls and cupping her head. His lips pressed tightly to hers, moving hungrily, gently demanding more. Her breath escaped her in a soft sigh and her lips parted, allowing him to slowly slide his tongue along her lower lip.

Her hands flexed against his chest, then slid up and around his neck. When her tongue tentatively touched his, a bolt of lightning rushed through him. How could such a little woman disrupt all his senses? She smelled as if she had just been rolling in Texas wildflowers, and her lips still tasted like fresh cherries. Everything about her seemed to call to him on a primal level. He wanted her more than he knew he should, yet he couldn't deny the way his body reacted to the feeling of her curves pressed along him.

Worried she would run if she knew exactly what he wanted to do with her, he reluctantly pulled his head back. Her breasts rubbed against his chest, their bodies fitting together so perfectly. Looking down, he could see her nipples pressing against her work shirt, and he wanted to groan.

"Phantom?" she asked softly, her voice husky with desire. Good. At least she felt a little of the same passion he did.

He drew in a deep breath and realized his hand still

held her long tresses. He had known her hair would be incredibly soft and enjoyed the way it seemed to wrap around his fingers in a lover's embrace. "So...I think you were trying to suggest some sort of arrangement before we got a little distracted." He struggled to draw in a deep breath.

"What makes you think this wasn't the type of arrangement I was trying to suggest?"

"Elena..." He wondered if he could go insane with the desire pulsing through him. "Do you realize the way you tempt me? You're playing with me."

She leaned back against the stall behind her and watched him with eyes full of curiosity and desire. "Do you think I'm playing?"

"I think I may be losing my mind, that's what I think. Either that or I'm asleep right now. Because you only look at me like that in my dreams." His heart pounded so hard he felt certain she could hear it.

"Do you really dream about me? Because I dream about you. I've been wondering if the kiss we had a few days ago was just in my imagination. I've never had a kiss make me feel the things I felt when we kissed. It had to be my imagination working overtime. But now..." Her voice trailed off and the corners of her mouth lifted. "Now I know another kiss from you can be even more amazing than that first one."

He still hadn't pulled his hands away from her, and he stood close enough that he could still feel her enticing body pressed along his, something he knew would haunt him in future dreams of her. "Elena, you can't realize the things you're saying right now." Oh, but he wanted her to mean every single one.

She blinked and swallowed hard. "You don't feel the same way?"

Aw, hell. He couldn't stay away from her even if he tried. And he wanted only to get closer. His lips fell to hers again as he crushed their bodies together, pushing her back against the stall wall. There was nothing gentle or coaxing about this kiss. It was demanding and urgent, and when her lips parted, his tongue slid inside, tasting her depths.

She responded to his urgency with her own, her tongue sliding against his, and he couldn't contain his moan of pleasure. His hand slid from around her waist to cup her ass, lifting her slightly. She made a small sound of surprise and he smiled against her lips, then trailed kisses across her cheek until he reached her ear. "Do you have any idea what you do to me, Elena?" he whispered.

Her arms circled around his shoulders, and she flexed her hips. The air rushed out of him as her lithe body rubbed against him. Her lips brushed against his ear, just as his had brushed against hers. "I have a general idea," she whispered back.

Phantom wanted nothing more than to take her right then and there, up against the stall. But he wouldn't. She had suffered a terrible trauma in the barn where they stood, and that realization dampened his raging desire. He would make sure their time together would be memorable and special. If only his body would get the message and calm down.

Slowly, he let her slide down and freed his hand from her curls, settling both his hands on her waist. She looked up at him in confusion, her beautiful brown eyes full of questions. "Phantom?"

His eyes searched her face. This woman wanted him. And he was about to tell her no. He was either the biggest fool in the world or deserved to be granted sainthood for the strength of his resolve. "You deserve…" His brows pulled together as he heard his own words. She deserved a man far better than him. She deserved a man who would be there for her all the time, someone who wouldn't vanish on her at a moment's notice.

An ache he had never felt before settled in his chest. He wanted her to have everything she deserved, and he couldn't offer any guarantees. He clenched his jaw, his muscles tightening as he fought what his body craved. "You deserve far better. I'm sorry, Elena, I never should have taken advantage—"

This time she did shove him, her hands pushing against his chest. Where there had been confusion and lingering desire a moment before, fury had taken over. "You didn't take advantage of anything. I took what I wanted. And I would've taken more." She shook her head. "I thought what just happened between us was…" She drew a deep breath and ran her trembling fingers through her curls. She schooled her features as she lifted her eyes to his face. "I thought what just happened was absolutely incredible, and I'd do it over again in a heartbeat if I had the chance. But not if it's going to leave you making lame excuses about what you think I need or attempting to protect me from you. I started it. And you can certainly consider it finished."

Chapter 8

PHANTOM RARELY CRAVED ALCOHOL, BUT AFTER HIS RUN-IN with Elena the day before, he wondered if a good shot of Texas moonshine would help his wayward emotions. He wiped at the sweat on his forehead with his forearm. Instead of burying his head in a bottle of Texas Jalapeño Spirits, his favorite from the Hill Country Distillers located southwest of Austin, he had thrown himself into work in the barn.

The plan had backfired on him. He thought he would be so invested in his work—mucking out stalls and doing minor repairs that had been needed for a long time—that he wouldn't be concerned with Elena. He hadn't counted on the way his memories of their passionate embrace would consume him every time he walked past the stall where he had held her.

Phantom had no doubt in his mind that he had hurt her, which had been the last thing he intended. His actions had been purely for the sake of protecting her from a situation that could only lead to heartache. He had seen the flash of pain in her eyes, though, and knew he had approached it all wrong. He wondered if he had hurt the fragile trust he had started to build with her.

They needed to keep things professional. He had been telling himself that since Elena left the night before. It still didn't sit well with him. He couldn't deny any longer that he felt something for her, more than he could afford to feel. Ever since she had left, his mind had kept yelling all the reasons a relationship with Elena could hold her back from pursuing her dreams and, worse, expose her to heartache if one day he didn't return alive from a mission.

He finished hammering in a board to replace one a horse had kicked out of the stall while hyped up on the sweet feed Phantom had given all the quarter horses when he first joined the ranch. Elena had pointed out the error of his ways, and he had dismissed her as his trainer. He smiled to himself. He had convinced her to take him back, and he had to stay on as her client. She was his direct connection to information about the human trafficking.

He enjoyed a long shower, looking forward to a cold beer and to relaxing after a long day of hard work. He had just entered the kitchen when he heard Buzz's heavy footsteps enter the room. "For a SEAL, your stealth needs some serious work." Phantom smirked, turning to face the large man.

Even though Phantom stood over six feet, Buzz stood a couple of inches taller. With arms as large around as most big men's thighs, he certainly intimidated most people. "I figure you have enough stealth to make up for me." Buzz grinned.

"I think I'll tell Stryker that's what we need to work on in our next set of drills."

"Great. You've given me something to look forward to." Buzz's smile slowly faded. "You know the paperwork Haslett sent over to you? We've hit pay dirt."

Phantom lifted his eyebrows. "You found something?"

"More than just a little something. I'll wait for you in

the conference room. It's going to take some explaining to get us all on the same page."

"Let me grab Santo and Stryker. They're going to be the ones running this mission on the ground when and if we go into Mexico."

"Oh, I'd bet my left nut you're headed to Mexico."

"I wouldn't make that kind of bet if I were you." Phantom grinned. "You never want to bet something that valuable."

A few minutes later, Phantom gathered in the conference room with the top two men he wanted with him in this fight—Santo and Stryker. He trusted all the SEALs, but Stryker was his friend and team leader, and Santo had been his closest friend since his first day in BUD/S training. If it hadn't been for Santo, Phantom didn't know how he would have made it through Hell Week. Phantom grabbed Derek "Brusco" Delgado and Snap as well, wanting the entire team brought up to speed.

"What have you found out, Buzz?" Phantom asked as they all sat down.

"Several of the pages that you received have the same code we discovered while tracking the drug cartel in Mexico. I've been digging into the dark web to find the forums these messages could have been posted to, but I haven't found them yet. The information from these files paints a grim picture, though."

"What have you been able to decipher so far?" Santo asked.

"The discussion gives instructions about moving a large group of victims, women and children. The traffickers operated somewhere near the border, but they moved frequently, making it virtually impossible to pin them down. Two days after they crossed the border, their holding facility was found in Matamoros, Mexico, right across the border from Brownsville, Texas. The victims were hauled in box trailers from there to Austin. The team in Mexico had been hot on their trail, but reached the facility too late."

"They weren't able to track them?" Phantom asked, feeling as if his hands were tied behind his back.

"They only got so far. Once the traffickers entered the United States, they split up, driving off for Austin in different directions. I have to say, they carefully orchestrated the plan to get these victims delivered." Buzz sighed.

"Are you picking up any chatter about a future transaction taking place?" Phantom asked, craving the liquor even more strongly than before.

"I came across a hit just before I went to find you. It's minor, but there's a new discussion posted about gathering women and children to bring into the United States. There's no disclosure on a location, but I think I've finally found the right thread to start watching."

"I need to pull Haslett into the loop and find out if he's heard anything else on his end." Phantom knew this mission had many innocent lives at stake. The fate of those lives lay in his hands and the success of the mission.

"You know you can come to me if you need anything," Stryker said, clapping a hand on Phantom's back as he stood. "You're doing a great job running with this already."

Phantom nodded and watched the others leave the conference room so he could place the call. With a heavy sigh, he pulled out his cell phone and hit the quick dial for Haslett. He hoped the admiral had been able to gather further intel. They needed to take action, and quickly. The countdown had already started for this newest batch of victims.

———

"It's Thursday night, and you know places are bound to be hopping. I need to move. I need to dance. I need to hang with my two best friends!"

Anya's call couldn't have come at a better time. Elena had finished a long day working at the ranch in Corpus, and even though she felt she could fall asleep standing up, she needed to escape the thoughts that continued to whirl through her mind. She needed to take some time for herself, and what better way than a night out with her girlfriends?

"Have you already talked to Evie?"

Anya laughed on the other end of the line. "Evie's idea of a night out is getting takeout for dinner instead of eating a frozen meal. Of course she's in. Now, I won't take any excuses from you. I don't want to hear that you're too tired, or that you have to get up early in the morning or any of the other thousands of things you've said the last five times I've asked you for a girls' night out."

"It has not been five times!" Elena sputtered, digging through her closet for something to wear. She gnawed on her lower lip. It *had* been a long time since they had gone out together.

"Evie and I are picking you up in less than an hour. You better be ready."

"Yes. Fine, yes, I'll go with you. But I really *do* have

to get up early in the morning, so we can't stay out too late."

"Did you just say yes? I think I'm going to die from shock. Evie's never going to believe this. All right, I'm going to go now before you start rethinking your decision and change your mind. See you soon. Bye!"

Elena chuckled as she tossed her phone on the bed and began to get ready. A distraction was exactly what the doctor had ordered. She needed to be with her girl-friends to laugh and talk and not remember how morti-fied she'd been that she had misinterpreted Phantom's reaction.

He *had* kissed her back. He *had* grabbed ahold of her and made it very obvious to her how his body felt about the idea of sleeping with her. His mind, on the other hand, seemed to be the problem. Why? His beginnings of an excuse that she deserved someone better had been a bunch of bullshit. It had been an easy cop-out, and it ticked her off.

She didn't know why it made her so angry. If he wanted to keep things between them strictly profes-sional, fine. She could understand that logic. She just wanted him to come out and say that was the reason he didn't want to be intimate with her, not give her trite excuses that only made her feel worse about the whole thing.

Truth be told, she had come on to him. She had initi-ated the flirting and even the kisses. But he had certainly followed through. Up until the point he had stopped everything.

Elena chose a silk blouse she hadn't worn in years and had found hiding in the back of her closet. Showing more cleavage than she normally did, it hugged her curves and defined her narrow waist. She wore a pair of black, starched jeans along with it, and a pair of boots she saved for special events, so they didn't have a scratch on them. She had never been the type of woman to wear heels to go out and wasn't about to start.

Anya and Evie arrived less than an hour later, knocking on her door and chattering loudly. Elena swung the door open and gave her friends a disapproving look. "You know the Bells go to sleep early. Don't wake them up." The Bell family lived in the main house, renting out the apartment over their garage to Elena since all their children had moved out.

"Sorry," Evie whispered. "I forgot."

Evie made Elena think of pixies or fairies every time she saw her. With blond hair and bright-blue eyes, she was petite and had a delicate bone structure. Elena and Anya had met Evie in college and had bonded with her almost instantly, even though Evie was a couple of years younger than they were. With Anya fast-tracking through veterinary school, Elena had graduated around the same time Evie had. It had been incredible for them all to end up in the same small town.

Trying to be as quiet as possible, Elena locked up and they hurried down the stairs from her apartment and into Elena's truck. "Since I have to be up early tomorrow, I'll be the designated driver and watch the two of you get drunk." She grinned as she backed out of the drive.

"You aren't the only one with responsibilities, you know." Evie sighed. Then she winked at them. "But I requested a personal day for tomorrow, so I can have as much fun as I want tonight."

The women laughed. "Then let the fun begin!" Anya cheered.

Hebbronville and the surrounding small towns didn't have much of a night life, so they headed for Laredo, an hour away. The entire drive, Evie kept them entertained with stories of the latest antics she'd witnessed at the courthouse where she worked as an assistant to the county judge. From bizarre crimes to insane pleas of innocence, the stories kept them laughing nearly the entire way, and Elena could feel the tension in her shoulders easing.

Since it was a Thursday night, their favorite club wasn't as crowded as usual, and they found a booth right away. While Elena sipped on a Coke, Evie and Anya chose mixed drinks. Anya sighed with pleasure at the first sip.

"I've been needing this for so long! Being surrounded by men all the time has its perks, but I needed my girls!"

Evie fixed her blue eyes on Anya in a way they all knew meant inescapable questions were coming. "Since you seem to hardly have any time for us anymore, fill us in on this love of your life. What's he like? Tall, dark, and handsome?"

Anya grinned. "Ask Elena. She's met him."

Evie turned her attention to Elena. "Spill. Tell me all. I want to know if he's suitable enough for our girl here."

Elena laughed. "I like him. And, yes, he's tall, dark, and handsome. In a rugged kind of way. He only has eyes for Anya when she's in the room."

"I know you met him as the veterinarian for his ranch, but how did it lead to love?" Evie sipped on her drink.

With a whimsical smile, Anya shrugged. "We spent a lot of time together and got to know each other. He is kind and caring, and even though he's a big man, he's so gentle."

"All of them are big men," Elena muttered, thinking about Phantom and the way he had held her, the feeling of his muscles bunching under her hands. *Damn it! He's not a part of girls' night. Forget about him.*

"What do you mean by 'all of them'? Exactly how many guys are there?"

"Six," Elena and Anya said at the same time.

"No wonder you needed a break." Evie shook her head. "That much testosterone is bound to be unhealthy to be around."

Anya laughed. "I can hook you up with one if you'd like. They're all really great guys."

"I'm sure they are, but you know I don't do the whole dating thing." Evie waved her hand dismissively.

"Just because you had one relationship go sour on you doesn't mean all guys are bad," Elena said gently.

"Tell me—if the man you had been dating since high school left you standing at the altar a month after graduating college, would you be that eager to date again?" Evie raised her eyebrows when they didn't respond to her. "I didn't think so."

"You know, if I remember correctly, after that happened we all agreed to swear off relationships—including you, Anya," Elena teased, reminding Anya of the pact they had made.

"Are you going to let that go? I'm in love. Y'all should be happy for me!"

Elena reached across the table and grabbed her friend's hand. "I am. I really am. But you can't blame me for wanting to give you a hard time any chance I get."

Evie reached over and grabbed both of their hands. "From here on, let that pact be null and void. We deserve to find happiness someday. Anya, I'm glad that day has come for you."

"Thanks." Anya smiled brightly, then turned her attention on Elena. "What about you? Any of the guys at the ranch catch your fancy now that you've met them all?"

Elena swallowed hard and shook her head. "No. They're all great guys, don't get me wrong. I just don't think any of them are meant for me."

Anya shrugged. "You never know. Just give it time." At that moment, "Boot Scootin' Boogie" began to play over the speakers, and Anya's eyes lit up. "All right, girls, let's dance!"

Elena didn't get home until nearly two in the morning. Fortunately, Anya barely drank and was able to drive herself home after they dropped Evie off at her apartment in town, saving Elena the extra drive. She groaned when her alarm went off a handful of hours later. She made herself a thermos of coffee and got ready to head out to the Bent Horseshoe.

Her emotions fluctuated between firm determination to forget what had happened between her and Phantom and nervous anticipation about how he would act around her. She stared in the mirror as she pulled her hair into a high ponytail. "You've got this," she said to her image, giving herself a pep talk. "You're a professional. Now act like one."

For the first hour out at the ranch, Phantom was nowhere to be seen. Could he be deliberately avoiding her? It wouldn't surprise her. She couldn't help but feel disappointed, though. She wanted him to start showing the horses. She knew it would not only be good for his business, but hers as well.

After mucking out all the stalls and giving each horse a quick brush, she pulled out one of her favorites and began to saddle him. She concentrated on her work, trying her best to block out all thoughts of Phantom. She couldn't help it, though, as her eyes kept wandering over to the stall where she had experienced the most passionate kiss of her life.

"Good morning."

His voice startled her and she jumped, which spooked the horse. The gelding danced sideways, pulling on the lead line that held it tied to the side of the stall, and slammed into Elena, knocking her backward. She frantically tried to maintain her balance, but the world tilted and she landed hard on her back, the air knocked from her lungs. Still fighting the line that tethered it, the gelding moved in her direction, and she realized she was about to get stomped on.

Strong arms that she remembered all too well wrapped around her and yanked her away from the horse. She struggled to draw air into her lungs, furious with herself for letting just his voice affect her so strongly. Slowly, she regained her breath and realized she was in his lap and he was rubbing her back soothingly.

"I'm sorry. I didn't mean to scare you." He looked contrite.

"No, no," she said, shaking her head. She pushed herself up and away from him. "I've just had more coffee than usual this morning, and it's made me jumpy. It's not your fault." She shoved herself to her feet and walked to the gelding—who had begun to calm some—and patted him on the shoulder, murmuring gently to him.

Phantom stood as well and raked a hand through his hair as he watched her. She flashed him a smile. "Seriously, it wasn't your fault. Besides, your timing is perfect."

"Really? Why is that?"

"Because today we start your training to show the horses. This gelding would be the perfect one for you to show."

Phantom gazed at the horse skeptically. "You were being serious about the idea of training me how to show?"

"The sooner we get started, the sooner you'll be able to enter competitions. I think you're going to really enjoy it." She turned back to the horse, unable to make eye contact with Phantom. She hoped she had the strength to get through the rest of the day. How was she supposed to train him when just looking at him reminded her how incredible their kiss had been?

Chapter 9

"THE WAY YOU SIT ON THE HORSE GIVES IT CUES ON HOW TO move. I've spent a lot of time with these horses, training them to respond the right way."

"It sounds similar to racing. We'd lean forward over the horse's neck to cue it to go faster and lean one way or another to guide it through turns or to pass another racehorse."

"That's exactly right. It can be even more precise with show horses. Just the lightest, smallest shift of your weight can cue your horse to pick up a jog or a lope, come to a stop, and even back up, without you using your legs or even the reins. I try to use the reins as little as possible. They should only come into play if your horse isn't responding to the cues your body is giving it." *Kinda like the way I misread the cues your body was giving me Wednesday.*

Elena forced her mind on the task at hand. She had spent extra time at the ranch in Corpus to keep her mind occupied instead of dwelling on their kiss and the way he had pushed her away. The owner of the ranch had been thrilled that Elena had spent extra time with her horses, as long as it didn't cost her extra.

"Is this going to cost me extra?"

"It might. Are you a difficult student?"

"I'm always difficult."

"Perhaps we can work out some kind of arrangement."

Focus! Focus! Focus! *It's over. It's done. You're a grown-ass woman. Move on already!*

Phantom stood near his horse, holding the reins loosely in his hands as he listened. He had gone back to giving her the expressionless face—no more smiles, no sparkle of warmth.

She had to remind herself that this was a good thing, this was what she really wanted. He was her client, and things needed to stay professional between them. But there was tension now, and she hated knowing it was all her fault.

"Are you ready to give it a shot?" she asked, forcing a smile to her lips.

"Absolutely." He mounted Black Out, the gorgeous specimen of a black gelding that had been one of the first offspring of Phantom's stallion. Standing over seventeen hands, the horse had a midnight-black coat that seemed to shimmer in the sunlight. Tall for a quarter horse, Black Out moved with grace.

Elena stepped forward and tried to clear her mind as she grabbed ahold of Phantom's leg and tipped his toe up slightly, forcing his heel down. She adjusted the stirrup on each side, breathing deeply through her nose to try to calm her nerves. Just being near him made her stomach tie into knots. *No, nope, this is not going to happen. I'm not going to obsess over this man.*

She cleared her throat and shaded her eyes as she looked up at him. Yes, the black gelding was the perfect horse for him to ride. With Phantom's height, he needed a large horse. "Now, roll your hips slightly. Just a little bit so that you… There, that's it. You've got the posture and stirrups down. Now let's see if you can get him to respond to your cues."

For over an hour they worked in the arena as Phantom and Black Out came to know each other. By that point, Elena had expected Phantom to be getting frustrated. The heat of the day beat down on them as they worked and Elena felt sweat trickle down her back as she instructed him. Black Out was one of her finest trained horses, more sensitive to body cues than any of the others. To his credit, Phantom hadn't complained once, even though it was taking a long time for man and horse to sync together.

"That's good for today. You both need a break. I'll get Strawberry ready for you to practice the showmanship routine."

Phantom dismounted with grace and began to walk to the barn with Black Out, but Elena quickly intercepted him. "Go get some water. I'll take care of Black Out. That's part of my job."

His eyes searched her face for several long moments, and he looked like he wanted to say something. She held her breath. In the end, though, he just nodded and handed her the reins. Elena sighed heavily as he walked off, almost relieved. Calling the new vibe *tension* seemed like an understatement.

She worked quickly to take off the saddle and brush down Black Out, before grabbing a halter for Strawberry from the tack room. The showmanship division of quarter horse shows required learning the delicate balance between a person on the ground—instead of in the saddle—and the horse on a lead line.

She had just stepped out of the barn and back into the blazing sunlight, leading Strawberry, when she saw a plume of dust on the road leading up to the ranch.

Moving rapidly in front of the dust was a large, nice-looking truck.

"I'll need to take a rain check on the showmanship training for today," Phantom said softly from behind her.

Her heart nearly leapt into her throat. How could a man as big as him move so silently? And how had she not even seen him when she came out of the barn? She strongly suspected she knew how he had earned his nickname.

She turned to face him, forcing herself to smile. "I totally understand. You don't usually get visitors to the ranch, so this will be a nice change of pace for you."

His face was unreadable. "This isn't a visitor. This is a new part owner of the ranch. He's moving in today."

"Oh. Wow…I didn't know y'all were still expanding. That's a good thing."

Phantom didn't reply. Instead, his eyes were fixed on the approaching truck. Finally, he glanced back at Elena. "I'll see you Wednesday, then?"

"Same as always," she replied, but doubted he even heard her, since he was already walking toward the area where they had parked their trucks.

The new truck sported a deep maroon color and had a small lift kit, a mean-looking grill guard, and mud flaps behind the dually wheels. The driver backed the truck up next to the others, between them and the road, and Elena wondered if he was preparing himself for a quick escape. If he had met the rough group of men that ran the ranch, he probably had good reason to be ready to take off.

Phantom walked up to the truck as another man stepped down. He looked pale compared to Phantom, but his skin still carried a smooth caramel color that looked flawless from where Elena stood. He looked young, and Elena guessed he could be around the same age as Snap. While not quite as tall as Phantom, he exuded strength, with defined muscles outlined in his T-shirt and jeans. He almost made Phantom appear trim—though she knew firsthand he had enough muscles to make her weak in the knees.

His dark-brown hair was slicked back, and he sported a pair of Wrangler jeans and scuffed-up boots to go along with his casual T-shirt. From the way he moved and carried himself, he had "cowboy" written all over him. He grinned broadly and extended his hand to Phantom, who took it and gave it a firm handshake.

And then Elena saw *her*. She bounced down from the other side of the truck, her long, pale hair blowing in the breeze. It reminded Elena of a commercial—someone somewhere had cued the fans at the perfect time for the woman to shake out her beautiful hair and come sliding around the front of the truck.

She was tall compared to Elena. Hell, anyone was tall compared to Elena. But she had incredibly long legs that were displayed to advantage by the cropped shorts and cowboy boots she wore, and Elena could only dream of being able to move so gracefully. Her excited laughter floated on the air as she launched herself at Phantom, and Elena couldn't tear her eyes away.

The beautiful woman threw herself into Phantom's outstretched arms, wrapping hers around his neck. Phantom's laugh hit Elena like a punch in the gut. That was *her* laugh. Somehow, she had come to believe that his laughter belonged to her. Yet this incredible beauty had earned the laughter as well. Elena swallowed hard as Phantom's arms wrapped around his visitor while she planted kisses all over his face.

The little bit of food that Elena had eaten earlier in the day was suddenly burning at the back of her throat, and she worried she was going to be terribly ill. This was the real woman he wanted. This was the woman he craved and desired. No wonder he had rejected Elena's advances. He already had a woman to fulfill his needs.

She felt like she was watching a tragedy, and her sense of morbid curiosity wouldn't let her look away. Phantom patted the beauty's back, and she slowly untangled herself from him but slid her hand into his and interlocked their fingers. She smiled up at him and, from the looks of it, talked a mile a minute.

Suddenly, as if sensing Elena watching him, Phantom turned slightly and looked over at her. She tried to look away but she wasn't fast enough, and she saw the remnants of the smile on his face quickly fade. Then he turned and began to walk the two newcomers into the house.

Elena felt as if someone had just cracked open her chest and beat violently on her heart. She turned toward the arena, Strawberry in tow, and focused on breathing in and out. She suddenly felt every ounce of exhaustion from her lack of sleep the night before. She wanted nothing more than to go home and forget the entire day had ever happened.

"Admiral Haslett seems to think great things about you." Stryker sat at his usual place at the head of the table with the rest of the team placed around the sides. Unlike at their usual team briefings, Anya sat to Stryker's left, watching the newcomer with curiosity.

Damian "Lobo" Almeda met Stryker's gaze with pale eyes. Despite his young age, he already had a light feathering of gray hairs mixed with the slicked-back dark brown. That and his angular features almost made him look like the wolf of his nickname.

"To be honest with you, sir, I don't know Admiral Haslett that well. I'd heard of him, of course. I doubt there's a SEAL in the service who doesn't know about him." His eyes darted over to Anya, then slid back to Stryker. "He tapped me on the shoulder and told me I was being pulled for a new assignment, and that you run the command. Then he gave me the folder and told me I needed to be here today and no later."

Stryker was silent for several moments. "And your thoughts?" he finally asked.

Lobo leaned back in his chair, and his gaze scanned the faces watching him silently. "On paper, it sure sounds like a great operation."

"On paper." Phantom's expression didn't change as he repeated Lobo's words. Phantom's comment wasn't a statement or a question. It was a judgment.

Lobo leaned forward, resting his forearms on the table. "On paper just about anything can look great. But reality can be a shit show. You all have already been here for some time, have already run a mission together. You've had time to get to know each other enough to read each other's body language blindfolded."

"Sailor, you know that you have to learn those things coming on to any new operation." Brusco spoke, his voice rough as always.

"I do know that. The question was asked about my thoughts, and I'm shooting straight with you. I want to make an impact with this team in all the missions that come our way."

"Just because your role might not be breaching a stronghold every mission doesn't make it any less important." Snap was chewing on a toothpick as if it were the tastiest thing he'd found in years.

Lobo was silent for several moments, his face as expressionless as the rest of the team's. "You asked my thoughts. I want to be here. I want to be a part of taking down the machine that's crippling the relationships we need with our neighbors to the south. And I'm ready, willing, and able to perform whatever role it takes to help with that."

"Even if it means you're going to be my babysitter?" Anya spoke up, her voice wavering slightly. "Knowing that you're going to be with me while some of the team runs critical missions that I am unable to know anything about?"

"I don't like to talk about my missions much, ma'am. But some of the most rewarding ones have been the ones where I was protecting someone from all the bad shi— excuse me, bad *stuff*—that came their way through no fault of their own."

Stryker's lips twitched. "I think you'll fit in here just fine. Welcome to the team, Lobo."

―⁓―

"How are you even here?"

"It has been far too long since I've seen you. Given that the admiral owed me a favor or two…"

Phantom waved his hands back and forth and shook his head. "Wait, wait, wait. Exactly how does Haslett owe you a favor?"

"You know, big brother, for someone who knows so much and has seen so much, you sure can be clueless." Amber sat down on his bed cross-legged, watching him with a large smile plastered on her face.

"You know how much I hate it when you play these guessing games with me. And why the hell did you dye your hair?"

"When you were sent on your last mission, I…um…I left home."

"You—I'm sorry, what did you just say? You just graduated from high school! What happened to going to Texas Tech?"

"I enlisted."

Phantom's stomach flipped violently, and the room suddenly felt very, very small. He drew in his breath slowly—*in through the nose, out through the mouth*. One breath at a time, he had to swallow down the bile. He really needed something to punch. He latched onto a thread of hope that burst into his mind.

"How long ago? It isn't too late to back out of this. If you need me to pull some strings, I can just make a few calls—"

"Enrique. Enrique! I've already completed boot camp. I've started my first assignment."

He concentrated on breathing. *Just breathe. This is all just one horrific nightmare.* His sweet, innocent baby sister was not in the military. She couldn't be. It wasn't right. She was supposed to be getting her degree at Texas Tech, living her dreams. He wanted to go to the gym in the other wing of the house and punch something. His two-hour workout that morning seemed like nothing compared to the steam he needed to blow off now.

"Where are you stationed?"

"Corpus. I'm working for Admiral Haslett."

"You're… Okay, Amber. This has been a fun little joke, but you can cut it out now. I don't want to hear any more of this insanity."

Amber's face fell and she stared at him, brown eyes wide. "I-I thought you would be proud of me. I worked hard for this! I work with several others managing all the correspondence and schedules for Admiral Haslett and his staff. I've done a few small things that impressed him. So, when I told him that I needed to see you, he put me with Lobo to head out here, just to see you. I thought you could take me back tomorrow, if you don't mind. As you know, the navy doesn't really hand out leave easily."

"Good grief, Amber! You're in the fucking navy? What the hell possessed you? You know your orders could change at any time. You could be on a fucking ship tomorrow headed overseas to who knows where!"

"There's no reason to raise your voice at me," she snapped, standing up, her fists clenched by her sides. "You left us, Enrique. You made the choice to go into the navy. To become a fucking SEAL, no less!"

"You better watch your mouth, Amber. If Dad heard you talking like that—"

"I'm a fucking sailor, now, Enrique. I can say whatever the fuck I want, and there isn't a damn thing you can do about—*mpf*!"

Phantom's hand clamped down over her mouth. "Stop it, Amber. Just stop it!" He released her and stepped back, shaking his head. "You didn't have anything to worry about. As soon as you graduated, the account that Mom and Dad set up for you kicked in and all your expenses were covered. They were there to support you with anything you wanted—"

"They still are. Unlike you, they're proud of me. I wanted you to be at my graduation from boot camp, but you were on another one of your missions. You've been gone a long time, Enrique. I'm not the same little sister you left behind. And I haven't lost my dreams either. I'm going to school through the navy. I want to become an officer."

Phantom ran a hand down his face and stepped away from her, sitting down heavily in her spot on his bed. Amber had always been his ray of sunshine. While his father had been so occupied with the business and his mother so consumed with being the perfect wife, Phantom had found himself taking care of Amber more often than not. He had resented the responsibility of looking after a kid nearly ten years younger than him at first. But Amber had quickly wrapped him around her little finger and always found a way to make him laugh, to bring joy no matter how tough the day had been.

That had continued when he went into the navy. Whenever he had leave, she always wanted to be with him and hear his stories about the crazy antics of the men he worked with. He never told her the horrors that he'd seen or the truth about what he'd done. But he always brought her gifts. And he always made sure that he had new stories for her.

Shit.

It was his fault. He had given her an impression of the navy that was far from the truth. She thought she was signing up for something fun while she went about getting her degree. If anything happened to her...

"Say something. Please."

He looked up at her and felt as if he had been punched in the gut. Large tears streaked her beautiful face. "I-I'm sorry, Amber. I am proud of you. I'm always proud of you. You've just dropped a lot on me. I never expected to see you, let alone hear this from you."

He stood and used his thumbs to wipe at the tears that lingered on her cheeks. "I haven't told you what this life is really like. I only told you about the good times. If anything ever happens to you because you didn't realize what you were getting yourself into...because you listened to the stupid stories I told to make you laugh...I wouldn't be able to handle it. I can't—"

"You give me very little credit, Enrique. You think I didn't know what you were doing all these years? You think I wasn't aware that you've been protecting me...that you've always been protecting me? I watch the news. I read the paper. I know what's going on in the world. I know that the men you work with call you 'Phantom,' and that it isn't just part of that old joke from high school. I've watched you change over the years. I can guess what you've had to do to earn that name. I went into this with open eyes. And I'm happy. I know I made the right choice."

Phantom swallowed hard and pulled her into his arms, holding her tight. He was supposed to keep her from the scary things in the world. Instead, she was running directly into a military life that could send her into the seething fury of their crazy world. As long as he could, though, he would make sure she stayed safe in the office.

Haslett. The son of a bitch had him by the balls now. He was fairly certain it was no accident that Amber had been selected to work as part of his large office machine. It was another way for Haslett to keep Phantom under his thumb.

He finally pulled back from Amber and gave her the best smile he could muster. "So, can you get any information on Haslett for me to use to my advantage?"

She chuckled and gave him a watery smile. She *had* changed. She wasn't his baby sister anymore. She had grown into a woman while he had traveled the world.

"Who was the woman you were with when we got here?" Amber asked, drawing his mind away from the dark memories of previous operations that constantly haunted him.

Elena. Just the thought of her conjured up the scent of wildflowers. Another woman he had hurt without intending to. "She's... That's Elena. She's the horse trainer."

One of Amber's sleek eyebrows arched dramatically. "Since when do you need a horse trainer? Or are you just keeping her around because she's so beautiful?"

Phantom schooled his features, stepping back into the guarded role he had built and maintained over many years. "Quarter horses are a bit different from racehorses. She's helping me make this ranch profitable."

Amber's lips twitched. "You've been using that face on me since you were a teenager. And all it tells me is that there's more to this than you want to let on. But that's okay. I can always do my own investigating. You aren't the only one who has hidden talents, you know."

She looked around his room and frowned. "So, is this your newest mission? How long will you be here? Don't worry, I won't ask you what you're doing. I know that's classified. But it sure is nice to have you so close. It would be nice to know if this is something that is going to last a while."

Phantom shook his head at her. "You're incorrigible. You haven't changed since I found you going through my duffel bag after my first deployment."

She wiggled her eyebrows dramatically at him. "Well, when there are secrets to be uncovered…"

Phantom threw his arm around her shoulders and turned her toward the door. "I can smell dinner. You're in for a treat. Snap is an incredible cook."

"Deflecting."

"While we're on the topic of poor choices, let's discuss you dyeing your hair and dressing like a cowboy's fantasy. How about that?"

"Now, Enrique, I can explain."

Chapter 10

"YOU KNOW WE WISH WE COULD SPEND MORE TIME WITH you. It feels like we hardly ever see you anymore."

Elena blushed at Mrs. Bell's words, guilt gnawing at her. While Mr. and Mrs. Bell were her landlords and she rented the apartment over their garage, they treated her as if she were one of their children. They doted on her, often bringing her fresh-baked pies and leftover meals, and always inviting her to visit their home.

"You work too hard, my dear," Mrs. Bell said as she patted Elena on the hand. The older woman's hands had grown shaky in her older years and were covered in liver spots, but still had strength as she squeezed Elena's hand tightly. "Mr. Bell and I worry about you. You leave as soon as the sun comes up, and you don't get home until after the sun goes down. That's just not safe for a young woman."

Elena smiled politely at the elderly couple. "I love what I do. I'm happy. It doesn't even feel like I'm working." *Most days. Most days I don't watch the man who has convinced me to trust—to feel—embrace the woman he loves, and it wasn't me. For the first time ever, I didn't want to spend time with the horses.*

"You aren't smiling like you usually do." Mr. Bell frowned at her. "I like to see you happy."

Elena chuckled. "You just need to get better glasses. Are you even able to see anymore? You know, at your age—"

"All right, young lady, make fun of me as much as you want. But I can tell something is bothering you. It isn't our place to pry. We just want to see you happy at all times."

"Is it the apartment, dear? Is something wrong? Do we need to have someone come fix something?" Mrs. Bell rapidly fired off questions. Even at the age of eighty-three, her mind was just as sharp as most twenty- or thirty-year-olds Elena knew.

"No, the apartment is terrific. I can't thank you enough for the incredible deal you are giving me on it. I can't believe I've already lived here for nearly five years."

"Nice try, missy. You aren't going to get out of this conversation so easily. Mr. Bell may not want to pry, but I hold no such qualms." Mrs. Bell winked at her. "What's going on in that mind of yours? I've known you long enough to read your emotions. And if Mr. Bell is picking up on something, you know you're wearing it all over your face."

"What is that supposed to mean?" Mr. Bell feigned annoyance and held a stern face for several seconds before he broke into a wide grin and leaned toward Mrs. Bell, pursing his lips dramatically for a kiss.

Mrs. Bell giggled like a schoolgirl and leaned toward him and pressed a kiss to his lips tenderly. They grinned at each other for several lingering moments, and Elena realized she might as well not even be in the room. To be so deeply in love for over fifty years must be an amazing experience.

Elena shifted in her chair to pour herself some more coffee and instantly felt Mr. and Mrs. Bell return their attention on her. She wanted to sigh heavily, but she didn't want to give them the impression that she wasn't thrilled to spend a beautiful Saturday morning in their backyard, watching the birds play in the birdbath. She needed the quality time with them more than she had realized.

She took a long sip of her coffee and lifted her eyes slowly to find them watching her with expectant expressions. "Maybe I am working a little too hard," she said, grasping for something to say. "I haven't been getting much sleep lately, and it's taking its toll."

"Why aren't you getting enough sleep? Are you worried about something? Do you need help, Elena?" Mr. Bell asked gently. Again, for the hundredth time, it struck her how parental he was with her and how much she had come to care for him. She thought of Mrs. Bell as her second mother.

"Well…" Elena began hesitantly, searching for the right words.

"It's a man, isn't it?" Mrs. Bell said eagerly.

"Martha! Let her tell us about this man at her own pace."

Elena couldn't help but laugh, even though she felt the heat of a blush creeping up her neck and into her cheeks. "I suppose you can say it's a man. You remember the Bent Horseshoe Ranch, right?"

"Of course. We were so sad when Daniel sold and moved away. He often came by to help Mr. Bell with some of the more difficult chores. We miss him."

"A group of men bought the ranch together."

"A group? Oh, don't tell me we have a cult brewing in Hebbronville." Mr. Bell shook his head. "What is this world coming to?"

"No, no," Elena smiled. "It isn't a cult. Not at all.

They're best friends and decided to go in on running the ranch together. They're determined to make it a success without having to hire ranch hands."

Mrs. Bell's eyes widened. "On that large of a ranch? It's thousands of acres and has hundreds of cattle. How many men are there?"

"Six. Well, seven now, I suppose. They brought on someone new yesterday. They're all extremely hard workers. I think they just might be able to pull it off."

"Seven? And? Which one of them do you like?" Mrs. Bell's eyes sparkled.

"I like all of them."

"Oh!" The older woman's eyes went wide. "I can certainly see your dilemma."

Elena grinned at her. "I said I *like* all of them. I didn't say I felt anything other than that."

"You can't fool me. I can tell someone has captured your interest." Mr. Bell smirked.

"I wouldn't say he's captured my interest as much as he's captured my irritation."

Mrs. Bell picked up her cup of coffee and leaned back in her lawn chair, a smile brightening her features and making her look ten years younger. "That's one of the ways it starts."

Elena shook her head. "No, our relationship is purely professional. We got off to a very rocky start, but we seem to be in a better place now." She spent the next half hour telling them about meeting Phantom, him terminating their relationship, and her ability to win him back. She omitted the part about their two kisses, knowing that would only fuel Mrs. Bell's interest in digging into a relationship that didn't exist.

"He likes you." Mr. Bell nodded.

"How do you know that?" Elena asked, startled.

"I know how men think and act around a woman they are interested in. The way he spends time with you, is willing to learn from you, always taking the opportunity to ask you questions… If he didn't like you, he'd find out the answers some other way."

"It *is* what he's paying me to do." Elena sipped her coffee. "I'm meant to be there for him, to help him grow his business and answer his questions. We work well together. But I need to keep it professional."

"Oh, so that's the excuse you're going to run with?" Mrs. Bell rolled her eyes and waved her hand in the air. "What's wrong with having a little fun outside of work? I can see it in your eyes. You like this man. And I believe Mr. Bell is right for once. I think this man likes you too."

"Right for once?" Mr. Bell sputtered. "Do I need to remind you of all the—"

"Old stories, Harold. Old stories. I'm sure you've bored Elena with them too many times to count." Mrs. Bell winked at Elena, who had to hide her smile behind her coffee mug.

They spent the rest of the morning talking about the Bells' children and grandchildren, and Elena learned they were expecting their first great-grandchild in a handful of months. She insisted that she wanted to help with the baby shower in any way possible before finally excusing herself.

At their beautiful glass front door, Mr. and Mrs. Bell hugged her affectionately. "Don't worry about any of this anymore. If you want something to happen with this man, it will happen. It isn't worth worrying about." Mrs. Bell kissed her cheek.

"And if he does anything to hurt you, let me know. I've still got my shotgun, and I may be old, but I can still aim straight." Mr. Bell winked at her.

Elena chuckled. "I'll have to keep that in mind. Thank you for the coffee and the visit. I've missed spending time with you."

"Then make more time for us!" Mrs. Bell scolded. "All you have to do is come down those stairs and knock on our door, and you know we'd love to see you, no matter what time of day." Her features softened, and she placed her hand on Elena's cheek. "Be safe out there, my dear. We *do* worry about you and how hard you work."

Elena smiled and embraced the woman one more time. "Thank you. I may hold you to that. Let's see how you feel when I come knocking on your door at ten o'clock one night."

"We'll just be watching the news at that hour. You won't be a bother at all. Though you may have to put up with listening to Mr. Bell's snoring. He always falls asleep in his recliner before the weather report comes on."

Elena smiled and waved goodbye to them before walking the short distance to the detached garage and climbing the stairs to her apartment. She wasn't surprised when she looked back to find them watching to make sure she made it into her apartment safely. She felt better after spending the morning with them.

Their love was a beautiful thing to see, and the way they cared for and fretted over her reminded Elena of her own parents. They lived far up in north Texas, and she didn't get to see them very often. She needed to call them and hear their voices and know they were doing okay. Once the shows slowed down, she'd even travel to see them.

She smiled to herself. She could move on from her passionate encounter with Phantom. Things were already beginning to look better.

———

"Latest intel indicates they are gathering more victims than usual for this haul," Haslett said over the speakerphone.

Phantom sighed and ran a hand down his face. "We know that a normal haul is around twenty victims. Most of them women, some of them children."

"Good to hear you've been doing your studying."

"What do we know about this code being linked to our last mission? Have you been able to discover who is running things in America?" Phantom asked Buzz, who sat with him in the conference room.

"Nothing solid yet. We're turning over every rock we can. There's a connection to the two missions, that's for sure. The same coder who worked for the drug lord obviously is working for this human trafficking ring as well." Buzz frowned.

"Is he working for them, or could he be behind the steering wheel and pointing them in the direction he wants?" Phantom asked.

Haslett sighed. "You think he may be running these operations?"

"Have you ever heard of someone referred to as the Puppet Master?" Phantom tossed out the question, his body tense as he waited for an answer.

Haslett paused for several moments, and Phantom gripped the edge of the table tighter. He needed answers. They needed mission details. The longer they waited, the higher the chance that these traffickers got away with selling many people into a life of slavery.

"Where did you hear that?" Haslett asked.

"You asked me to dig, and we did. What's going on here?" Phantom didn't want to waste any time getting to the truth.

"That term came up recently. It involves a fanatical group we've been trying to track whose members seem to harbor unpatriotic views and could be considered terrorists." Haslett sighed.

"Terrorists? Do you have anything substantial to back this up?" Stryker asked, jumping into the conversation.

"Not yet. Which is why I haven't told you anything about it yet. We're still digging on our end. You keep digging on yours. Don't worry, Phantom. We're going to stop these bastards no matter what."

"Yes, sir." Phantom frowned into the phone. He didn't like the unknown, and the Puppet Master added a whole new level of strange to their investigation. "We'll keep at it. I'll be in touch."

He ended the call and leaned back in his chair, rubbing his eyes wearily. He had driven Amber back to the base on Saturday and taken advantage of the time to visit with Haslett in person and compare notes. There wasn't much more to add than what they had already discussed.

During Sunday morning's breakfast, his eyes continued to drift to where Elena had sat just the week before, bringing her bright attitude and warm smile with her. He enjoyed being with her, probably more than he should, and he needed to work on changing that. He couldn't allow himself to get into a relationship with complicated emotions and expectations that he probably would never be able to live up to.

After breakfast, Buzz had come to him about the latest message he had deciphered on the dark web from the "Puppet Master." There wasn't much information in the line of communication, only a statement that arrangements were being made—certainly nothing Phantom's group could take action upon, even if they knew who the person or group of people were.

Twelve hundred hours had come and gone, and Phantom needed to head out to the barn to tend to the horses. Just thinking about them took his mind off the dangers of the mission ahead and to his other concern—Elena. The woman must have magical abilities, because every time he thought of her, saw her, or came close to her, all he could think about was feeling her body fit so perfectly against his as he tasted her cherry-flavored lips. The right thing for both of them would be to give in to those desires, right? *She wants you. You want her. Why are you denying both of you something that could be amazing?*

He shook his head. He had to get a grip on his emotions when it came to Elena. Otherwise, he could end up doing something they could both come to regret.

Chapter 11

"YOUR MOTIONS SHOULD ALWAYS BE VERY SMOOTH AND fluid when you're presenting a horse for the showmanship class. Hold your head up high, make sure you are poised and in control so the horse moves comfortably at your side, and walk forward with confidence."

Elena stood in the center of the arena, acting in the role of the judge as Phantom walked Strawberry in. She should have known he would be a natural at the showmanship class. He effortlessly moved with confidence and a commanding presence, something the judges would certainly notice, and he would definitely earn a blue ribbon if he remembered the patterns and different movements he had to make.

"When I step back, go ahead and lead her into a jog. Remember how I showed you earlier. There! That's a perfect transition. Keep going to the first orange cone, then stop and execute a three-hundred-sixty-degree turn."

Phantom didn't say anything as he moved through the course to her directions, and she wanted to shout for joy at how quickly he had picked up everything. When he set up Strawberry for her to do the walk-around, Elena's heart beat a little faster. When passing at the head of the horse, she came close enough to him that she could almost feel the heat radiating off his body.

She wanted to get even closer, to touch him, to wipe the sweat from his forehead, and more than anything, she wanted to kiss him. She realized she couldn't stop her desire for him or her burning interest to know more about him. But she had to be realistic. He had a woman who he obviously cared deeply for, and she had come to terms with it. She would just live in her daydreams and stay professional about everything else.

"I'm about to cross by the horse's tail. Where should you be standing?"

"Exactly where I am until you cross. Then I make my move."

She beamed at him. "Very good. I think you're ready."

He narrowed his eyes, a look of doubt on his face. "Ready for what?"

"Your first horse show—as a competitor."

"No, no, no. I need a couple more months at least—but I certainly want to come with you to any show you decide to attend. I want to pick up as many pointers as possible."

"There's nothing better than jumping in and getting your feet wet. It's the best way to learn." Elena smiled at him and stepped up to take Strawberry's lead line from him. She found herself incredibly close to him, staring up into his gray eyes. She couldn't remember what they had been talking about. All she could think about was the fact that his head only had to dip down to hers and they'd kiss.

"I'm not sure I'm ready for this," he murmured thoughtfully, but she noticed his eyes had dropped to her lips.

Snap out of it! She shook herself. She needed to stop fantasizing about what would never be. Yes, there seemed to be something between them, but she had tried to travel down this path once before, and he had turned her away. Lesson learned.

She stepped away from him, taking Strawberry with her. "You're going to do great," she said as cheerfully as possible.

"Elena, I..." She paused and looked back at him when his voice trailed off. His gaze searched her face for several long moments, then he shook his head as if dismissing what he had been about to say. He gave a half-hearted shrug. "I just wanted to thank you for all the time you've spent with me and the horses. You really are an exceptional trainer."

"Thank you." She had hoped he was about to tell her he had made a mistake, that he really wanted her and never should have pushed her away. The compliment kept things exactly as they should be—professional and courteous. She needed to remember that, and the very important fact he already had a woman in his life.

She turned back for the barn. "Your first horse show will be this weekend. I've already made all the arrangements. I think you're going to find competing in horse shows addictive. I know it is for me."

Phantom followed behind her silently, and she wondered what he was thinking. Was he nervous about his first horse show? Or was he feeling just as conflicted as she was about the undeniable attraction between them?

They worked together to put Strawberry in her stall and give her fresh oats and hay. The sun had started to set, creating long shadows down the aisle of the barn, as Elena stepped out of the feed room and nearly collided with Phantom. Then he surprised the hell out of her with his question. "Would you like to stay for dinner?"

—⁓—

Phantom didn't know why he had asked her to stay for dinner. It had been impulsive. He hadn't wanted his time with her to be finished already. With her around, all the ugly and dark things he knew existed in the world seemed far, far away, unable to enter the circle of joy and excitement that seemed to follow Elena everywhere she went.

She wiped her hands on her jeans and gave him a hesitant smile. "I'd enjoy that."

The dining room and kitchen were loud and boisterous as the team gathered to eat dinner. Elena turned to Phantom before stepping into the room and crashed into his chest. He caught her by the shoulders to steady her and felt the warmth of her skin through her shirt. His heart kicked up.

"Sorry," she mumbled. "Where can I go to freshen up?"

He cleared his throat. "There's a bathroom just around the corner."

She nodded, a blush staining her cheeks as she took a half step back. He realized belatedly he still held her shoulders, and he released her quickly. She turned and headed in the direction of the bathroom, and he swallowed hard. His resolve to keep a safe distance from her was in serious jeopardy.

He quickly went to the bathroom in his bedroom and washed up, returning to the hallway just as Elena emerged. Together, they walked into the dining room, and the team greeted her enthusiastically. Anya pushed through the group and embraced her friend. "I wasn't expecting you for dinner tonight! This is a nice treat."

"Phantom asked, and I couldn't say no to some of Snap's cooking."

"Thank you!" Snap called from where he hovered over the stove in the kitchen. "It's nice to know that someone appreciates all my talent and hard work."

Santo approached Elena with a big grin on his face. "It's good to see you again. You hang out at the barn too much."

Elena shrugged as she smiled up at him. "It *is* where I work, you know. You could always come out and say 'hi.'"

"When we aren't working the ranch, I'll have to keep that in mind."

Phantom scowled at Santo. *What kind of game is he playing? We've already talked about Elena. Is he seriously going to try to pursue her? Fuck, I'm the one that invited her to stay for dinner.*

"What's for dinner, Snap?" Phantom asked, stepping farther in the room. Santo glanced up at him, and they stared at each other for several moments before Santo turned from him and picked up a conversation with Brusco.

"Enchiladas, my specialty. You couldn't have picked a better night, Elena." Snap chuckled.

"See what happens when you compliment him?" Phantom asked, moving to stand near Elena.

She looked up at him with the bright smile that made him feel as if his stomach was turning flips. "He's harmless. Let him have his fun."

Her words nearly made him laugh. If only she knew the kind of harm Snap could cause. He was a deadly force to reckon with. He wondered how Elena would react if she knew the truth about who they all were. Would the trust between them be broken completely?

"Elena, I'd like you to meet the newest partner here on the ranch," Stryker said, and Lobo stepped forward. "This is Lobo."

Lobo extended his hand to her. "Anya speaks favorably about you."

Elena smiled at him. "Don't believe everything you hear. It's nice to meet you."

"Soup's on!" Snap announced. "Grab it while you can."

Elena hesitated, and Phantom urged her forward before the guys could beat her to it. "Guests first."

After grace had been said, they all dug into the delicious enchiladas Snap had made. Phantom knew Snap was an exceptional cook, but it was too much fun to pick on him. He glanced over at Elena, who seemed to be enjoying the food the same as everyone else.

"So," Santo said, pausing in his eating for a moment, "when you aren't training horses and wayward cowboys, what do you do, Elena?" Phantom hadn't failed to notice that Santo had elected to sit directly across from her.

She finished chewing and smiled. "Puzzles."

"Puzzles? As in the thousand-piece monsters that take the patience of a saint?" Santo quirked an eyebrow at her.

"Sometimes I'll do those, but not often. No, I like puzzles of all kinds."

"What other kinds of puzzles are there?" Brusco asked.

"Well, there's my favorite, the Rubik's Cube, but I've already got that one figured out, so I only fiddle with it when I don't have another puzzle handy. Then there are grid puzzles, riddles, and math puzzles."

"Wait, did you just say that you've figured out the Rubik's Cube?" Brusco asked.

"Don't even get her started on all this," Anya groaned.

"No, this is getting good," Phantom argued. "I'd like to know how she figured out the cube."

"Most puzzles are all about math and patterns. The Rubik's Cube can be solved with an algorithm. There's a really simple pattern to making it happen, and you can do it in just a handful of moves."

"Sure. I'll believe it when I see it," Stryker said, chuckling.

"I'll have to bring my cube with me next time I'm out here to prove it to y'all."

"See what you started?" Anya glared at Santo. "You won't be able to get this to stop now."

Elena laughed and elbowed Anya. "Yeah, you make a lot of noise about something you brag about being able to do too. And who taught you?"

Anya rolled her eyes. "Yeah, yeah. Rub it in."

"What about cards?" Santo asked as they began to wrap up the meal. "Do you enjoy playing cards?"

Phantom wanted to growl at Santo. He wasn't getting the chance to have any type of conversation with Elena. He didn't know exactly what he would talk to her about in front of the entire group, but he didn't have a chance with Santo dominating the table.

"No, no, no. Bad idea, Santo. Seriously. You think it's crazy that she likes puzzles? Did you miss the part where she talked about math? That's what cards are all about." Anya shook her head at Santo.

"So you think you're good?" Santo asked, his gaze never leaving Elena's face.

A smirk crossed her lips and she shrugged. "I win from time to time."

"Good. Let's get this stuff cleaned up and play. What's your poison?"

"I suppose it depends on how many people are playing. Personally, I prefer spades."

"I'm playing," Phantom said instantly. He had invited Elena to stay for dinner to be with him, not to hang out with Santo.

"Count me out," Anya said. "I know what's coming."

"I'm in," Buzz said.

"Perfect. Elena and I will be one team," Phantom said quickly before Santo could speak up.

"Game on," Santo grinned. They cleaned the dining room and kitchen in record time, and Phantom led Elena to a part of the house he knew she hadn't seen yet—their game room.

"Must be real hard on all of you when you have downtime," she said sarcastically as she looked around.

"Yes, it's nice to have. To tell you the truth, though, we hardly get to use it. There's always work to be done."

"That's what happens when you have seven men trying to manage such a large ranch all on their own. Lots of work to be done and never enough time in the day to take care of it all." A curious look crossed her face. "Why did you ask me to stay for dinner?"

Phantom nearly choked on the beer he had been sipping, completely caught off guard. He studied her face for several moments, trying to think of the best way to approach his answer. "I like having you around. You're always happy, always optimistic. It's nice."

She watched him intently, then opened her mouth as though she was about to say something, but Santo and Snap came into the room, followed by Brusco and Lobo. "From the way Anya's talking, you two are about to die painful, merciless deaths," Brusco teased Santo and Snap.

Elena turned from him and sat at the table, a grin once more on her face. Phantom sat across from her and wished he could ask everyone to leave so he could talk to her in private. He wanted to know what she had been about to say.

"I think Anya's just trying to scare us away from the game to make her friend look good. We've got this," Snap said smugly.

Several hands later, Snap wasn't anywhere near as smug, because Elena and Phantom were stomping them in the dirt. "Okay, new rules," Santo said, sighing heavily. "From now on, Elena and Phantom aren't allowed to partner up. They are an impossible force to conquer."

"You're just being a sore loser." Phantom laughed and out of the corner of his eye saw Elena's face light up. He must have done something right.

Just a few hands later, Santo and Snap conceded defeat, much to the laughter and cheers of Brusco and Lobo. "That has to be the best game of spades I've ever seen," Lobo chuckled.

"I've learned my lesson," Santo groaned as he stood. "I'm never going up against someone who loves math again."

"Math may play a role, as I work out the probability of each hand we've been dealt. More than anything, though, it depends on having a great partner who's ready to jump in and run the hand with you," Elena said, smiling at Phantom. His heart did a somersault.

Elena stood with the rest of them, and Santo gave her a brief hug. "Good game, Elena. I think you missed your true calling and should have gone to Vegas."

She chuckled. "I'm much happier with horses than gambling. Thanks for the great night, guys. I need to get home, though. It's already past my bedtime."

Phantom glanced down at his watch, startled at the late hour. He had been so enthralled in watching Elena's talent with the game and trusting her with every move they made that time had slipped away. "I'll walk you out."

The sound of crickets and cicadas filled the otherwise quiet night air. Their boots crunched on the gravel as they walked to her truck, and Phantom felt he needed to say something to fill the silence. *What do you tell her? That you want her even though you pushed her away, even though you're all wrong for her?*

"I enjoyed tonight. It was a nice change of pace." Elena broke their silence as she stopped in front of her truck door.

"Different than your usual night of puzzles?"

"I like a simple life. What can I say?" She shrugged.

"Elena, about the other day… I need to explain…"

"No." She shook her head. "No explanation necessary. It's in the past, and we should just forget about it and move on. That's what I'm trying to do."

Trying? Did that mean she was having a hard time

forgetting how it felt to be pressed together, tasting each other, same as him? "Be careful driving home. You know the deer out here can be bad late at night."

She grinned. "I know. I've been out here longer than you have, remember? You're still a newbie as far as I'm concerned."

He opened the truck door for her and waited until her taillights disappeared down the road before turning back to the house. He found Santo in the kitchen, and his temper flared. "Just what the hell do you think you're doing?" he demanded, storming up to Santo.

Santo raised an eyebrow at him. "Debating on a snack. You have a problem with that?"

"You know what I'm talking about. What are you trying to do?"

"She's a strong, beautiful woman. Someone here should try to win her over, if possible. If you won't, I might as well try."

Phantom's hands curled into fists at his sides. "Elena deserves everything good life has to offer. What exactly do I have to offer her? I could be the worst thing to ever happen to her."

"Fine. You think you aren't good enough? Then I'll try."

"And exactly what do you have to offer her? None of us are good enough for her. We'll be handing her a life of anxiety and uncertainty. She doesn't deserve that."

"Is that what you think Stryker is giving Anya?" Santo asked, his tone tense. "You think she doesn't deserve better? Or you think Stryker is giving her a raw deal? It's one or the other."

Phantom took a step toward Santo, his muscles

bunching with the need to strike out at his friend. "I don't believe either of those things. It isn't the same. Anya's comfortable with the life we live, and Stryker is going to bend over backward to give her the world."

"You saying you wouldn't do the same for Elena?"

"You're deliberately twisting this around, and you're starting to piss me off," Phantom growled.

"If we need to step outside so you can throw a few punches and feel better about yourself, I'm game." Santo's eyes were narrowed, a muscle twitching in his jaw.

"Elena is off-limits. If I need to pound that into your brain to get you to understand, then I'll do just that."

"Excuse me, guys," Buzz said, stepping between them and heading for the freezer. "I'm in need of some ice cream. Don't stop fighting for my sake. It's been rather entertaining so far."

Phantom stepped back to give Buzz room, and the ridiculousness of the situation hit him. Santo had been by his side through some hellish times over the years, and he knew his friend would never try to do anything to hurt him. He looked away from Buzz and back at Santo and gave a half-hearted smile. "Shit, man, I'm sorry."

Santo smiled. "I'm not. I hoped some healthy competition would get you to see the light."

"You mean you were deliberately trying to tick me off?"

"I was deliberately trying to get you to see the prize you are letting slip away right underneath your nose. Snap was right the other day when he said she only has eyes for you. It's clear to everyone she's interested in you. Why are you fighting it so hard?"

Buzz finished fishing around in the freezer and emerged triumphantly with a tub of ice cream, grabbed a spoon, and nodded to them with a broad smile on his face as he left the room. Phantom shook his head. "She's special, bro. She's so strong and independent and stubborn as hell. She needs a good man at her side, and I don't know that I can be the partner she deserves."

"You'll never know if you don't try. The two of you work well together. It's obvious you get along by the way you were in sync throughout the entire game tonight. It's worth a shot."

"If things get serious enough, I'll have to tell her the truth about why we're really here. She's all about trust. That alone could be a deal breaker."

"All of us know the risks we're taking out here. If she can't come to terms with what you're doing, it wasn't meant to be in the first place."

Phantom sighed heavily. Everything Santo said made sense. He couldn't bear the thought of another man being in Elena's life. Still, he didn't know if he could handle losing her once he finally had her. "Shouldn't I try to keep my relationship with her professional? Hell, I'm her client."

Santo began to laugh so hard he nearly doubled over. "Yeah, good luck with that," he said when he gathered his breath. "Once you fail miserably, and you will, you owe me a steak at that really expensive place in Laredo."

Phantom smiled at his friend. "I don't think I'm willing to take that bet."

Chapter 12

"I STILL CAN'T BELIEVE YOU MADE THE CHOICE TO LIVE out at the ranch," Evie said.

Anya wiped refried beans off her lips and took a big sip of sweet tea before responding. "Is there a reason I shouldn't have?"

"It just seems so fast. I know, I know." Evie held up her hands. "You said you know when it's right, it's right. Given my past, I have a hard time putting my faith in that."

Elena glanced back and forth between her two friends and shrugged. "If it's what makes you happy, I say go for it. I'm glad you're finally back at work, though."

"I'm glad to be back too. I was going stir-crazy at home."

"Home. You do realize you just referred to the ranch as your home." Elena bit down into her potato, egg, and chorizo taco, enjoying the heat from the spices as she chewed. It was almost hot enough. She reached for the pica sitting in the middle of the table and slathered some generously over her taco. She glanced up when she realized Anya was taking too long to reply. Evie also watched Anya closely.

Anya wore a sappy smile, and Elena knew they were about to hear about Stryker. "It's where he is. That's home for me. Wherever he is."

Elena tried not to choke on her taco. Her best friend

had never been the type to go moony over a guy. She was a successful veterinarian, had built her business from the ground up, and had always joked that she would never need a man. She was independent, and fierce and… everything that Elena had thought had made all three of them so similar. Which now had her doubting herself.

Elena looked down at her half-eaten taco, her appetite gone. "Well, I'm happy for you."

"You could've fooled me." Anya's voice dripped with artificial sweetness.

"Anya, you know Elena and I both want to see you happy," Evie offered. "We just don't want to see you hurt. I need to meet this Stryker guy. Elena has a better pulse on your relationship with him than I do."

"I think he's a good guy," Elena said. "I think if he's everything Anya says he is, he really could be the one. I was just with them last night, and he was completely attentive to Anya."

"Speaking of last night," Anya said, one eyebrow raised, "is there something going on between you and Phantom?"

Elena's half-finished lunch suddenly seemed to weigh ten pounds in her gut. "What do you mean?"

"He's different when you're around. He seems to hang on your every word. And the two of you spend a lot of time together."

"Of course we do. I train his horses. And now I'm training him so that he can show. He has some big plans for the business."

"Are you sure that's all it is? He seems to light up when you're around."

He does? No, not Phantom. Maybe Anya was

misreading what was actually a look of dread on his face. Elena ran her hand through her curls, smoothing them away from her face. "If anything, you're seeing his excitement at working with the horses. He has a real gift with them."

"Oh." Anya looked disappointed. "I had just hoped… Well. The two of you seem to be ideal for each other. You both love horses, you both have a bit of a wild side, even though Phantom rarely shows his, and I thought the two of you were working together really well."

"We are!" Elena replied, almost too fast from the startled expression on Anya's face. "I mean, he's been a great student. He's going to be competing in his first show this weekend."

Evie had a skeptical look on her face. "You would tell us, right, Elena? If something was going on between you and this guy, I mean." She waved a hand in Anya's direction. "It seems love is in the air."

Elena chuckled. "There is no love to be found between me and Phantom. I won't deny he's a good-looking guy, and we do get along well. It's in our best interest, though, to keep our relationship purely professional. Going beyond that could just make things difficult."

Evie groaned. "You might as well wave the white flag. I can see where this is heading."

Anya smiled. "You *do* like him!"

Elena felt the heat of a blush in her cheeks. "Yes, I like him. But there's no chance of anything happening between the two of us. He already has a woman. Happy now?"

"What are you talking about?" The confusion on Anya's face nearly made Elena laugh.

"I saw the beautiful woman who came to the ranch the other day. Tall, graceful, with long, pale hair—she embraced him as if they hadn't seen each other in years. She made him laugh. I could tell he loves her."

Dawning understanding brightened Anya's face. "Of course he loves her! And it's hard to say exactly how long it's been since they've seen each other. Their schedules have kept them apart for a while. You don't need to worry about her, though."

"I'm not worried about her. Like I said, I'm not considering a relationship with him. It won't benefit either one of us."

"Of course, if you *were* interested in a relationship with him, I'm sure you'd be happy to know the beautiful woman you saw is Amber, his sister."

Elena had been taking a deep sip of her tea and sputtered, coughing as she tried to catch her breath. Evie patted her on the back roughly until she finally stopped coughing. "His sister?"

"Yep. Glad it doesn't mean anything to you, though." Anya watched Elena with a smirk on her face.

Elena chewed on her lower lip, absorbing the news before shaking her head. "He's not interested. At all."

"I think you may be misreading his signals. Seriously, Elena, he's different when you're around. Happier."

Elena shook her head and pretended to be preoccupied with the ice in her glass. "No. My love life still revolves around a bowl of Froot Loops, milk, and ice."

"Ugh. You don't still eat that, do you? I thought that was just a bad college habit." Evie made a face.

"I'm never lonely when I have that sweet treat to enjoy." Elena forced a smile to her face.

Anya didn't seem to be buying it. "Are you certain there isn't even the smallest spark between you guys?"

Elena's mind wandered back to the heated kiss they had shared in the barn. She could still feel his hand cupping her ass, lifting her so that she could hold him the way she wanted, feel him the way she'd craved. There hadn't been a spark; there had practically been an all-out fire blazing between them.

Thinking about it made her heart beat faster. Still, he had pushed her away and made it clear he didn't want to continue as she did. "No. There's nothing there. I'm not his type. And he isn't mine. How's your migas plate?" She asked Anya.

"Wow. And I thought the guys were good about changing the topic. It's great. Want some? I can't eat all of it."

Elena waved her hand to signal no. "Is your new assistant the guy who showed up at the ranch the other day? Phantom said he's a part owner at the ranch. If that's the case, why is he taking you to work and staying at the clinic with you?"

"Lobo is a part owner, but he also had experience working in a veterinary clinic when he was in high school. He offered to help me for a short while as I get things back up and running. And…it's kind of a security blanket for me. I was pretty rattled by the break-in."

"I can imagine," Evie said.

"Speaking of being rattled, do either of you know Jonas Franklin?" Elena asked, already dreading her trip out to his ranch as soon as lunch was over.

"Ugh. Don't even get me started on him." Evie groaned.

"I try to avoid him at all costs. I still tend to his animals. I can't turn them away because I feel responsible
for them since I'm the only veterinarian in the entire
area. But I try to avoid interacting with Jonas as much
as I can. I don't even ask him to pay when I'm out there.
I just send him bills in the mail."

Elena gnawed on the inside of her cheek. "Why?
What is it that you don't like?"

"I interact with him at the courthouse frequently."
Evie sighed. "He's always meeting with Judge O'Connor.
Usually it is because he believes he should legally be
cleared to do whatever he wants on his land and
shouldn't need to get the appropriate clearances from
the county inspectors. For some reason, he seems to
have latched onto Judge O'Connor, and I have to deal
with him more than I'd like. I've lost count of the
number of times he has asked me out. And he constantly hovers around my workstation. I get the feeling
he is trying to find any documents he can get his sneaky
eyeballs on."

"He's asked me out before too," Anya said. "He wants
to know everything he can about my schedules and the
people that I work with. It's like he wants to find out
any secrets about his neighbors. There's something off
about him. That's why I try to avoid him. Why are you
asking?" Anya watched Elena with concern in her eyes.

Elena tried to suppress a shudder as she thought about
Jonas. "That man strikes me as being wrong in many
ways. He's asked me out, and I've told him repeatedly
we aren't compatible and tried, in the nicest way, to let
him know he's not my type. He still won't take the hint.
Both of you know what happened a few years back and

how certain things bring it all back with a terrible feeling of helplessness. The last time I saw Jonas, he came up behind me and began to massage my shoulders. I thought I was going to hyperventilate."

Anya shook her head fiercely. "No man should think it is okay to initiate such intimate contact, regardless of your past."

"I thought I might have been overreacting because of the attack." Elena stared at the tablecloth, fighting back nausea at both the memories of her past and the knowledge she would have to encounter Jonas soon.

Anya's hand covered one of Elena's hands, and Evie's covered the other. Elena glanced up at her two closest friends and saw the way they were watching her—not with pity, but with support. They had taken turns camping out in the hospital room as she recovered from her injuries, making sure she never woke up alone. The moment she shifted in her bed, Evie or Anya jumped up from the cot the hospital had brought into the room and helped her with anything she needed. She couldn't have asked for better friends.

"I think he knows what happened to me and likes to put me in a position to make me uncomfortable. I think he gets some sort of pleasure from making others feel weak. I just have a bad feeling about him. I've decided to try to find another client that will cover the loss, and I'm going to drop him."

"Good for you." Anya nodded firmly. "If he makes you that uncomfortable, the money isn't worth it."

"Now you've made me curious to know more about his interactions with Judge O'Connor. I don't understand why she tolerates him," Evie said thoughtfully.

Elena drew a deep breath. "Well, I can't put it off forever. It's time to go visit his ranch. Thank you both for joining me for lunch. This has been nice."

"Yeah, I better get back to the clinic before my guard dog sounds the alarm."

"Don't you mean your guard *wolf*," Elena chuckled.

Anya smiled. "Lobo is a great guy. He's a good addition to the team, and I'm incredibly grateful to him for helping me out until I feel a little more secure."

"At some point you need to invite me to the ranch," Evie said, giving Anya a pointed stare. "I want to meet all these men you two keep talking about."

"Be careful what you wish for." Anya chuckled. "If these guys decide they like you, they just might try to keep you."

Sherman's skills were still in improving. Elena took him though a more complex reining pattern, and he struggled with a few of the directional changes. She worked him for hours, determined to get him to fly through various patterns without getting set into any type of routine. When it came to higher-level championships, a horse and rider had to be ready for any type of pattern thrown their way.

The sun had started to set by the time she finished bathing Sherman, cleaning the tack, and setting everything in order in the barn. She sighed wearily and ran a hand through her long, curly hair, dreading the unavoidable meeting with Jonas. She had to share with him the wins from the other weekend.

"Elena! It's so good to see you again. I regret that it

has taken us so long to meet up." Jonas walked toward her from the direction of the main house, and she hoped she would be able to get through her meeting with him quickly.

"You've been a very busy man, Jonas. Your business must be doing well."

He smiled broadly but attempted to shrug as if her words meant nothing. "It takes a lot of work to get things to run fluidly in my business. I'm glad I caught you out here in the barn. I wanted to get your help with some transfer paperwork on a new horse I bought."

"Is it the bay mare? She's absolutely gorgeous."

"I'm glad you approve! I think she may actually be a better competitor than Sherman."

Elena raised her eyebrows in surprise. "Sherman's a tough act to beat. I look forward to working with her."

"Good, good. I look forward to watching you train her. Join me in the barn office so we can work on these transfer papers."

Elena drew a steadying breath and followed him to the barn office, an area Jonas seemed to rarely use. He shouldered open the door that seemed to be perpetually stuck no matter how often Elena worked on it. The hinges squeaked, and she made a mental note to bring her WD-40 with her the next time she came out.

"So are you done for the day?"

"Yes. Sherman got quite the workout today. He still needs training, but I'm fairly certain we're going to have a top contender for the show. I wouldn't take him if I didn't think we had a good shot at winning the Grand Champion."

Jonas grinned at her as he sat down at the desk and

clicked the button to power on his docked laptop. "I know you're going to bring me the Grand Champion prize. You've yet to disappoint."

"Speaking of which..." Elena began, positioning herself close to the other door in the office that led to the tack room, giving her space from Jonas. "I brought you the ribbons for the wins the other weekend." She pulled an envelope out of her back pocket. "Here are your winnings for the cutting event. There was no prize money for the reining event."

Jonas nodded and reached for the envelope, deliberately rubbing his fingers over the back of her hand as he took it from her. She pulled back quickly and fought the urge to wipe her hand on her jeans. She felt as if she had been tainted by his touch.

"Let me show you something," Jonas beamed, gesturing for her to walk around the desk to his side.

She hesitated for a few moments, then forced her legs into motion and went to stand behind him. The computer had pulled up the log-on screen, and she stared at the puzzle depicted on the screen. "What is that?"

"You and I have a lot in common, my dear," Jonas said, still staring at the locked screen. "We both have a love of puzzles. In order to get into my computers, you have to solve one of my cryptic puzzles. All the answers are to be given in a question format to point to a location on the ranch. You have to use the clues provided in the puzzle to formulate the question."

Elena didn't want to tell him she was impressed, even though she was. Not many people were so engaged in puzzles that they had the ability to create their own. Her eyes roamed over the graphics on the screen, and she began to see words hidden within the extensive artwork. Her mind worked quickly, gathering all the information and thinking about the layout of the ranch.

The answer struck her, and she couldn't resist blurting it out. "Where on the back eighty acres is the watering hole located?"

Jonas lifted his eyebrows. "Impressive. I should have made it more difficult knowing your skills with puzzles."

"Did you create this log-on specifically with plans to keep me out? I have no desire to go digging around in your computer, Jonas." Elena folded her arms over her chest, wishing she could leave. Her level of discomfort increased every extra moment she was near Jonas.

"No, of course not. I simply hope no one else is able to break my puzzles as quickly as you." He typed the question into the log-on screen and the internet screen popped up, showing an online form to request transfer of ownership through the American Quarter Horse Association. Jonas pulled out a pair of glasses to help him read the small type and began to chicken-peck at the keyboard. "Can you read the information off to me and I'll key it in?"

Elena wanted to tell him no. Just because she had finished her responsibilities for the day didn't mean she wanted to spend her spare time with him. But she didn't have a good reason to deny helping him, when she knew she wouldn't hesitate to do it for any of her other customers.

After ten minutes of painfully trying to read the information to him while he attempted to navigate the form, she lost her patience. "Why don't I fill out the form? I've done it plenty of times in the past, and that way we can move through it quicker."

He glanced up at her. "Am I keeping you from something?"

"You know me. I like to be as efficient as possible, and I think we'd use our time much more effectively if I filled out the form."

He nodded. "Very well. Have at it." He stood and gave her the chair. It wasn't until she was seated at the computer and working on the form that she realized she had put herself in a vulnerable spot. He stood hovering over her and could easily take advantage in such a position.

She decided to keep his mind on business and finish the form as quickly as possible. "How did you hear about this new horse?"

"I have several connections that keep me updated whenever a talented horse comes on the market. My business dealings have had me so busy I haven't been able to focus on building my horse enterprise as much as I'd like. Things are running smoothly, though, and this was too good an opportunity to pass up."

"Has the mare won in competitions already?" Her fingers flew across the keyboard, keying in the information rapidly.

"Yes. She's made it all the way to state quarter horse shows, but can't move past that level. That's where your expertise will come in handy."

Elena sighed with relief as she finished the application and clicked the submit button. She could feel Jonas close behind her and stood, turning to face him, her heart pounding in her chest. "All done. You should get the new registration certificate in the mail soon."

He smiled approvingly. "Good. Now, since you've finished up for the day, I can finally show you the display for all the trophies and ribbons. We'll add the new ones you earned from the other weekend."

Elena nearly groaned. She didn't want to be around the man any longer. He was still her client, though, and she needed to set aside her personal discomfort around the man. She would keep a safe distance and pray that he didn't try to cross any boundaries with her—again. "Absolutely. Lead the way."

Jonas had a beautiful home. With a small entrance foyer that held a chandelier casting a warm glow through the space, it welcomed her inside. She had been in his home a handful of times and had always appreciated the simple and tasteful design. To the right lay the expansive living space, and she instantly saw the large display case full of trophies and ribbons set in a central spot in the room.

"It's beautiful," Elena said, stepping farther into the room to get a closer look. "Did you have it custom-made?"

"Of course. I only want the best to be able to display the fine work you do with my horses."

Elena paused in the center of the room, unwilling to go any farther. She didn't want to get stuck in a tight spot with Jonas. "Thank you for showing me, and thank you for giving me any credit, but your horses are very talented. It's my pleasure to be working with them."

Jonas scoffed. "You're easily the best horse trainer in south Texas. I wouldn't want anyone else working with my horses, and I know the only reason they're gaining notice in the industry is because of your abilities with them."

Elena smiled at Jonas. He hadn't tried to invade her space and seemed to be on his best behavior. She was grateful for it. "Thank you, again. I'd best head home. I've got another horse show this weekend with another client's horses, so I'll be up early again tomorrow."

"Before you leave, there's one other thing I'd like to show you. It's in my office." He turned and began to head down a hallway off the living room, and Elena hesitated for several moments before reluctantly following him.

The office was large and clearly where he spent the majority of his time. Maps covered the walls, and his desk held two monitors and a docked laptop. To the side of his desk stood a large credenza with blueprints spread out on it.

"This is a project I've been working on for quite some time. It's very near completion."

Elena approached the credenza and looked over the blueprints with curiosity. "Is this another barn?" she asked, growing excited at the prospect of working in a new facility.

"It is. But not just any barn. You inspired part of the design."

His voice was incredibly close to her and she took a step sideways, pretending to concentrate on the drawings and calm the unease building within her. "How could I inspire your design?"

"Your love of puzzles is what got me to think creatively about it."

Elena looked up at him, hating that he was so close to her. "I meant to ask you this earlier, but I was drawn in by your puzzle. How do you know about my love of puzzles? I don't remember ever telling you about it."

"You forget that we live in an incredibly small town. Some people have talked about your passion for puzzles, and I became interested. I did some research and found all the different kinds. I think you'll be impressed by the way I incorporated them into the design of the new facility."

Elena's level of uneasiness increased. "What do you mean?"

"I'll save that answer for when you first get to experience the facility. I'll just tell you it adds a lot to the beauty of the design."

"Puzzles can be cosmetically attractive. Many artists incorporate a puzzle in their work without it being obvious to the common eye. I'm sure your barn will be impressive." Elena shifted to a position so that she was closer to the door than Jonas.

"I'm glad you approve."

"It's very creative, Jonas. I don't know why you focused on my hobby to help you with the design."

He smiled and moved closer to her, and she forced herself not to step back. She wanted to get away from him. He had taken his interest in her much further than she had ever feared. Gathering information about her interests felt far too much like he was stalking her. "This facility will be an area where you'll spend a majority of your work. I wanted to make it interesting for you."

"I-I appreciate it, Jonas. I didn't even know you were building a new barn. Where is it on the property?"

"I'll show you as soon as it is finished. There will be many surprises for you."

"Then I have something to look forward to," she said, forcing a smile to her numb face. "I'll see you next week, Jonas."

She turned to walk away from him and gasped in surprise when his hand caught hers and pulled her back toward him. Instantly, she yanked her hand free from his grasp and took several large steps back from him. He held up his hands defensively. "I didn't mean to frighten you, Elena. I just wanted to thank you for all your work."

"We've talked about boundaries before, Jonas. You continue to push them with me, and I don't like having to remind you that we don't have that kind of relationship. The only relationship I want is one where you are my client and I provide my knowledge to the training and showing of your horses. It isn't anything other than that."

"It doesn't have to be, Elena. Daniel told me what happened to you a few years ago. I can't imagine anyone wanting to hurt someone as beautiful and exquisite as you. I can understand your hesitation, but surely you know I'd give you anything your heart desires."

He did *know! The bastard has been deliberately trying to put me in uncomfortable situations for his own enjoyment, just as I suspected.* "If you really knew what happened to me, you would never put me in these difficult positions. You would respect me and not continue pushing a relationship on me that I clearly don't want. I know about your wealth and influence, Jonas, but that isn't what my heart desires. You can't buy my love."

"What do you want, Elena? I'm already building a

state-of-the-art training facility you'll get to use. I'll get you horses in your name. I'll support all your efforts to become the best trainer in the state—hell, in the nation—if that's what you want. I want you, Elena. I want you to be a part of my life, and not just appearing once or twice a week as my horse trainer."

Elena moved closer to the door. "It isn't going to happen, Jonas."

"Give me time. I'll prove to you I can make you a very happy woman."

"I'm already happy. Don't attempt to touch me again. I don't want to have this conversation with you again." She turned and walked through the house quickly, afraid if she looked behind her she'd find him pursuing her to force her to continue the conversation.

Once she had left the house, she broke into a run, sweat running between her shoulder blades in the late-evening heat. She jumped into her truck and quickly guided it away from the ranch and out onto the road. It wasn't until she finally hit the main paved road that she realized she was shaking violently.

She swallowed hard and brushed her hair away from her face. Jonas had finally gone too far. The most recent contract he'd signed expired in three weeks. When she returned the following week, she'd try to avoid Jonas completely, gather her personal tack and gear and leave. A simple email giving her two week's notice should sever any thought he had to extend his contract.

They were getting close. The Congressman knew they were. It was just a matter of time before they discovered who had killed his friend. Yes, Benicio had been an ass most of his life, an arrogant ass on top of that, but that arrogance had allowed him to become one of the youngest drug lords in Mexico. Now his vibrant life had been snuffed out.

The Congressman already knew that the navy was behind the placement of the vigilante group that had done it. Were they active duty, or something else? Civilians? Veterans? Whatever the answer, the navy had been given too much leeway to meddle in international affairs.

Which was why getting this congressional task force nomination was critical. He could take some of the pressure off his southern connections under the guise of investigating criminal activities and use the power of his position to generate loopholes for his connections to continue their affairs, gathering the money he knew waited for them.

But it would all be a waste if the navy's wonder team continued to interfere in his affairs.

By destroying Benicio and his cartel, they had essentially crippled his drug operations. Every day that he didn't have enough manpower, thousands upon thousands of dollars slipped through his fingers. He had helped Benicio set up a system for smuggling the drugs into the United States, as well as an elaborate communication system, and the implementation of both gave him huge kickbacks.

Another congressman nearby droned on and on, while he sat and stewed over his own problems.

This next transaction with his connections was critical. The operation had been in the planning stages for months. The Border Patrol would never even know what had happened.

And if he could uncover the whereabouts and identities of the Texas team, he could get rid of all his problems at once.

"All those in favor of passing Bill…"

He glanced around at his fellow party members to see which way they were voting. Damn these navy men! They were costing him money and causing him to lose focus. His fellow party members raised their hands, and he joined with them. He sighed with relief when one of the older party leaders smiled at him and nodded approvingly. He'd find out later what he had voted for.

In the meantime, south Texas needed his attention. There would have to be a total kill of his enemies for things to work out in his favor, but he wouldn't be the one to get his hands dirty.

He was already lining up the right people to handle the things he needed to keep at a distance. He had a new point person working for Haslett, and he knew the information he needed would come through any day.

Yes, he just needed to bide his time. Soon he would destroy the men who had come so close to destroying his carefully crafted enterprise. He smiled to himself. Things were beginning to fall into place, just like a well-designed puzzle.

"We'll take Black Out and Strawberry to the show. With the two of us, there is a chance we'll take Grand and Reserve Champion."

"Or I'll look like a total fool, fumble my way through

things, and no one will ever want to bring their business to us—I mean, to the ranch."

To us. Almost as if they were in this endeavor together. Subconsciously, he realized he *did* think that way. In reality, his ranch would benefit the most from the high-profile show. Any profit made went to the ranch. It didn't impact her.

But it should. She had been busting her ass for a long time, and he didn't want to let her down. He wanted her to be proud of all he had learned. He knew that the exposure of her expertise in the show ring would help further her dream of becoming a coveted trainer in Texas, and she saw that as her reward. He felt she deserved much more than that.

"I'll be back here tomorrow. The grooming and prep work takes a little longer, so I'll need Thursday and Friday to get them in the best condition."

"Are you talking about the horses or me?" Where had that come from? It was a flirtatious remark, and he hadn't planned to behave in such a way around her. He needed to talk to her, needed to explain why he had tried to put distance between them and find out if any chance existed for a rekindled spark between them. He had become so comfortable around her, though, and the temptation to watch her reactions to his flirting or teasing seemed natural when he let his guard down.

A hesitant smile tipped up the corners of her mouth. "Both, I suppose," she replied softly. "You'll finally get to experience all the work that goes into getting ready for a horse show."

He rubbed the back of his neck as she walked away from him, leading Strawberry back to her stall. They were finished for the day, but he didn't want to see her go yet. Working with her—hell, just *being* around her— brought him a level of excitement and pleasure he hadn't experienced in a long time and easily classified as the highlight of his day. Even though tension still crackled between them, he always felt relieved—yes, even happy—when he saw her truck heading up their dusty road.

It meant that at least for the time she worked with his horses, he could keep her safe from the mad world they lived in. He knew he shouldn't feel so protective of her, but he couldn't help it. With each day he worked with her, she made him long for more, and he wanted to make sure she never felt any discomfort, any sadness, any disappointment. Knowing *he* had been the source of some of her recent disappointment left a bitter taste in his mouth.

When he saw her truck coming up their road, he knew he would have her all to himself for several hours. He hated the idea that other ranchers were enjoying time with her. He didn't want anyone else to receive her glowing smile or see the twinkle in her eyes when a horse or the person she trained performed well. He treasured his time with her and wished she only worked at his ranch.

"You certainly are deep in thought. Are you really that worried about the show?" Elena had left the barn and was wiping her hands on her jeans as she walked toward him, concern on her face.

He shook his head, unable to find his voice for the moment. His experiences with women had never included thinking about what he wanted long-term.

Early in his career he had experienced the frog hogs, the women who jumped from one SEAL to another, putting more pride in their lists of conquests than in the feelings of the men they were involved with. At the age of nineteen, he hadn't turned down the opportunities for a good time.

But he had known going in that none of those flings would last. The women hadn't wanted anything more from him than a couple of wild nights.

When it came to Elena, he suddenly had the desire to have her love and support wrapped around him. He wanted to have her waiting for him every time he came home from a deployment, there to take care of his bruises and aches and pains and be strong enough to let him have his time with the team before he could come for her and seek the sweet solace he knew he would find with her.

He wanted to be there for her, to give her a strong shoulder to lean on if she ever needed it. He wanted to show her that she could trust him and rely on him, and that he would support her and help her grow with all her dreams. He wanted to put her on a pedestal where she belonged.

"Phantom?"

She stood in front of him, and he looked down into her eyes. That warm brown seemed to hold a little bit of sparkle, but it could have been just the glint of the sunlight hitting her. "No, no. I'm not that concerned about the show." He threw out the first answer that popped into his head and realized with surprise that he really wasn't. Elena had trained him and the horses well. The show would be fine.

"You're going to do great. Well, I-I suppose I'll

see you tomorrow. I have another ranch to visit this afternoon."

"You're hitting another place today? I thought we were your only stop on Wednesdays. Since when did your schedule change?" *She belonged to me on Wednesdays.* The possessive thought took him by surprise.

"Just this week. I have to go see them today because I'll be back here tomorrow. Don't worry, Phantom. I'm not going to shortchange you."

Her voice seemed tense and the expression on her face veiled. Did she really think that he counted her hours to make sure he got what they'd agreed to in the client contract they'd signed?

"Elena, we need to talk." *What am I doing? How do I fix what I broke between us? Santo is right. I won't ever know if there's a chance for us if I don't try. But, damn it, how do I even approach this? An apology is weak. I have to show her I want to try to build something between us. I need to have a plan.*

Elena had already started walking to her truck when he spoke. She stopped in midstride, and her back went ramrod straight. Very slowly, she turned her head to look at him, and the apprehension on her face deeply disappointed him—in himself. His actions had created the tension between them. Only he could fix everything.

"I thought everything for the show has been planned. What else do we need to talk about?"

He crammed his hands down into his pockets to keep himself from reaching for her. He wanted nothing more than to cup her face in his hands and try to find that heat again. He shook his head instead. "Never mind. It can wait." He needed to hit the gym again to take out his frustrations. And when that failed, he'd take a very long, cold shower.

She tilted her head to look at him with curiosity, but stayed silent for a very long time. Oh, how he wanted to touch her wind-tossed curls and bury his face against her neck, inhaling her wonderful scent.

"I'll see you tomorrow, Phantom." She left so quickly, he didn't get the chance to say how much he looked forward to it.

Chapter 13

DRIPPING SPRINGS USED TO BE A LITTLE SECRET, A SMALL town outside Austin that few people knew about. The secret had been spilled, though, and Elena stared at all the changes with wonder. Now boasting tall apartment buildings, exclusive million-dollar neighborhoods, a thriving commercial sector, and its own exquisite indoor arena, Dripping Springs was an extension of the massive Austin scene.

Elena hadn't shown in the Austin area in a couple of years and couldn't have been more excited to be back in the central Texas region. Known for having some of the most talented trainers and horses, the central Texas region would allow her to see how her skills and the abilities of Phantom's horses measured. Her body hummed with both excitement and nervousness. With it being Phantom's first time showing, she wanted him to have a great experience he would always remember with fondness.

Dripping Springs sat west of Austin, and the drive, complete with pit stops and traffic, had taken them nearly five hours. By the time they had the horses stalled, fed, and secured, it was edging close to midnight on Friday night. Many activities were occurring that weekend in both Austin and Dripping Springs, and most all the accommodations that were remotely close were booked, except for one.

The B and B didn't have an updated website, but when Elena had called and talked to the owner, he'd guaranteed he would hold the last two cabins for her. He said the cabins were old homesteads they had lovingly restored and kept as authentic as possible. Elena was looking forward to the cozy comfort of the cottage and the soft mattress after the long day they'd had.

She also looked forward to a chance to take a deep breath away from Phantom. Being around him for hours on end had her nerves wildly aware of every move he made. The sound of the steering wheel sliding through his hands as he turned into the drive of the B and B reminded her of the feeling of his palms cupping her ass. She squirmed in her seat, eager to get out of the truck and take a large gulp of fresh air.

"Do you know if anyone will even be awake to check us in this late?" He cast a sideways glance at her, and she could feel the tension radiating off him. She wanted to laugh. Clearly, he shared her feelings after being trapped together on the long drive. She hated that he didn't want her as she wanted him and knew she would be thinking about him sleeping in a nearby cabin, wondering if he slept in the nude or not. Her cheeks burned at the thought.

"I told the owner we'd arrive late, and he assured me someone would be available to give us keys. I think the office is over there." She pointed to a small building set slightly back from the historic cabins.

"I don't see a light on in that building." A muscle near his eye twitched.

"Don't worry. Maybe they dozed off, but I'm sure someone will come to the door as soon as we knock."

She lifted her chin when he cast her a dubious look, hoping she looked confident. She'd never stayed at a B and B before and hoped the owner proved as professional as he'd seemed over the phone.

Phantom threw the truck into park, the headlights shining on the tiny building, and Elena breathed a sigh of relief when she saw a light flip on inside. She quickly unfastened her seat belt. "I'll be back soon."

He said nothing, but joined her at the front of the truck near the stairs leading up to the hut serving as an office. His desire to make certain she stayed safe didn't surprise her. She only wished his desire extended beyond the chivalrous idea of protecting her.

The soft click of the dead bolt being unfastened sounded just before the door swung open and an older man faced them. He ran a hand through his gray hair and down his wrinkled, drowsy face. "You must be Elena."

The slight anxiety that crossed his features made her nervous. "Yes. You're Adam, right? I let you know we'd be arriving late today."

The elderly man glanced at the clock on his desk as he stepped back so they could enter. "Technically, it's already tomorrow. When you said 'late,' I thought you meant ten o'clock, not the next day."

Phantom closed the door behind them. "Sorry for the delay. We were held up at the barn longer than we expected. I'm sure you want to catch some sleep as much as we do, so we'll sign whatever papers are needed and take the keys off your hands."

Adam lowered his head and shuffled his boots on the hardwood floor. "Yeah, about that…" He lifted his head and looked at Elena, then Phantom. "Since it was so late, I thought you might not turn up. I had a last-minute customer show up, and I gave them one of the cabins you reserved."

Elena blinked rapidly, certain she must be so tired she had misheard him. "You did what?"

"If I hadn't fallen asleep at the desk, I wouldn't even be here. You're lucky we still have one cabin left."

"Wait—you only have *one* cabin available in this entire place?" The muscle near Phantom's eye twitched again.

"You're lucky we have that, son. It's a very busy time of the year in Austin, and as big as Dripping Springs has become, people take advantage of our little home-away-from-home atmosphere here too. I really didn't think y'all were coming."

Elena tried to control her rising ire with the man. He had a business to run and had made a decision to make sure he capitalized on the busy weekend. She couldn't fault him for that, tired and annoyed as she was. "We'll take the last cabin."

Phantom didn't look at her as he pulled out his wallet and paid for the rental. She strongly suspected she would hear his thoughts on the situation once they were out of Adam's earshot. After a quick transaction, the older man handed Phantom an old-fashioned key on a key chain with the B and B logo and escorted them out of the hut, locking it up behind them.

"We usually put out a breakfast spread about seven in the morning in the main house." Adam didn't offer any further information, just gave a curt nod, then strolled on the rock-paved path toward the large house in the dark distance.

Phantom glanced at the key chain, then searched their surroundings. "We're in that cabin over there." He pointed to their left, and Elena could just barely make out the shape of a small building. She didn't say anything as they jumped back into the truck and drove to the cabin set a few hundred yards from the next old homestead.

She hopped out of the truck before he killed the engine and grabbed her overnight bag from the back seat. Drawing a deep breath, she leaned against the truck for a moment. She had to pull it together to get through the weekend with him.

He waited for her by the front of the truck, a simple backpack slung over his shoulder. When she began to charge forward toward the cabin, his finger hooked in one of her belt loops, pulling her back. He shook his head at her. "I'll lead."

Her heart stuttered. She could feel the warmth of his fingers as they grazed her side when he removed his hand. While she took pride in being independent and taking care of herself, his strength and control over the situation made her feel safe.

In the faint moonlight she watched the way his eyes scanned the area before he led them up the three short steps to the door. "Wait here," he said, his tone indicating there was no room for her to question why or argue.

He moved into the small cabin slowly, silently...a phantom in the night.

After a minute, the lights flicked on inside and he opened the door fully, his eyes boring into her. "'Small' is a compliment for this cabin. Jail cells are larger."

"Oh, you're being overly dramatic. It only *feels* small.

You're just oversized." She flashed him one of the forced smiles she had been perfecting and slid under the arm that he had braced in the doorway, entering the cabin.

She instantly fell in love with its charm. There was nothing fancy about it, but it wasn't supposed to be. Being a genuine cabin that had been built in the 1850s, it showed the labor and hard work that had gone into its construction. The hand-cut wood had been layered with plaster made from a mixture of mud to make walls. A king bed placed off to one corner and a small table under the window were the only pieces of furniture in the room. Had it not been for the flat-screen TV mounted on the wall, Elena would have thought they had stepped back in time.

A soft smile lifted the corners of her mouth as she turned back around, but it dropped quickly at the look on Phantom's face. "Right. So it isn't what we thought we were getting, but we'll make the best of the situation."

He glanced at the bed before looking at her again. "I'll sleep on the floor."

Elena frowned at him. "We're intelligent, rational adults. We can sleep in the same bed for one night. Or are you offended by the very idea?"

Phantom clenched his hands at his sides twice before responding. "It's awkward, and I won't put you in such a position."

"I don't think so. We should just share the bed. There's no need to argue about it."

Imagining what it would be like to be in the same bed with him brought a blush to her cheeks. She wanted to know what it would feel like to rest her head on his chest and listen to his heartbeat after they had passionately made love. She wanted to explore every inch of his body. Her wayward thoughts made her blush even more, and she was grateful there wasn't much light in the cabin.

She had fought her desire for him ever since he had pushed her away in the barn, but she hadn't succeeded in erasing the emotions he stirred in her. Now, with him standing so determined and strong in front of her, she couldn't stop her mind from traveling such a path. He represented the traits she found appealing in a man, but not just superficially. Yes, the man held his own when it came to an impressive male physique, and handsome hardly seemed a sufficient word to describe his features. But he represented patience, caring, generosity, and a good heart.

After their first meeting weeks ago when he'd told her he didn't need her services, he had surprised her over and over again. He had shown her his kind and gentle side, something she hadn't thought she could ever find in a man. Her mind wandered back to the moment at the diner after the Edinburg horse show and the way his fingers had so gently wiped away her tears. There had been sincerity in his expression and in his words.

He had been humble enough to admit he needed her help with the horses. On top of that, he had allowed her to enter his personal world, inviting her to have dinner with his business partners and showing his fun side when they had played spades the other night.

She liked everything about him, even though he didn't seem to share the same feelings. But if he really didn't enjoy her presence, why had he asked her to stay for dinner and insisted on being her partner when they played spades? Could he have emotions for her after all, emotions that, for some reason, he didn't want to acknowledge?

He took a step forward and stood so close she could smell his musky cologne as well as the lingering aroma of the fresh hay they had fed the horses before leaving the show barn. She had to tilt her head back to see his eyes darken as he watched her slightest movement. "If I tell you what's running through my mind, if I tell you the things I'm *really* thinking about when I consider lying in a bed with you, you'll beg me to sleep on the floor."

"What happens if that only makes me more determined to have you sleep next to me tonight?" she whispered.

He raised a hand as if to stroke a strand of hair off her cheek, then clenched his fingers into a fist, slowly lowering it back to his side. "We may both lose sleep tonight if I join you on that bed."

"That's a risk I'm willing to take."

"Elena…"

She could tell by the expression on his face he didn't want to agree with her. She shrugged. "I'm going to get comfortable." She turned her back on him and walked over to the bed. Setting down her overnight bag, she slowly drew a deep breath. Her hands trembled as she reached for the zipper on the bag.

A small bathroom had been added to the back of the cabin, obviously not part of the original structure. There wasn't a door on the bathroom, just a small curtain to divide it from the room. She could tell the curtain didn't close all the way, which meant he could see in if he looked in that direction. Her heart began to race, and her palms began to sweat. She wasn't about to be a prude and ask him to look away until she finished changing.

Suck it up, buttercup. I didn't expect to be put in this situation, but it's what we have, and we'll make the most of it. Or, at the very least, I will. He can sulk all night if he wants, but he's sleeping in the damned bed!

She headed into the bathroom and closed the curtain as far as she could, leaving a large gap that refused to shut. She swallowed, even though her mouth was dry, as she tugged her T-shirt out from the waistband of her jeans and quickly whisked it over her head. The faster she got into her pajamas, the better. She had just slid the straps of her bra down her arms when she heard the door open and close again behind him. She should have been grateful he'd stepped out.

Instead she felt disappointment. She wanted him to desire her the way she desired him. She wanted him to be interested in her and unable to take his eyes off her. She sighed heavily. She might as well ask for the moon.

The air in Dripping Springs was cooler than in Hebbronville. It was still humid and muggy, but nothing like it was back home. Phantom stood on the porch, his hands crammed in his pockets and his mouth turned down in a frown. Home. He hadn't had a home since he was a kid. Even as a teenager he had felt out of place in his parents' house. He had felt restless and unwanted, even though he knew his parents loved him tremendously. They just hadn't known what to do with him.

But now, out of nowhere, his mind had identified the ranch as home. He had fallen in love with the ranch and the town, and that left him in uncharted territory. He had started to feel comfortable in his own skin. He had never felt more at peace than when he worked in the barn with Elena.

Elena. Good grief, the woman would be the death of him. She was too stubborn for her own good. He had been unable to tear his eyes off her when she entered the bathroom. When she had pulled her T-shirt over her head, the incredible lines of her body had become obvious. She had her hair piled on top of her head, exposing her long neck and the way it curved down to her shoulders.

She wore a navy-blue bra, and the contrast of the color against her dark skin could only be described as exquisite. Her breasts were rounded enough that, even standing behind her, he could see the swells from the side. Adding in his vibrant memory of the way she had felt pressed into his chest during their passionate kiss, his imagination quickly painted a picture of what her breasts would feel like if he slid up behind her and cupped them in his hands. Then his imagination had caused sweat to break out between his shoulder blades, overwhelming him with an idea of the way her nipples would become erect and stab into his palms.

Her waist tucked in gradually from the swells of her breasts, and he remembered how she had felt when his arm had wrapped around her. Her tiny frame and luscious curves seemed built precisely to fit his needs. He'd heard the zipper of her jeans, and his eyes had slid down to where her hips flared out slightly to her heart-shaped ass—and it had suddenly become hard to breathe.

He hadn't even realized he had left the cabin until the

soft breeze hit him. He stood on the porch, breathing in the night air, and tried to calm his body. What the hell was he supposed to do? He needed to find self-restraint so he could lie next to her through the night without giving in to the desire to hold her sweet body against his.

Heaven help him. That bed wasn't large enough to put the kind of distance between them that he needed to keep his sanity. He wanted her with every cell in his body, but he needed to make things right between them. He had to confess to her that he had wanted her all along but had made the mistake of assuming what would be best for her instead of letting her decide for herself.

He had no doubt he would be able to pleasure her. In his dreams, she cried out his name as he brought her to ecstasy. More than one night, he'd woken up so hard that even the light touch of the sheet across his skin felt like torture. He knew that being with Elena would be different than what he had experienced with any other woman.

But then what? After the pleasure, after they were both satiated, he had nothing to offer her. He could be deployed any day, and he would have to leave her without explanation—with the added strong chance that he wouldn't be coming back home. He couldn't put her through that. She deserved a man who could give her added stability in her life, not leave her questioning whether he would return alive.

Feeling calmer, he drew in a deep breath and turned back to the cabin, entering through the door with barely a sound. He froze. She had let her hair down and wore a simple pair of silk pajama pants and a tank top. She had a hoodie on the bed waiting to be pulled on. Her breasts, freed from the constraint of her bra, pushed against the fabric. She had just set her bag in the corner and had turned to face him when he entered, and her large eyes settled on him. She arched an eyebrow, obviously wanting to know his decision.

Heaven help him. His body had made the decision before he had even stepped into the room. To his surprise, his mind completely agreed.

Chapter 14

ELENA'S HEART BEGAN TO POUND FASTER AS PHANTOM didn't break eye contact. He started to pull his T-shirt out of the waistband of his jeans. Her breath hitched as he pulled it over his head, and his muscles rippled as he tossed it over into the corner where he had set his backpack.

Her imagination had not done him justice. His shoulders were broad and thick with muscle. His arms were as big around as one of her legs, corded and powerful, not bunched like a bodybuilder's. Covered with a light spattering of brown hair, his chest had definition that made her hands itch to touch. She had heard of six-pack abs, and based on the muscles that rippled with every move, he made an average six-pack look weak.

Elena suddenly became aware she had been staring at his body and forced her eyes to travel back up to his face. To her shock, he had lost his closed-off expression. Desire flared in his eyes, and a muscle jumped in his tight jaw. Surprise and hope made her nervous, and she almost squeaked when he took a step toward her.

With only a couple of long strides, he stood in front of her, one hand sliding into her hair as the other slid over the silk of her pants and cupped her ass. He hauled her up against his body and closed his fist around her hair, pulling her head back. "Oh!" she gasped, just before his lips came crashing down on hers.

This wasn't a slow, gentle kiss like they had shared in the barn a couple of weeks ago. This kiss demanded, took, and claimed. A shudder rippled through her. Deep within, her body clenched with excitement and need. Her hands reached for his chest, and he sucked in a deep breath when her fingers brushed over his pecs.

He let go of her suddenly, and her knees wobbled, but his hands grabbed hers before she could fall. He forced her hands up above her head as his thighs pressed against her, driving her backward until her back slammed against the wall. With their bodies locked together, she felt the evidence of his desire pressing hard against her lower belly, and excitement hummed through her.

She moaned into his mouth as he devoured her. He paused briefly to suck on her lower lip before sweeping his tongue back into her mouth, tasting her everywhere. She breathed rapidly through her nose, tangling her tongue with his. She could smell the musky scent of his aftershave and the ever-present aroma of horses, leather, and man, and knew she would never get tired of his scent.

He kept her hands pinned above her head with only one of his large ones. His other hand slid down her arm, following the curve of her body, until it settled on her hip. She stood on her tiptoes, trying to taste even more of him, and was rewarded by him crushing her hard against the wall.

With a harsh groan, he ripped his lips from hers, kissing and suckling at her skin as he made his way along her jaw to her neck. His teeth nipped at the tender flesh below her ear as his hand slid up underneath her silk top. Her breath rasped in her ears, her chest heaving with each gasp.

Then his hand was lifting her breast, cupping it and molding it. "Is this what you want, Elena?" His voice thick with passion, his lips moved against her ear as he spoke. "I've imagined holding you like this. Do you think about us together? Is this what you imagine? Is this what you want?"

She moaned, arching into his hand. The ache between her legs had started the moment he touched her, but it had become a throbbing need, demanding satisfaction. He moved against her, and she cried out when the hard length of his desire rubbed against her where she ached the most.

"Answer me, Elena," he demanded, his breath hot and harsh against her neck. His hand on her wrists stretched her arms higher above her head, forcing her breast to arch further into his hand. His finger flicked her pouting, aching nipple, and she cried out in pleasure. "Is this what you want?"

"Oh, Phantom, yes!" she exclaimed and wrapped one of her legs around his waist, gasping as she rubbed against him. "Yes, please. Yes. Yes." She had imagined what it would be like to be held by him again, had fantasized about his rough hands touching her. Nothing compared to reality.

"Tell me what you want, Elena. Tell me what you want me to do to you." His hands released her briefly, only long enough to pull her tank top over her head. His gaze devoured the sight of her breasts, and her nipples tightened even more. His eyes returned to hers, and her breath caught in her throat at the blaze of passion burning there.

He switched hands, once again grasping both her

wrists. He held her wrists high above her head, forcing her back to arch and thrust her other breast into his hand. "Oh," she moaned as he manipulated her sensitive flesh. Her eyes slid closed in ecstasy. She became restless quickly, though, as her neglected nipple ached to be touched, so tight it became nearly painful.

Her eyelids fluttered open and his face was dark and intense, his eyes burning into her. "Tell me, Elena. Tell me what you want." She moistened her lips, and he watched her tongue hungrily.

"Touch me. Please, Phantom. Touch me."

His breath came as fast and rough as hers. "I am touching you, Elena." As if to prove his point, his hand squeezed her breast, lifting it, caressing it.

She couldn't control her own body anymore. She had never been shy when it came to sex, and she knew what she wanted with Phantom. She moved her body against him, her breath hitching as pleasure rippled through her core. He pulled back, then slammed his body back up against her, lifting her slightly off the floor.

"Oh!" she cried out in surprise and pleasure. He was so hard, so large. "Phantom...please... Phantom..."

She didn't think he could stretch her any further, but his hand squeezed around her wrists, forcing her body to contort the way he wanted. Her back was arched so far she could no longer touch the wall. His hand squeezed her breast again, and both exquisite delight and need pulsed through her veins. "Tell me, Elena." His rough skin rubbing against hers made her crave more. "Tell me what you want me to do to you."

She lifted her eyes to his and thrilled at the excitement she saw reflected back. He wanted her to tell him the things her body craved, and a thousand images of what he could do to her flashed through her mind. She hadn't known her desire could climb any higher, but her entire body quivered with it. "I want you to touch my nipple. Please, Phantom," she beseeched him.

His thumb lightly grazed across it. "Like this?" he rasped.

She shook her head. "No. Squeeze it. Make me really feel it."

The breath rushed out of him, and his eyes dropped to her breast. She looked down as well, and the sight of his fingers moving against her dark nipple made her heart race. He gripped her nipple, squeezing it slowly, tighter and tighter. She drew in a sharp breath as he continued to tighten his thick fingers, and she lifted her eyes to find him watching her closely. And then he twisted.

"Oh…" The moan was torn from within her, and she let her head fall backward, closing her eyes and thrilling in the exquisite pleasure he pulled from her body. His mouth landed on her neck, biting lightly, then lapping at the tender skin before biting again.

"Tell me, Elena."

Oh, good heavens. Every time he says my name, it's like he's stroking me inside. This can't be real. I must be dreaming. I never want to wake up.

"Tell me what you want me to do, Elena. I want to hear everything you want me to do to your beautiful little body."

His words washed over her, and her eyes slid open. She stared up at the ceiling, panting, her body twisted to his command. "Let me touch you," she gasped out.

His teeth bit her again, this time not as gently, and hot, pulsing desire coiled deep inside.

"No." His tone left no room for disagreement. He had taken control, though he still wanted her to tell him what she wanted and needed. "Answer me." He twisted her nipple again and she cried out his name. "That's it, Elena. You're mine. I'm the one doing this to you. Say my name again."

"Phantom...touch my mound. Touch me where I ache to feel you." She felt her cheeks run hot. His growl of pleasure against her throat made the embarrassment more than worth it.

His hand slid over her stomach and she trembled violently. His fingers dipped inside her pants, and he murmured in appreciation when he found her entirely without underwear.

His fingers combed through her carefully trimmed curls, and his teeth sank into the skin over her collarbone. "Oh, yes. Oh, yes. Please, Phantom." Her words were breathy whispers. His fingers slid slightly past her highly sensitized flesh and into the soft, wet folds of her sex. Any moment now, she would entirely lose control.

She didn't hesitate. Her other leg lifted and wrapped around his waist, exposing herself to his questing fingers. He stroked his fingers further within her core, and the tip of a thick finger lightly pressed up into her. "Phantom!" she cried out loud.

"That's it, Elena. That's it." And then his fingers circled where she felt the most sensitive. She threw her head back again, a hoarse cry tearing from her lips. He rubbed the inflamed nub lightly, then harder, and harder still.

"Phantom, Phantom, Phantom." She was gasping out his name as a mantra.

Then he stopped and just pressed his fingers hard against her throbbing nub. The coil of desire tightened, tightened, and held her on the edge of an incredible precipice. "Tell me, Elena," he whispered. "Tell me what you want me to do to your body. Tell me what to do to you."

He was torturing her, the sweetest torture she had ever experienced in her life. She drew in a quivering breath. "Take me, Phantom. I need you inside me. I need you to take me. I need—" Her words ended with a gasp as he released her wrists. His hands tore at her pants, and she heard them rip as he shredded them like tissue.

She became intensely aware of every motion he made as she suddenly stood without him supporting her hands. She wanted to watch every move his impressive body made. He pulled a condom out of his wallet, and she watched him tear the foil packet open. She held her breath as he rolled it on, trembling with anticipation.

He gripped her hands over her head once again and pressed a kiss to her lips. Pleasure exploded through her body as he thrust into her, slamming her into the wall. He seated himself fully inside her, and she gasped for air as her body contracted around him, trying to accommodate his length and girth.

She expected him to begin to move, but he stayed still, his body pressed firmly against hers, his mouth still moving against her lips, coaxing her to relax. He breathed heavily, and she trembled as she felt him pulse once inside her. His lips slid across her cheek, and she loved the feeling of his chest rising and falling against her chest, stimulating her already sensitive nipples.

"Elena?" He pressed a kiss to her temple. "What do you want?"

His need to please her made her feel more treasured than she had ever felt in her life. "Take me, Phantom. Take me hard. Take me—"

"Aw, hell," he moaned and pulled back, then thrust his body into her, before pulling nearly all the way out and again slamming back in to the hilt. His free hand grabbed hold of her breast, squeezing and twisting the nipple, massaging and crushing the sensitive tissue.

"Phantom," she moaned.

Her body tightened all over, and her toes curled as her inner muscles began to squeeze his length with a power she had never felt before. She lost the ability to talk, to think. She could only feel. And cry out his name so loudly she feared people in other cabins heard her. Then she didn't care.

"Elena…aw, hell, Elena!" He slammed into her one more time and bit down on her collarbone. She felt him pulsing inside her, his body straining against hers as he stood on the balls of his feet, thrusting as deep into her as he could possibly go.

Waves of pleasure washed over her. Vaguely she became aware that the rough wall no longer pressed at her back. The coolness of the soft sheets against her flesh told her she had been placed on the bed, and she slowly began to catch her breath.

Phantom was still inside her. He lay on top of her, breathing heavily against her neck. She could feel his tension, could feel him still pulsing within her. Her hands stroked his back in soothing circles. Slowly, slowly, he pulled out of her and went into the restroom briefly before returning to her. He pressed a kiss to her sweaty forehead and rolled onto his back, pulling her with him so she lay halfway across his chest.

She listened to the gradual slowing of his racing heart and felt him draw in a shuddering breath. She could finally touch him, and her fingers brushed over the light whorls of hair on his chest as they both slowly returned to earth.

She felt slightly exposed, as foolish as that was after what they had just done. She pressed a kiss against his chest and sighed. His fingers stroked lightly up and down her arm, and the silence of the room wrapped around them.

He pressed a kiss to the top of her head as they continued their lazy touches. But she felt a tension growing in his body, and irrational fear formed like icicles in her stomach. *Don't say sorry. Don't you dare say you're sorry. You wanted me, and I wanted you.*

"Elena, I didn't hurt you, did I? Everything happened so fast."

She let out a breath of relief. If that was all that was bothering him… "No. It felt wonderful."

His fingers came under her chin, tilting it up so he could look down in her eyes. "You'd tell me the truth, right?"

Elena's cheeks heated and she chuckled. "Yes. You were also right about me imagining us being together. It's just been a little while—maybe a year—since I've been with a man."

He squeezed his eyes shut and let his breath out

slowly. "I'm sorry, Elena. I should have… I'm just sorry."

No. Oh, no. Why? Why did he have to ruin what had been so incredible?

She began to pull away, not wanting him to know how much his words had hurt. But his eyes snapped open and he watched her intently. His arms tightened around her, refusing to let her leave.

"Phantom…you've said enough. Just let me go."

"No." He rolled so that she lay on her back again, and he leaned over her. "I don't think you understand what I'm sorry for."

"It's rather obvious." Her heart slammed against her rib cage and her stomach churned.

"If I had known… Elena, you're incredible. I would have made love to you. I would have kissed you all over. I would have treasured you properly—in a bed. You haven't been with a man in a year, and I'm so insensitive I take you standing against a wall!"

Elena's eyes searched his face. "*That's* what you're apologizing for?"

"Yes. I should have made our first time together far more special."

She smiled and traced his lips. "You made it more than special—you made it incredible. I enjoyed it. Every single thing we did. If I hadn't wanted to have sex like that, I would've stopped you."

He watched her thoughtfully. "I don't know if I could have stopped once I got to hold you the way I've wanted for so long."

She glanced down at his chest, trying to decide the best way to ask him the things running through her mind. "If you've wanted this for so long, why did you wait?"

"I want to make you happy. I don't want you to think this is meaningless to me. You are special to me. And I don't want you ever to think otherwise. Thank you for coming into my life."

"I think I'm the one who should thank you after the amazing experience you just gave me, Phantom."

"Enrique." He watched her closely.

Her eyebrows snapped together in confusion. "What?"

"You should know my real name. Phantom is my nickname, but you deserve to know my birth name. It's Enrique Ramirez."

"Enrique." She enjoyed the feel of his name on her lips. "It fits you. Would you like me to call you Enrique, or do you prefer Phantom?"

"I enjoy hearing you call me by either name. Phantom is what I'm most used to." He pressed a kiss to her temple.

"I like calling you Phantom. Thank you for sharing your name with me. Thank you for this incredible night."

He chuckled softly. "Let's see what you say in the morning. I'm afraid you're going to be sore."

She sighed and stretched, stifling a yawn. "Well worth it."

He shook his head and brushed another kiss over her lips. Then he stood and stripped out of his jeans and boots, then lifted her and slid her under the covers and joined her. "Morning is going to be here before we know it," he murmured against her ear.

"Mmm. Our first class isn't until ten thirty. We can sleep in for a little bit."

His arms tightened around her, and he dropped his forehead to hers. "Elena…I was so… You were so… I don't even know the right words."

She smiled, feeling light and heavy at the same time. As she began to fall asleep, she felt Phantom's lips press against her temple. "Good night, Elena."

They slept in on Saturday morning as she had promised, but they woke up far earlier than either one wanted. The horse show beckoned. His preference would have been to spend the weekend finding ways to make love to Elena gently, to show her exactly what he had been talking about.

If she was sore, she didn't complain. She went on to compete beautifully, exhibiting Strawberry in more than four different events. He competed with Black Out in showmanship and Western pleasure, and he felt every bounce in the saddle. He could only imagine what it had been like for Elena competing in jumping.

The drive back to the ranch had been full of laughter. The judges had taken everything in the competition far too seriously, and their attempts at covering up their confusion when something didn't work out perfectly—such as the announcer calling out the next program, or horses being called out of order—had been hilarious. The judges even confused one another at different points throughout the day, making for animated moments. Elena and Phantom enjoyed talking about the horses' performances and were bringing home new trophies to be added to the ranch's collection. Phantom had been both shocked and excited to win his first trophy as a quarter-horse competitor, tasting the addiction to win more.

They held hands as he drove, her small hand nestled in his, and she eventually dozed off. He knew she had to be exhausted, and he took every opportunity to glance over at her and admire her profile. He couldn't believe this beautiful woman had entered his life and turned it into an unexpected, delightful experience. He couldn't wait to see what happened next.

"That should be all the tack. I'll be able to clean it more thoroughly on Monday," Elena said to him as she closed the tack-room door behind her. She kept her voice slightly hushed, which only seemed right with the inky black of night surrounding them.

He nodded as he secured Black Out's stall. For some reason, he struggled to find words to say to her. How could he tell her he didn't know how to tell her goodbye?

He didn't have the right to ask her for anything. She hadn't asked anything of him. She acted as if she expected everything to continue as it had been. He wanted more. He didn't know what to say or do to make that happen, though.

Maybe she had just wanted to know what it would be like with him. Maybe she had sensed his passion for her and had wanted to catch fire with him for one night. She had given her body to him with desire that matched his and had made him burn hotter than he ever had before. Could one night be all she wanted?

He walked with her out of the barn toward her truck. It looked small parked next to the long row of giant trucks that he and his fellow SEALs drove. It seemed perfect for her, though. She walked up to the driver's side and he followed her. She reached for the door handle, but he grabbed it before her. He didn't open her door.

He moved around her as she turned to look at him, pressing her back against the truck and bracing his arms on either side of her. He studied her and she watched him in return, one eyebrow raised. Even exhausted from a grueling day at the horse show, two days on the road, and a very demanding man, she shone. Her lips turned up slightly in the hint of a smile, and her eyes were curious.

He couldn't say goodbye. He leaned forward, pressing against her as his lips sought hers. She came to him quickly and eagerly, her mouth meeting his.

He wanted to be gentle. He wanted to show her that he could be slow and meticulous, drawing out her pleasure. But she let out a shuddering breath, and the fire of desire clawed within him again. He had thought after the previous night his need would be satiated for a while, but he could hear her cries of ecstasy echoing around him as clearly as if they were back at the B and B.

His hand slid into her silky curls and he tugged, angling her head back. She submitted to him with another shuddering breath, her lips parting, beckoning for him to taste her as deeply as he wanted. She rested her arms on his shoulders, opening her body to him, letting him feel the weight of her breasts pressed against his chest. His jeans were almost instantly uncomfortable.

His tongue swept inside her mouth and he could taste cherries, sweet and oh so delicious. His heart began to beat faster and his mouth moved against hers, demanding more. She moaned and her tongue slid along his, teasing, tempting, tormenting. He felt her nipples pebble under her thin shirt, stabbing against his chest.

Her lack of a bra had been at his request. He had cornered her by herself in the women's restroom after they'd left the horse show and had locked the door. She had been just about to change out of her show attire and had looked at him with a raised eyebrow as he had advanced on her. But his request had been simple—for her to wear his thin undershirt, and once they were on the road, she would get rid of the bra. To his delight, she had also chosen to wear a simple jean skirt.

As they drove home, he had been shocked that she was able to remove her bra without taking the shirt off to do it. He had been anticipating getting to watch the gentle sway of her naked breasts while she changed, if only for a few seconds. But she had kept him from enjoying the show.

She hadn't completely disappointed him. She had delicately reminded him that she wasn't a fan of underwear, and when they had stopped to gas up the truck, she had wiggled her sweet ass down in the seat and allowed him to get a glimpse of the heaven between her thighs.

Now he grew full and heavy with need. His hand tightened in her hair, tilting her head further back to arch her chest against him. His other hand slid up underneath the thin shirt, and her round breast filled his palm, the weight heavy and...perfect.

"Oh." She drew in a breath against his lips and arched more fully into his hand all on her own.

Memories of the B and B swirled through his mind.

Her body reacted so perfectly to him, to his every desire. The way she'd given herself to him so completely was one of the greatest aphrodisiacs he had ever known.

His hand gently massaged her breast, caressing and teasing, and she began to move restlessly, her fingernails pressing into his scalp. Breathing was becoming harder. "Don't leave," he murmured against her ear. "Stay with me tonight."

He hadn't expected to ask her, but the words had poured from him on their own. He suddenly wanted it as much as he wanted air. Her eyes opened and she studied him with a hungry gaze. "I don't care what Anya thinks. But your friends…what will they say?"

"I don't care. I just want you with me."

"Yes. I want to be with you too."

Chapter 15

ELENA FELT A LITTLE BREATHLESS STANDING IN PHANTOM'S room. He had grabbed her overnight bag and brought it inside, and they had stumbled their way through the door and into his room between kisses. She doubted she'd be able to find her way back out since she had been so distracted by his warm mouth on her neck, her cheeks, her lips.

She stood in the center of the room as he locked his door, tossing her bag to the side. She didn't want to take her eyes off him even to look around at his bedroom. She didn't think she would ever grow tired of watching the way his muscles bunched with each movement.

He turned to face her and gave her a warm smile. With a couple of quick steps, he stood in front of her and pulled her against him, sliding his arms around her waist. She slid her hands up into his hair, pulling his head down to hers.

She pressed kisses along his jawline, enjoying the rasp of his light stubble against her lips. His hand slid up her back and into her hair, gently tilting her head back further. He pressed his lips against the pulse beating rapidly in her neck. She sighed heavily, her fingers tightening in his hair.

"Elena," he whispered, "I never should have pushed you away. I've been about to lose my mind with the desire to touch you since that day in the barn."

"I never knew a kiss could be as amazing as the one we shared that day. I've dreamed about it ever since."

"You and me both," he groaned. Then he kissed her with the same intense passion they had shared the night before, his lips moving sensuously, teasing her lips to part. She moaned when his tongue touched hers, and she copied his motions. She had never been kissed in such a consuming manner until Phantom.

He pulled her tighter against him, and she could feel his erection pressing into her lower belly. She moved her hands down slowly, caressing his chest as she went. She grabbed handfuls of his shirt and began to tug it free from his jeans, eager to feel his flesh.

He pulled back from her slightly, giving her room to pull his shirt up and over his head. He stayed still as her gaze roamed over his muscular form, drinking in the sight of him. He didn't restrain her hands as he had at the B and B, and she took full advantage of the opportunity to touch and explore him.

Her fingers danced across his shoulders and down his biceps, then back up to place her palms on his chest. She could feel the tension in him and knew he wanted to touch her too. She took her time, though, savoring the feeling of his warm skin over hard muscle. She traced the contours of his chest before her hands slid lower, caressing his taut abdomen.

When her fingers dipped slightly within the waistband of his jeans, he drew in a sharp breath and tightened his hold on her once again. In one smooth motion, he pulled her thin shirt over her head. He gazed upon her with gray eyes that seemed to sparkle in the faint moonlight spilling into the room.

Her body, already sensitized to his touch from their heavy petting out at the truck, felt flushed all over, her nipples tightening under his intense gaze. He brought one hand up to her collarbone and ran his fingers along it with a featherlight touch that caused her to shiver in anticipation. He lowered his head to place his lips where his fingers had been, his lips and tongue tasting her skin.

His hand dropped to her side, rubbing along her ribs, then sliding back up slowly. She drew in a shuddering breath as he cupped her breast, lifting it and gently squeezing it. When his lips began to kiss a trail down her chest, she thought she would scream in anticipation.

He looked up at her for a moment, his mouth hovering over her pouting nipple, and his breath was its own caress. Then he focused on her breast again and laved his tongue against her aching flesh.

"Oh!" She drew in a sharp breath and swallowed hard, her gaze fixated on his dark head.

He kept one arm wrapped around her waist as he wrapped his lips around the nipple and began to suckle. Gentle at first, he pulled harder and harder until her eyes rolled back and her head lolled over on her shoulder.

Her fingers flexed between them, caught between their bodies against his abdomen. She attempted to reach the button of his jeans, but he pulled back, releasing her nipple in the process. He straightened and pressed a fierce kiss to her lips. "Tonight we're going to take our time," he said hoarsely.

She gasped when he swung her up into his arms and carried her to his bed, placing her gently on the mattress and following her down. He lay at her side, and it felt as if his hands and lips were everywhere, teasing and tormenting her. He placed kisses down her neck and across her collarbone as his hands ran down her sides slowly, caressing every inch of her flesh as he went.

She reached for him, her hands exploring his body. They roamed over his chest to his back, pressing against his muscles. She lifted her head and pressed kisses against his chest when he was close enough, and he drew in a sharp breath when her tongue lashed across one of his nipples. Knowing she could tease him just as much as he teased her increased her pleasure.

He moved down her body, looking up at her as he took her nipple in his mouth again. She slid her hands into his hair and pulled gently, asking for more. He began to suckle again, and the tug pulled at her all the way to her core.

His warm breath traveled across her skin to her other breast, and still watching her, he pulled the other nipple into his mouth. She couldn't look away. She was too mesmerized by the heat in his eyes and the beauty of his body against hers. Her fingernails pressed against his scalp as he sucked harder, and her body moved restlessly, needing more.

His mouth released her and began to travel down her stomach, his hands moving up to cup and caress her breasts. "Phantom!" she gasped when he ran his tongue under the button of her jean skirt. Her entire body hummed with excitement.

Her hands tugged on his head, pulling him back up to her face, and they both met in a passionate kiss, breathing heavily. Her hands slid down his stomach to the button of his jeans, and he moaned against her mouth as she unfastened them and pulled down. She freed him from his jeans and boxer briefs, and her hand reached out tentatively to touch him.

He broke free of the kiss, sucking in a deep breath as her fingers wrapped around him, caressing as she explored. "Elena," he groaned, pressing his face against her neck, his body trembling with need.

Her hand stroked him slowly, driven by his murmured words of pleasure in her ear. His hands continued caressing her breasts, his fingers flicking over her hard nipples. She writhed against him, her hand tightening around him. "Phantom, I need you," she whispered.

His hands moved quickly to remove her jean skirt, whisking it down her legs. His palms traveled back up her thighs, then slid between her legs, gently parting them. He pulled away from her to completely shed his jeans and pull a condom from his wallet. His eyes stayed focused on her body as he rolled the condom on.

He lay back down with her, this time on top of her, settling between her thighs. She reached down and guided him forward, and he sealed his lips over hers as he pressed toward her center. He moved slowly, easing his way through her slick folds. She moaned against his lips and arched her hips, drawing him further inside her.

They both gasped in pleasure as he surged forward, seating himself fully inside her. He pressed kisses along her jawline to her ear, breathing heavily as he began to move. She moved with him, her hips meeting his with each thrust.

Her hands grasped his back, clinging to him as their movements became faster. Pleasure built within her with every motion, the sensation of his hard chest rubbing against her sensitive breasts only driving her excitement higher. "Phantom!" she gasped, feeling as if she were about to explode into a thousand pieces.

His movements became faster and harder, and she knew he was on the edge. Knowing his pleasure matched hers caused ecstasy to explode within her, and she cried out as she fractured, her body grasping his tightly. He groaned deeply, his voice raw with pleasure as he found his own bliss.

They were both breathing heavily, slowly coming back from the exquisite high they had experienced. He rolled to his side, taking her with him, his face still buried against her neck. "That," he said softly, "is what I consider making love."

She smiled into the darkness, her hands stroking his back. "I think I could get used to that."

—⁓—

Elena awoke slowly and lifted her lips in a lazy smile before she even opened her eyes. She stretched languidly, feeling rested and satisfied in ways she could never explain. There was also a tender ache between her thighs, her breasts heavy and sensitive.

"Quit trying to look so sexy."

His warm voice washed over her, tinged with humor and a hint of desire. She smiled fully as she opened her eyes. He lay on his side, propped up on one elbow, cradling his head with his hand. She took him in, from his sleep-mussed hair to the shadow of a beard covering his jawline, to the impressive torso that tapered down to his trim waist and narrow hips. The sheet covered him just below his hip bone, allowing her to see the dark strip of hair leading to his sex. She was suddenly wide awake.

"If you keep looking at me like that, you'll never get out of this bed."

She rolled onto her side and assumed a position similar to his. "What makes you think I want to?" She drew in a deep breath as his eyes darkened with desire. How could the slightest change in his features cause such an intense craving in her for him? She doubted she could ever have enough.

His lips twitched slightly, then his arm snaked out and wrapped around her waist. He hauled her against him, lowering his head and pressing his lips to hers. She felt his arousal against her hip and sighed with delight. His hand rubbed up and down her back, his kiss staying gentle. The previous night, he had taught her, in exquisite detail, his definition of making love, and she had never felt so treasured in her entire life.

He sighed against her lips and sat up slowly. "I can smell breakfast. We have one of two options. We go out there and mingle with the guys—and you'll get to see Anya—or I keep you locked in here all day and all night and explore your body like I've been fantasizing."

Her eyes widened slightly. "I think I may want to hear more about your fantasies."

"You have no idea how sexy you are without even trying. I can't believe I'm able to have you, to hold you, to experience how incredibly sensual you are."

Elena smiled up at him, her heart squeezing with excitement and unwanted anxiety. She knew what she had experienced with him had been incredibly special. He stirred emotions in her, and she knew she wanted him to be her one and only.

She had realized it after they were together at the B

and B, and she knew sex would never be as good with any other man. No one would be able to make her feel the things he did. The sex hadn't been the only thing to shape her feelings. With Phantom, she felt safe and happy and had never felt so treasured and valued.

"You carry just a little bit of appeal yourself, you know," she said in response to his comment.

"All smoke and mirrors." He smiled at her, then kissed her quickly on the mouth. "As much as I would love keeping you as my prisoner, I don't like the idea of doing it with everyone knowing exactly how terrible a host I am."

Elena chuckled and rolled onto her back, stretching. "And what makes you think I would consider you a terrible host for keeping me here?"

He nuzzled her neck, then rolled away from her. "You are far too much of a temptation."

He left her alone for some privacy as she showered in his personal bath. The warm water washed over her skin, still sensitive from their lovemaking, and she leaned against the cool tile.

How would she be received by his fellow ranchers? She knew Anya would be thrilled. She could almost see the smug look on her best friend's face.

Phantom showered quickly while Elena dressed, and together they left the sanctuary of his room and walked out into the main living area of the home. Her hands trembled slightly when she heard the sound of men's voices. Phantom's arm slid around her waist, pulling her back against him before they rounded the corner to the dining room.

"Remember that I don't care about what anyone else

thinks. I only care about you. If you feel uncomfortable at any point, I'll walk you to your truck—or to my room, whichever you would prefer."

She rested her head on his shoulder and looked up at him. "Now who's being too much of a temptation?" *How is it possible he can make me feel so good with just a look, a touch, a smile?*

He kissed her forehead and then lightly smacked her on her ass, propelling her forward into the dining room. Just as she did, Phantom's cell phone began to ring. She saw the men in the room jerk their eyes toward them, glancing at her briefly before settling on Phantom. He fished the phone out of his back pocket and glanced at the screen, cursing softly.

"I'll be right back," he said to her softly, turning and walking back toward his room as he answered the call.

She turned to face the men and drew a deep breath. They looked uneasy, exchanging glances with one another before looking back at her. "Good morning," she said, forcing cheerfulness into her voice.

"Good morning," Stryker said, standing up from where he had been seated at the dining room table and ignoring the plate of food that sat in front of him. "Elena…it's nice to see you."

Self-consciously, Elena ran her hand through her damp curls. "It's nice to see you too."

Slowly, the rest of the men said good morning to her and gave her half-hearted smiles. She wasn't feeling an overly warm welcome. "Is Anya here?" she asked finally.

"There was an emergency with a patient, and she had to go in to the clinic," Stryker replied.

Elena realized Lobo wasn't there, which made sense given that he always went in to the clinic with Anya. She was struggling to think of something else to say when Phantom came walking back into the room. Instantly, she noticed he held her overnight bag.

"I'm sorry, Elena, but an urgent issue has come up with the ranch. A colleague of ours just called me to give me the heads-up, and we all need to jump on it quickly. I hate to end our morning like this…"

"No. No, it's fine. Not a problem at all." She turned her back on the group in the kitchen. She had worried she would get an odd response from them, but had never expected such a cool greeting to her being there. She certainly hadn't expected Phantom to ask her to leave. She began to head for the door, but Phantom quickly caught her hand and held her close to him as they walked out of the house, preventing her from fleeing like she wanted to.

Once outside he looped his arm around her waist again, holding her to his side as they walked to her truck. They were silent as they went, and Elena had to fight against the tears that burned at the back of her eyes. She was angry and frustrated and, more than anything, extremely disappointed.

They reached her truck and she grasped for the door handle, but Phantom's hand caught her, stopping her and turning her to face him. "I'm sorry, Elena. I wasn't expecting this to happen."

Elena's gaze lifted to his, and her heart squeezed in her chest at the look of concern on his face. "You're the only one that matters, remember?" she whispered.

If only he knew how true that really is.

He gave her a weak smile and captured her face in his hands before dropping his lips to hers. She drew in a deep breath and returned his kiss, her fingers combing through his still-damp hair. "Phantom," she murmured against his lips.

"Mmm?"

"Thank you for giving me the most incredible weekend of my life."

Chapter 16

PHANTOM SIGHED HEAVILY AS HE STEPPED BACK INTO THE house. The morning had started off with great promise but had quickly gone downhill as soon as his phone rang. Admiral Haslett had finally gathered the intel from his contacts in Mexico, and the SEALs had a mission—an urgent one.

He wanted to explain to Elena why he was making her leave and that he didn't want to, but he couldn't. The expression on her face had been devastating. He knew she thought they didn't want her around, or more specifically, that *he* didn't want her around. He would need to find a way to make things up to her.

Grim faces greeted him when he walked into the dining room. The team knew something had happened. He nodded to them all. "It was Haslett. He's received confirmation from his contact in Mexico that there's a human trafficking ring operating north of Reynosa. Their facility is practically on the border."

"That fits with the chatter I uncovered yesterday," Buzz said, pushing away his half-eaten food. For Buzz to lose his appetite, the information couldn't be good. "The communication is going between Mexico and the United States and details a large group of people about to be shipped out. At least thirty women, twenty children, and ten men. It's going to be one of the largest groups of people they've taken into the United States—at least for this ring. They're getting greedy."

"Or overly confident. No one has stopped them so far. It makes sense for them to grow more aggressive." Santo sighed heavily and shook his head. "I've checked with Judge O'Connor, my friend here, and she hasn't heard anything that would prove useful to us."

"It's obvious their code is identical to the one the drug cartel used. That connection can't be a coincidence. Someone higher up on the food chain is pulling the strings," Buzz said.

"We have to be cognizant that we're working this from two angles. There are the traffickers in Mexico, but there's also a connection on the U.S. side we're going to have to identify," Stryker volunteered.

"Haslett is uploading a file to me, Santo, Buzz, and Stryker. Buzz, you'll be staying home on this mission and providing us with tech support. Stryker and Santo, we'll be headed into Reynosa early Tuesday morning. Haslett says they're moving the victims soon, so our window is small."

"Drug cartels will sometimes dabble in human trafficking. Could that be what we're looking at here? Could this be a branch of Benicio's group that we didn't know about?" Brusco asked.

Phantom shook his head. "With Benicio dead, the operation would have fallen apart. No, there's a different leader behind this one, and the deeper we look into this, the more I'm certain we're going to find that leader is operating from here in the United States."

"So, you're going to take down their compound in Mexico?" Snap asked, his eyebrows raised. Phantom mustered a weak smile, and Snap grinned broadly. "You'll need some explosives then." The men chuckled lightly at Snap's enthusiasm for his "arts and crafts" projects.

Phantom nodded, though he suddenly had a burning desire to rewind the clock and spend the day locked in his room with Elena instead. He was dedicated to his job and would serve with honor. But for the first time in more than ten years, he didn't want to take the assignment. He wanted to stay with Elena, at least a little longer. At least until they grew tired of each other. His gut twisted at the last thought.

"Team, we should have already received the file from Haslett. We don't have much time, so we need to work fast and get up to speed on what we're going into." Phantom rolled his shoulders. His mind drifted to Elena. He had very little time left to see her before they had to leave.

Stryker stood and put a hand on his shoulder, speaking to him so softly only Phantom could hear his words. A corner of Stryker's lip quirked. "She's good for you, Phantom. Don't fuck it up."

Stryker's words hit Phantom in the gut. Elena was the best thing that had ever happened to him. If it weren't for the new mission, he would already be on the road to get her in his arms again. But there *was* a new mission, and he needed to get his head in the game.

He returned his attention to the team. "This group is supposed to move the hostages in the next five days. That means we hit the ground Tuesday for reconnaissance and then take them down. We do whatever legwork we can from here until we leave Tuesday morning."

Tuesday. That meant he had one last day with Elena. Then he might not ever see her again.

––⁓––

Elena's mouth was dry and her hands were moist. She wiped her palms on her jeans, keeping one hand on the steering wheel as she headed up the dirt road. She hadn't been nervous before keying in the gate code, but once the large iron gate had swung open, all she could think about was how Phantom would receive her.

Would he be happy to see her? Would he have returned to his old, cold expressions? Worse still, would he try to avoid her altogether? Did he regret their time together?

She certainly didn't regret it. If she could, she would go back in time and relive the entire weekend. A part of her wondered if she should be embarrassed by the way she had responded to him so passionately. Should she be ashamed of how she had behaved, the way she had cherished their sweet lovemaking Saturday night? Just thinking about the way he'd talked to her when they were in the throes of passion made her nipples tighten into aching buds, and a warmth blossomed between her legs.

Even with her body craving him, she wanted a sweet kiss from his lips more than anything. If it became intense, even better. But she wanted to breathe in his breath, smell his heady scent, and feel the warmth and strength of his mouth on hers.

She pulled up to the long row of trucks and parked in her usual spot. She stepped out, her eyes drawn to the ground. A deep impression of a pair of boots lingered in the dirt, and her heart kicked up a beat. It was where Phantom had stood Saturday night, as he had caressed her and kissed her and driven her to a frenzy. Her lips twitched with a smile. It had been incredible.

She looked up at the house and her smile faded. She would never forget the odd reception she had received from his fellow ranchers Sunday morning. Something had changed in the way they viewed her, and the only thing she could think of was the fact that she and Phantom had slept together. She couldn't understand why that would be an issue at first, but the more she thought about it, the clearer it became. They didn't approve of her for their friend. They probably thought she would want more than a casual fling with him, and they were right.

She longed for something substantial with Phantom. She wanted to be able to laugh with him, share things with him, experience life with him. She wanted a repeat of that wonderful drive home from Dripping Springs when they had enjoyed each other's company, even when they weren't talking…just holding hands.

Phantom had passionate blood and certainly knew what he wanted and needed when it came to relations with a woman. No doubt he went through women quickly. She had already considered these things before sleeping with him, and it had done little to calm her desire for him. She had known before they had been together at the B and B that her feelings for him had grown beyond anything she had expected.

His friends had probably picked up on her wish for something more. If they felt she would inhibit his lifestyle, they certainly wouldn't approve of her. They would be ready to protect their friend from someone they saw as a problem.

If they knew she was already aware that her time with Phantom could be limited, they would think differently about her. She would enjoy whatever she could have with him, however long it lasted. Even if the past weekend would be her only magical experience with him, she would accept that and move on.

If it continued, she'd treasure every moment. She knew, though, that Phantom probably didn't feel anywhere near as strongly about her as she did for him. When the end came, life would continue as always. She held no grand delusions of a fairy tale come true between them. She would be able to handle it. She would have her moment of tears, she had no doubt. But it would pass, and she would be the same self-sufficient woman she had always been.

The day moved at a snail's pace, or at least it seemed that way to Elena. She cleaned the stalls, set the horses on the lunge lines, and even cleaned and polished all the tack they had used at the show. Every minute felt like an hour, and she kept anticipating she would see Phantom walking into the barn at any moment, the easy, handsome smile on his face that set her heart into overdrive.

By midafternoon she began to take the horses one by one into the arena to work on smoothing out areas that she had noticed at the show needed corrections. The hot sun beat down on her, and the horses were drenched in sweat within minutes. Even though exhaustion tugged at her, she took out two of the horses that hadn't made it to the show to train and prepare for another show a couple of months away.

By the time she finished training and bathing the horses, and getting them back into the stalls with their hay and oats, the clock had inched toward four. Phantom hadn't appeared all day. Her worst fear had been realized. He regretted what had happened and didn't know how to face her.

Halfway through mucking out the stalls, she heard someone walking into the barn, and her heart skipped a beat. Almost as soon as her hopes had been raised, they were dashed. Phantom walked silently—she would never have heard him coming. Whoever walked into the barn seemed hesitant, and his steps seemed too deliberate. She wondered if he wanted her to hear him walking.

She stepped out of the stall, wiping the sweat off her brow with the back of her hand. She arched an eyebrow at the man walking toward her. "Hi, Lobo. Why aren't you with Anya?" As far as she knew, he was supposed to be with her best friend every workday.

"Hi, Elena. How are you?"

He was smiling at her. It appeared to be genuine. Such a drastic difference from the reception she had received from the other ranchers the previous morning made her suspicious. Had someone sent him out to talk to her? Could it be Phantom wanted him to run interference until he could decide how to move forward with her?

She squinted at him. "I'm confused, if you must know the truth."

"Anya is out at one of the ranches today. The rancher is having trouble with his herd coming down ill. She says I just get in the way when I go on calls with her."

"Ah." Elena turned and secured the stall door. "That's not what I'm confused about, though."

When she turned back to him his face had gone passive, reminding her of the emotionless expression she had seen on Phantom's face so many times. Lobo didn't say anything, just watched her. It appeared he didn't plan to ask her what she might be confused about. He probably didn't even care.

She couldn't take the silence any longer. "I'm just curious. Do your friends suffer from some type of amnesia or something?"

His surprised expression nearly made her laugh. "Not that I know of. Why? Did they forget something important?"

Elena leaned on the rake and assessed him silently for several moments. "You weren't here yesterday morning to witness everything, so I suppose I'll have to explain. But let me back up so you can understand why I'm so confused. The other night—the first night when I met you—did you get the feeling we all meshed well together? I mean, your friends seemed to like me, didn't they?"

"We all like you. You're smart and funny, and you give Buzz a hard time about his Christmas carols, which earns major points in my book." Lobo grinned at her, but it gradually faded when she continued to pin him with eyes demanding answers. "I'm not sure what you want me to say, Elena. The short answer to your question is yes, we all meshed together great, and I know without a doubt my friends like you."

"Huh." Elena chewed on her inner cheek for a moment, shook her head, and grabbed the muck bucket.

She turned to the next stall, fully prepared to ignore him and keep working. As she began mucking the stall, he walked up to the door, and she could feel him watching her silently for several seconds. Her muscles were beginning to shake with exhaustion. The heat of the day had taken a toll on her.

When she looked up at him, he spoke. "Look, Elena, I heard yesterday morning might have been a bit rough—"

"Oh, so you *do* know what happened. Were you planning to just hang around until I broke down and complained? You'd have been out here all day, because that's not the type of woman I am."

One eyebrow lifted, quickly followed by his smile. While each man in the house had a unique appearance, they were all very handsome, including Lobo. Elena imagined he had broken plenty of hearts when he had chosen to come to Hebbronville. "I can see why he likes you."

His comment took her by surprise, and she wondered if she had heard him correctly. "What?"

"Are you always so straightforward??"

"Yes. It gets me in plenty of trouble. Do you always avoid answering questions by asking more?"

He chuckled. "You're a breath of fresh air. I think that's why we all like you so much."

She snorted and turned back to her work. She hesitated, though, and, after drawing a deep breath, pivoted back around to face him. "So if you know what happened yesterday morning, and you remember what things were like when I had dinner with everyone and we played cards, why did everyone treat me as if they'd never met me before? Why were they all so uncomfortable they couldn't even look me in the eye? That's the reason I asked if your friends have amnesia."

Lobo looked down at his boots for a few moments, then returned his gaze to her face. "I don't know everything that happened, Elena, so certainly it isn't fair for me to speculate."

"Did I do something wrong? Did I break some unwritten rule you all have about not keeping a girl over for the night?"

"No." He shook his head firmly. "It's nothing like that."

"Really? Because the only thing different, from what I could tell, is that Phantom and I slept together. I'm the same person I was the night I had dinner with y'all. Are y'all afraid I'm a gold digger or something? I hate to disappoint, but I've been propositioned by men at far wealthier ranches and always said no."

"Why?"

Elena blinked rapidly, startled by his question. "Do I strike you as that type of person?"

"To be honest, I don't know you well enough to know *what* motivates you. If you're looking for a man to take care of you financially for the rest of your life, I don't see anything wrong with that."

"Have you been out in the sun too long? I think you may have cooked your brains."

He laughed, stepping back as she pushed past him to head to the next stall. "I've never been one to judge. It's not my place."

"Clearly. You won't say anything about how your friends treated me, and you're completely comfortable with the idea I may be after Phantom simply for his wealth."

"Look, Elena…" He sighed heavily and ran a hand through his hair, his fingers leaving his carefully combed style ruffled and disarrayed. "Yesterday turned out to be a bit of a rough day for the entire group. I'm sorry for whatever they did to offend you, and I can promise you, they're sorry too."

"Who told you to come out here and tell me all this? Phantom? Stryker?"

"No one did. But I've heard the guys talking, and I've heard them kicking themselves for not treating you right yesterday morning."

"Lobo, look. I get it if all y'all don't approve of me. That's fine. You're certainly entitled to your opinion."

His lengthy silence made her look up. His face had gone unreadable again. "What makes you think we don't approve of you?"

"What other reason would all of them have for giving me the cold shoulder?"

"Is there a reason we shouldn't approve of you?"

She wiped at her forehead with the back of her hand again and felt a trickle of sweat run between her breasts in the summertime heat. She had been guzzling water all day but felt slightly dizzy. The heat and her increased blood pressure from their discussion weren't helping. "I don't know. I don't know what kind of woman you want to see him with. But I'm not here to change him or make him be anything other than the man he is. I'm not going to try to force him to fit into my life, and I don't expect him to make room for me in his."

"So you're just using him for a good time."

"No! I mean, are you kidding me? Is that what you think? I'm not using him for anything. I care about him.

I enjoy being with him. But more than anything, I want to see him happy. No matter what that might end up looking like. With me or not."

Lobo's eyebrow lifted again. "I've gotten the distinct impression Phantom is a difficult man to please, but you seem to be hitting all the right notes with him."

"Yeah. Sure I am," Elena muttered to herself under her breath, scooping more horse manure into the bucket. "That's why he hasn't even bothered to say hello to me today."

"Phantom is tied up in some critical work today. Otherwise he'd be with you in a heartbeat."

Elena's eyes shot to Lobo's face. "Do you have supersonic hearing or something?"

He shrugged. "Or something. Elena, I'm not just saying these things to make you feel better. I sincerely believe them. Everyone here likes you—a lot. None more than Phantom. I'm sorry about how things went yesterday."

"No reason for you to be sorry. You weren't here." She pushed past him once again, pulling the bucket out of the stall. With a heavy sigh, she turned and latched the door. She had completed her chores. She'd appear desperate if she lingered with hopes of Phantom coming to see her. She had almost bought into the fairy tale. Her heart ached.

"Elena?"

She realized she had been leaning against the stall door, her head resting against the wood. She had pushed herself too hard already, and the conversation with Lobo had only made things worse. She needed to go home, cool down both mentally and physically, and sleep. She felt she could fall asleep standing up.

"Well, everything is done for the day. I'll be back on Wednesday."

"I'll let Phantom know. Are you okay? You look really pale."

"Yes, of course. The heat is a bit much today." She gave a weak laugh. "I'm looking forward to the air-conditioning in my truck."

"It's definitely one of the hottest days we've had yet. Are you sure you're okay? Do you want me to take you home?"

"No, I'll be fine." She drew in a deep breath for strength. "Thank you for offering, though."

Lobo looked skeptical, and she hoped he wouldn't push her. He shook his head and sighed heavily. "I don't think you should be driving. I've seen plenty of people pass out from overexposure in the heat, and if something happens to you on the road—"

"I can take care of myself. Don't worry about me."

He frowned, but he didn't stop her as she began to walk past him. "Is everything good? You aren't upset with the guys, are you?" he asked before she moved too far away from him.

"No. I understand it's just been hectic for everyone. I hope everything gets fixed here at the ranch quickly. Everything's going to be just fine with me."

So far, all the intel from satellite images backed up the information laid out in the briefing packet Haslett had uploaded to them. The information in the packet had been even more disturbing than Phantom had anticipated. The hostages were being taken from the border to San Antonio where they would be sold in an auction.

Buzz had been able to go on the dark web and get a lead on the auction and found it had been scheduled for that very weekend. They needed to get to Mexico as soon as possible before the traffickers tried to move their captives across the border.

Phantom sighed heavily and rubbed his eyes as he stared at the grainy photo of one of the suspects. He had a scar on his right cheek, a mole over his right eyebrow poorly covered by a small eyebrow piercing, thin lips, and shaggy, limp hair. He wore a large ring on the left hand. Phantom could see the man with his eyes closed, the same as he could picture the four other men that were identified in the packet. He had to know them perfectly. His infiltration plan depended on it, and that plan would let them take down all the traffickers and save the hostages.

The scale of the hostage rescue mission could be one of the largest they had encountered, and they were tasked to kill any identified enemy agents on sight. Since the mission was completely black, they still didn't know who they would be partnered with in Reynosa. Phantom knew they had a good group there that took care of human trafficking, and he fully expected some of them to be on the mission.

That would leave his group to find out who managed the operations and facilitation on the U.S. side. There had to be a main contact point, and that person would have a crew working for him.

The team had to be on point—a precise, fine-tuned instrument of destruction.

He glanced up at the clock and saw the day had

slipped away from him. It was five in the evening. *Shit!* Where had the time gone? Elena usually wrapped up around five, and he needed to see her. He had to see her. He felt as if a fever raged inside him, and only Elena could bring him a sense of peace.

Everything about her represented the good things in the world. Her innocence, kindness, and gentleness reminded him why he fought the ugly battles. He left his room and hurried toward the front door, nearly crashing into Lobo in the hallway.

"Oh, hey, Phantom," Lobo said, turning around. Phantom paused, glancing over his shoulder at the other man. He didn't need the interruption. Not now. Elena probably wondered why he hadn't come out to see her yet. "I talked to Elena a little while ago. I apologized to her about the team's behavior yesterday."

That grabbed his attention. "And? How did she respond?"

"I sure do hope you're serious about her."

"Why do you say that?" Phantom hadn't intended his voice to come out as cold as it had, but he didn't want to hear any man talking about Elena.

"Because she's a good woman. You're lucky as hell."

"Thanks."

"She already left for the day. I think she may have been put out you didn't come out to see her."

Phantom clenched his fists. He had to see her. He would lose his mind if he didn't. "I'm going out," he said curtly, heading to the drawer where they kept the key fobs for their trucks.

"You deploy in the morning," Buzz said as he passed them, a knowing look in his eyes. "Good luck."

Chapter 17

PHANTOM CALLED HIMSELF A FOOL A THOUSAND TIMES OVER as he drove. To ignore her like that so soon after they had been intimate seemed a classic rookie mistake. He could only imagine the thoughts running through her head.

Now all he wanted was to hold Elena close and prove to himself he hadn't lost her altogether. Anya had been startled when he had asked where Elena lived, but she was obviously used to Stryker's strange questions, because she'd only hesitated a moment before telling him.

His truck had roared down their dirt road as he had driven away, and the tires had peeled out on the highway as he headed toward town. It seemed to take forever to get to the sleepy little town of Hebbronville but he made record time, arriving in twenty minutes when it usually took thirty. He was just glad the sheriff wasn't out writing speeding tickets.

He slowed the truck to a crawl as he turned onto the quiet, house-lined street. Some had seen better days, while others, like the one Anya had identified for him, had been meticulously maintained, with a beautifully decorated front yard and a detached garage. Elena's apartment was above that garage, and he was relieved to see her truck in the driveway. He parked on the street and made his way to the stairs on the side of the building. He sent up a silent prayer, drew a deep breath, and knocked on the door.

———— ∿ ————

Not even Froot Loops were appealing to Elena. When frustrated or upset, she had to keep busy, and she decided scrubbing her tiny apartment until she felt numb would be the best thing to do. She always kept her apartment tidy, so it didn't need to be cleaned, but it gave her something to do.

She hurried up and down the stairs to the laundry room, washing all her sheets and blankets, a throw blanket, and small rugs. As the laundry cycled through, she busied herself with scrubbing out her nearly empty refrigerator, then swept and mopped. As clean as she kept everything, she moved through the steps much faster than she wanted and hadn't achieved the numbness she wanted. She almost wanted to call Anya or Elena but knew she couldn't tell her story without giving in to the tears burning the backs of her eyes. At least the dizziness and budding headache from her long day in the heat had abated some after a long drink of cold water and time in the AC.

She had just finished her final load of rugs and began to gather her dirty clothes, but paused at what she found. Stuffed in her overnight bag was the torn pair of silk pants. The pants Phantom had ripped off her as he had conquered her body—and her heart.

She had been a fool. She had let herself fall for him, and when she'd been in his arms, she had believed they both had found something special in each other. She never thought she could feel about a man the way she felt about Phantom.

Just a couple of weeks ago she had been teasing Anya for falling for Stryker. Had she fallen for Phantom? The ache in her heart told her the answer. How could she have let it happen?

She had told herself not to fall in love with him. But the strong, quiet man had affected her long before he had touched her body, long before their very first kiss so many days ago. His laughter, his smile, the warmth in his eyes, the strength of his presence—all of it had drawn her in, and she only wanted to get as close as possible.

She was about to head downstairs to grab her clothes out of the dryer when a knock at her door echoed through her tiny apartment. It startled her. She hadn't heard anyone coming up the stairs. Frowning she moved to the door, peered through the small peephole, and instantly began to tremble. She didn't know if she could open the door.

"Elena, I need to talk to you." His voice wasn't raised… Clearly he knew she stood directly on the other side of the door.

Why is he here? What does he want? Keep it together. Remember, you're a grown-ass woman. You don't need him. Elena drew a deep breath. It didn't help the trembling. *Heaven, give me strength.* She flipped the deadbolt lock and pulled the door open slowly.

"Oh, hi," she said, feigning mild surprise. "Please, come on in."

She opened the door wide enough to let him in and turned her back on him, stepping into the small kitchenette. "I wasn't expecting any company. I might have a beer if you want it?"

"Elena. Elena."

Elena ignored him and pulled open the refrigerator door and peered inside. "I'm out of beer. But I have a bottle of white wine I haven't opened. It's nice and chilled. Would you like that?"

Suddenly he stood beside her, his hand at her waist. The warmth of his touch seemed to burn through her clothing, through her skin, and touched her soul. She couldn't let him touch her. When he did, she forgot the ache in her chest.

She stood quickly, backing away from him. She reached up to run a hand through her hair. Her fingers were blocked by the band she had used to pull her unruly curls into a ponytail while she cleaned. She didn't know what to do with her hands. "I should have some glasses around here somewhere."

"Elena, I don't want any wine."

"Right. Okay, no wine. Is there something you needed? Did I forget something out at the ranch?" She couldn't make eye contact with him.

"Are you so mad at me you can't even look at me?"

Slowly, she lifted her eyes and saw many emotions exposed on his face. "I'm not mad at you," she whispered.

"You should be mad at me. Hell, I'm mad at myself. We shared an amazing weekend, and instead of coming to see you today, even if just to get a small kiss and let you know I can't stop thinking about you, I left you alone. I wanted to see you today. I *needed* to see you today."

She swallowed hard. "Then why didn't you?"

He took a half step closer to her. "I got so wrapped up in the issue brought to our attention yesterday that I lost track of time. By the time I headed for the barn, Lobo told me you'd left."

He took another step toward her, and she felt riveted to the spot. Her heart pounded in her chest. She could smell him, and she shoved her hands in her back pockets to conceal the trembling. "I wanted to see you today, and when I found out you'd already left, a simple phone call wouldn't be enough. I need to hold you and make sure this weekend really happened."

She rubbed her forehead. "What we had this weekend was—"

"Special. Incredible. Unforgettable." He took a final step and stood directly in front of her, so close she had to tilt her head back to look up into his eyes. The movement caused everything to tilt, and his arms wrapped around her quickly.

"Elena, what's wrong? Are you sick?"

The genuine concern in his voice tugged at her heart, and she loved the feeling of his arms around her. "I'm fine. It's just been a long day. I overdid it in the heat today."

She gasped when he lifted her in his arms and carried her to the bed. He set her down gently, his fingers tracing her face. "Have you been drinking a lot of water? Have you passed out at any point today? Can you see clearly?"

"I'm fine, Phantom. I don't want you to worry about me. Is this why you came over here? Did Lobo tell you what happened in the barn?"

Phantom became very still. "What happened in the barn?"

Elena's cheeks suddenly felt hot, and she tried to sit

up in the bed. "I shouldn't have said anything. I struggled in the heat, and he saw it. I assume he told you about it. Which would explain the real reason you're here."

Phantom ran his hand down the side of her face and shook his head. "I've already told you the real reason I'm here. I couldn't go any longer without seeing you."

Her heart began to beat faster. She suddenly remembered the way he'd slid his hand in her hair, grabbing a fistful to pull her head back to meet the onslaught of his mouth. A shiver of awareness covered her skin in goose bumps. "Phantom—"

His eyes darkened as he looked at her. "From the look on your face, I'd say you feel the same way." He helped her sit up further on the bed. "You probably have heat exhaustion. Have you been drinking a lot of water?"

"Yes. You don't have to worry."

He frowned. "You should eat something."

He leaned forward and pressed a firm, quick kiss to her lips. Then he stood and went to her kitchen, rummaging through her cabinets. Elena leaned back against her headboard.

He returned moments later holding a granola bar, a glass of water, and a bottle of Tylenol. He handed her the water and shook out two Tylenol pills. "This will help with the headache."

"How do you know I—"

"I can see the pain in your eyes. I know some of that pain is caused by me and the way I've disappointed you today. But I know you well enough to know it's related to something else too. From the way you've been rubbing your forehead, it didn't take much to come to the obvious conclusion."

"You're far too observant. Even though I know how to play very well, I'll never go up against you in a game of poker. You'll be able to read my face like an open book."

He gave her a smile that warmed his eyes as she tossed back the pills and drank the water. "Now eat a little something. It will give you the energy you need, and you won't be dizzy anymore."

She took a large bite of the granola bar. "You didn't have to come here. Am I disappointed you didn't come out to the barn today? Yes. Does that give me any right to have expectations for you? Absolutely not. We had fun this weekend. Besides, I seduced you, remember?"

"I never do anything I don't want to do. Never. You might have tried to seduce me, but in the end, I'm the one who claimed you."

A tiny shiver slid down her spine at his comment. The tone of his voice, the unspoken control and power that had made her fall apart in his arms and slowly rebuilt her, made her crave him with every fiber of her being. That didn't change the fact that he might not be interested in continuing their relationship any further. *Then why is he here? If he doesn't want more with me, would he really have driven all the way from his ranch to tell me how much he needed to see me?*

Her heart pounded, and she placed the empty granola-bar wrapper on the stand next to her bed. "You're right. I feel much better. I also haven't given myself a chance to sit down and catch my breath since I got home, and I'm sure that only made things worse."

Phantom shook his head. "Elena, do you realize how much you've come to mean to me? The thought of going two days without holding you, kissing you, treasuring you, felt like agony. That's why I'm here tonight. And if I've read this entirely wrong, I'll walk out the door and never bring this up again. You deserve the absolute best, and I don't know if I can give you what you deserve. Just look at this weekend! I lost all control with you."

Elena's breath caught in her throat at his words. "I *gave* myself to you. You didn't take anything. And I would do it again in a heartbeat, exactly the same way. Or up against the truck. Or anywhere else where you'll have me. Because I love you, and I want to be with you in any way possible."

Air rushed out of his lungs and he reached for her, pulling her up against him, feathering kisses all over her face. "Say it again. Please, say it again."

"I love you. I love you with my whole heart. I think I have since I first heard you laugh."

He drew in a deep breath, then let it out in a shudder. "Elena," he whispered. "Don't push me away. Don't ignore me if I've done something to hurt you. I want us to work on this, to build it even stronger. Will you promise me?"

Elena nodded, her hands sliding into his hair as she swallowed hard past the lump in her throat. She had just confessed to him that she loved him, and he hadn't run from her. In fact, he'd held her, kissed her, and begged her to repeat the three simple words. *I love you.*

His gaze searched her face and slowly, slowly, for the first time since he had arrived, he smiled. "You're all I'm able to think about. Ever since you left yesterday. I couldn't sleep last night because my pillows and sheets smelled like you. And like us making love."

Her mouth formed an O shape as her breath rushed out of her. This was what she had wanted. She had wanted him to be happy to see her and to still crave her the way she craved him. From the flame building in his eyes, his desire for her had started to climb as rapidly as hers.

She could see his pulse beating at the base of his neck, and she nervously licked her lips. His gaze dropped to her tongue, and she felt the incredible power he gave her when they made love. She had the ability to make him feel things—to make him desire her.

She slowly licked her lips again and watched his eyes as they followed her movement.

"All I've been able to think about is you," she confessed. "From the moment I left the ranch yesterday morning, my thoughts have been dominated by you."

"Elena," he whispered, and ran his knuckles down the side of her face. "I belong to you. Only you."

Her gaze roved over his face, drinking in everything about him. "All of me belongs to you, Phantom. My mind. My heart. My body. I'm yours."

His eyes slid closed briefly, and she watched his Adam's apple bob as he swallowed hard. When they opened, his eyes burned with an emotion she hadn't seen before. She trembled with the power of it. He dropped his head and his lips landed softly on hers, barely caressing them with his breath, then the faintest touch of his skin. Her eyes slid closed as she sighed against him. The kiss was so incredibly gentle, she felt tears burning in her throat.

His callused hand caressed the column of her throat before weaving into her hair and pulling off the band that held her curls. He smiled against her lips as the unruly mass tumbled down. "Have I told you how much I love your hair?"

She couldn't contain her chuckle. "No. You've never said anything about it."

"It's like an extension of you. It curls around me like a lover."

She drew in a deep breath at his words. If only he knew how much she desired him. Her heart pounded in her chest. If their weekend together had taught her anything, it had taught her she could say anything to him—that all he wanted to know was how to please her.

"Phantom," she whispered.

"Hmm?" His voice rumbled in his chest.

They weren't in the dimly lit B and B. They weren't in the inky blackness and solitude of the ranch at night. Twilight had fallen outside, casting the room in shadows, turning her apartment otherworldly. "I want you." The words tumbled from her trembling lips against his, a boldness she could only have with him, and she felt him draw in a sharp breath.

"Elena," he moaned softly, pulling back slightly to look down at her. Passion flared in his eyes as he searched her face.

"I need you," she said, her gaze meeting his. She saw the pulse in his neck beat faster. He trailed his knuckles down the side of her face again, but she shook her head, and he looked at her in confusion. "I don't want you to be gentle with me, Phantom. I want to feel your desire and know that it's as overwhelming as mine. I want you to take me. I want you to claim me. I need you to do it."

"Elena," he groaned. The hand that had been tenderly

playing with her curls grasped a fistful of her hair and pulled. She gasped and couldn't stop the smile that crossed her lips before his fell upon her. With him, reality always proved to be far better than anything she could imagine.

His kiss was rough and demanding, and she eagerly parted her mouth under his, granting him the access he expected. His tongue swept inside and she moaned, moving closer to him. Much to her surprise, he kept her at a distance, one hand in her hair and the other cupping her face. She wanted to feel his body against hers, craved the feeling of his muscles.

When he drew back, he nibbled lightly on her flesh until he was breathing in her ear. The rough rasp of his breath told her that he wasn't as fully in control as he was trying to pretend, and her own breath seemed harder to catch. "Do you know what you're asking me to do?"

"Yes. I'm yours. I want to feel you claim me the way I need to be claimed by you, and you alone."

He growled against her ear, a deep, passionate rumble. But then she felt him pull his hand out of her curls, and she nearly pouted in disappointment. Maybe she hadn't been clear enough. Maybe she needed to take charge and show him exactly what she wanted.

Anything she might have thought next vanished as he grabbed the plackets of her blouse with both hands. The sound of ripping fabric filled the room, followed by the bounce of several tiny buttons scattering across the floor. Cool air washed over her breasts and her nipples pebbled in reaction. She opened her eyes and smiled with satisfaction at the hunger on his face as he stared at her bare breasts.

His eyes lifted to hers and he raised an eyebrow. "I should come visit you more often."

Her lips twitched with a smile. "I'm going to need to buy more clothes if you keep this up." Her smile faded slowly as she saw the desire in his eyes. His expression alone ramped up her excitement.

She tried to draw in a deep, steadying breath, which made her breasts tremble, and he smiled with an animalistic hunger. Still keeping her at a distance, he lowered his head and ran his tongue lightly over her right nipple, then moved his head and lapped at her left one the same way. Her hands clenched on his arms, and she arched her back to show him just how much she enjoyed the attention.

"I need you," he said, lifting his head to look at her. "I need you like I've never needed a woman before, Elena. I'm on fire and you're my only salvation."

His words washed over her. She grabbed the edges of his T-shirt and pulled it over his head, drinking in the sight of his muscular body. She knew what his raw power was capable of.

He hesitated, and she didn't know why but didn't want to wait any longer. She moved in against him and wrapped her arms around his chest, practically purring as her stiff nipples rubbed against the whorls of hair on his chest. His muscles bunched and flexed in response, and she leaned her head against his chest for a moment, listening to his rapid heartbeat. But only for a moment.

She squeezed her arms around him and tipped her head, her long curls brushing against her back as she looked up at him.

The air seemed to rush out of his lungs as their gazes locked.

His arm snaked around her waist and hauled her body up against his. "Phantom," she gasped. She arched her body against him, feeling his need pressing against her hip from where he sat next to her on the bed, and her eyes slid shut with excitement.

But instead of claiming her mouth in another one of his passionate kisses, he skimmed her chin and jaw with his lips, barely tasting her. She whimpered with impatience before his warm hands slid down across her bare stomach in slow and gentle stroking. The sensual caress made her heart hammer against her ribs.

She had asked him to claim her. Obviously, he would do it at his speed and by his rules. "Tonight belongs to me," he whispered.

Chapter 18

PHANTOM SMILED AS HE SAW THE SHUDDER THAN RAN through Elena at his words. He couldn't contain his joy. She loved him. When everything else in his world seemed uncertain, he could hold tightly to her words. *I love you.*

But would she still love him if she knew what he really did? When she learned who he was and why he was really in Hebbronville—could her love survive the revelation?

Everything he had told her and shown her had been the truth, to a certain extent. He was a horse rancher who was wild about his trainer. But he had an additional responsibility, a critical one, and he didn't know what she would think if she ever learned about it.

For now, though, he knelt beside the bed, turning her so her legs dangled off the end, and her hands grabbed his shoulders. He ran his hands slowly over her back, then down her legs until he came to her boots. One by one, he removed them and slid his fingers up again until he had returned to the waistband of her jeans. Working deftly, he unfastened the button and pulled down the zipper.

Her breath rushed out as she lifted herself so he could slide the jeans off. To his delight, she wasn't wearing underwear. Her hands clutched at his shoulders, and he looked up to see her staring down at him with a passion that rivaled his own. "Phantom?"

He closed his eyes and tried to draw in a deep breath. She was the most exquisite thing he'd ever seen. Leaning forward, he pressed a kiss to her carefully trimmed mound, and his hands tightened around her waist when she gasped in surprise and delight.

Slowly, he raised his head, looking at her from head to toe, drinking in her appearance. "You are gorgeous," he whispered, finally connecting his gaze with hers. She stared back at him with desire and…love. He would never get enough of it. He wanted to drown in her eyes.

"Kiss me, Phantom," she asked so sweetly he couldn't even consider denying her. He angled his head over hers and breathed in the scent of wild flowers. Elena. *Mine.* He had never thought he could feel so possessive over another person. He wanted her to be his in every possible way.

His lips moved as a whisper over hers before kissing her firmly. He ran his tongue along her lower lip, and she opened for him. One of her hands slid up into his hair, gently tugging him closer, as the other moved onto his chest. The feeling of her nails digging into his skin made him draw in a deep breath.

His need for her clamored through his body, making it hard to think straight. One of his hands slid up from her waist to cup her breast, weighing and lifting it as his other hand reached around and massaged her inner thigh, moving closer to the center of her need. He tugged her against his body, breathing heavily as he pressed his desire against her leg, letting her know how badly he wanted her.

He moved to join her on the bed, but she pushed up onto her knees, forcing him to remain standing. "You aren't playing fair," she said to him, a mischievous grin on her face.

He raised an eyebrow, then drew in a sharp breath as her fingers moved along his waistband and unbuttoned his jeans. "Elena," he growled low in his throat, but he didn't stop her. The feeling of her skin moving against his made all thoughts vanish. In the silence of the room, the sound of the zipper of his jeans sliding down seemed incredibly loud. Struggling to concentrate, he grabbed a condom from his wallet as she peeled open his clothing.

He stepped back from her by a few inches and took it upon himself to kick off his boots, quickly followed by his jeans and boxers. And then he was as naked as she was, and her eyes moved over him with hunger. When she licked her lips, he knew he wouldn't be able to take much more anticipation.

He moved onto the bed and nudged her legs apart with his knee. She was breathing heavily as he settled himself between them. Her legs wrapped around his waist, drawing him closer to the pleasure her body offered.

"Tell me what you want, Elena."

"I want you, Phantom. Always. I want you."

His eyes closed for a moment, her words going straight to the heart of him. He lowered his head to her chest and drew one of her taut nipples into his mouth, scraping it lightly with his teeth before suckling on it.

"Oh!" she cried out, arching off the bed, her hands moving restlessly from clenching his hair to clawing at his back.

He moved from one nipple to the other. She whimpered and her hands slid down his back to forcefully grab his rear, making it apparent what she wanted. But he wanted to hear her say it.

He lifted his head and stared down into her desire-crazed eyes. "Talk to me, wildflower. Tell me what it is you need from me."

She shuddered beneath him. "Make love to me, Phantom. I want to feel you inside me. I want to know that I belong to you completely."

He swallowed hard and quickly rolled on the condom, then began to move forward, pressing into her sex. He pushed in further, her body incredibly tight around him. She moaned, her legs clenching around his waist.

Finally, he filled her completely. He stayed still for several moments, trying to gather his breath. "You feel so incredible," he whispered to her.

"I was about to tell you the same thing." Her sexy voice stirred his desire, and her expression full of bliss nearly made him lose control. She drew a deep breath and flexed her hips, and he slid in slightly further.

He withdrew nearly all the way, exquisitely slowly, then pressed back into her, flexing his hips and driving deep with each thrust. Her hips moved with him, matching his rhythm, and his body trembled with the strain from holding back.

Breathing heavily, Elena rocked her body against him, encouraging him to take her more forcefully. "Please. Phantom, you know what I need."

"You're mine," he growled, staring into her eyes. He thrust into her with such passion and strength that her body scooted up the sheets toward the headboard.

"Yes," she murmured. "I'm yours, Phantom. Completely. I belong to you and you alone. You have my heart, my mind, my body. I am yours. Oh!" She cried out as he began to move even faster, her bed creaking beneath them.

He dropped his head to nuzzle her neck. "Tell me, wildflower. You know what I need to hear."

"I love you. Oh, I love you so much, Phantom. I love you!" The last word ended on a slight squeal as passion overtook her and her body arched into him.

He felt her orgasm rip around him, and he couldn't hold back any longer. He thrust faster until his entire body stiffened and a long, low moan was torn from him. They panted for air as they slowly came back into their own bodies, their skin slick with a fine sheen of perspiration.

Phantom rolled to his side and pulled Elena with him, holding her snugly against his body. He placed gentle kisses over her face, and she sighed contently. "Thank you," she murmured, kissing his chest. Then she tilted her head backward and looked at him teasingly. "How are we going to get any work done together when we know we could be doing this instead?"

Her words suddenly brought him back into the real world, and a light frown touched his lips. "I have to go out of town for a few days, wildflower."

Her eyes had started to droop with exhaustion in the aftermath of their passionate lovemaking but flew open to focus on him. "When?"

"I leave tomorrow morning. But I'll be back to you as quickly as I can." His own words startled him. He hadn't said that he would hurry home. No, he had said he would get back to her as quickly as he could.

"Why do I have the feeling that I can't ask you anything more about your trip?"

Phantom closed his eyes and pressed a kiss to her forehead. "You're right, I can't talk about it. Someday… someday maybe I'll be able to tell you everything. But right now, it's best for your own safety."

He could feel her eyes on him as he stood and went to her bathroom to dispose of the condom. He freshened up quickly and glanced in the mirror briefly. He hated that he couldn't tell her where he was going or why, but it was the way life went for a Navy SEAL. Even if she was his wife, he wouldn't be able to tell her about the mission. He swallowed hard as he realized the path his mind had been wandering.

She watched him with curious eyes as he returned to the bed and slid under the thin blanket, pressing a kiss to her forehead. "Why can't you tell me anything?"

He lay on his back and closed his eyes, wondering how to handle the conversation. "I still do some strategy work," he said. It wasn't the complete truth, but it wasn't a lie either. "A delicate situation has come up, and I'm needed to handle it appropriately." He opened his eyes to find her lying on her side, her head propped up by her hand, watching him closely. He could tell from the expression on her face that she was struggling with what to say next.

She frowned and ran a hand through her hair, brushing it back from her face. "I made a commitment to you that I will trust you. I know you aren't telling me everything. I hope that someday you will trust me enough that you will."

"I *do* trust you, Elena. It's…complicated. The entire operation is confidential."

"It isn't anything illegal, is it?"

"What?" Her comment startled him, then made him chuckle. If only she knew. "No. There's nothing illegal about it."

"Is it dangerous?"

Why the hell did she have to ask that? He caught her face in his hands and leaned up, pressing kisses to her forehead, eyelids, nose, cheeks. "I'll be extremely careful. You don't need to worry about me."

She arched a slender eyebrow. "So it *is*. Why can't you tell me more, Phantom? Why are you keeping secrets from me?"

"I don't want to, but the situation requires I be discreet. One day I'll explain things." When he returned from this mission—*if* he returned from this mission—he would tell her he was a Navy SEAL. He wasn't prepared to break that news to her right before he left for a dangerous assignment.

"You don't even know when you'll be back?"

"It should be within a handful of days, maybe less. I'll let you know as soon as I return."

She sighed heavily, and he could see the disappointment on her face. He needed to switch the conversation to something different, anything to take her mind off the answers he couldn't give. "There's something I've been wanting to ask you to do for me."

Her gaze searched his face. "What?"

He gave her a mischievous smile. "Teach me how to solve a Rubik's Cube?"

Her face relaxed and she gave him a weak smile. "Promise you won't share my tricks?"

"Cross my heart."

"Good. It won't take long. Because I intend to make

the most of tonight. The next few days are going to be torture."

—◊◊◊—

They only had one day on the ground to evaluate the intel from the briefing, and initially, it didn't seem like enough time. The city of Reynosa was a bustling tourist hub with a fluctuating population of over a million, making it easy for them to cross the border and disappear. No one would look twice at a few guys on the prowl for cheap tequila and any entertainment Mexico could offer.

Reynosa was a seething, moving city that seemed to have its own pulse, its own breath, and Phantom felt unease as soon as they arrived. The area they were targeting was far northeast Reynosa, practically on top of the border between Mexico and Hidalgo, Texas. The area held many different shops and even a mall, with the heavy traffic of customers and business people creating the ideal situation for the SEAL team to blend in.

First, though, they had to meet up with their counterparts on the mission. They were staying at a hotel near the shopping district. Stryker took up post outside the hotel to watch those coming and going. Santo held a position in the lobby of the hotel, and Phantom waited in the room they had chosen on the ground floor, keeping his eye trained outside the window to watch for the people they were to connect with.

They had been told that each person would wear a simple lapel pin with the Mexican flag, something for them to distinguish them by. They had been waiting for nearly an hour when Stryker spoke over the coms.

"Three friendlies approaching. One woman and two men."

"Copy," Santo said. "They're headed your way, Phantom."

Phantom knew that Stryker and Santo would be slowly following the trio, ready to take them down at the first sign of trouble. Even though they wore the lapel pins, that didn't guarantee they were the right people. The meet could have been compromised at any point, and they couldn't take any chances.

There were two light knocks, three heavy, then two more light knocks on the door. It was the signal they had established through Haslett. "Who is it?" Phantom asked, standing to the side of the door, his rifle aimed at it.

"Housekeeping." A heavily accented voice came through the door.

"I have everything I need."

"We brought fresh towels directly from the laundry." The code was correct. So far, everything appeared to be in order.

Slowly, Phantom stepped forward and opened the door, his gun still raised. The three people lifted their hands to show they didn't carry any weapons, and he gestured for them to enter. Santo and Stryker slipped in quickly behind them, patting them down for wires or guns.

Not surprisingly, each one of them had concealed handguns. "What can I say, my friends?" One of the men wearing a baseball cap spoke. "Reynosa isn't the safest place to be these days."

Phantom's eyes narrowed. The voice was familiar.

He pulled the baseball cap off and was momentarily caught by surprise, then laughed. "Javier! I didn't expect to see you here."

Javier Ortes, a high-level leader in the Mexican navy, smiled. "Nor was I expecting to see any of you." He quickly shook hands with Phantom, Santo, and Stryker. "This is Clara," he nodded toward the stout, petite woman with them. "She is an integral part of the Mexican federal government's operations to stop human trafficking. She's been trying to bring down this ring for nearly a year now. The ring's last shipment into the United States was nearly stopped by her agents, but there was a leak. Three of her men were killed, and two more crippled. That's when this special task force was created."

"How did you come to be involved?" Stryker asked Javier.

"I've been working with Clara for over six months now on special assignment. My skills have been helpful to her team."

"He's being modest," Clara said, her voice carrying a firm, authoritative ring. "He's been integral to stopping the actions of several traffickers. This ring, though…" She shook her head. "It's very different from what we've been up against so far."

She turned to face the other man in the room. He was average height, muscular, and dark-skinned. "This is Arturo. He also has military training, but works for us full-time now."

They shook hands in greeting. "We've all been given the file on this mission. Our target is within the shopping center near the border, correct?" Phantom asked, jumping into the details of their mission.

"Yes. We've had eyes on the location for the past few days and have confirmed all five of the traffickers are staying in that location. We also have infrared set up on the building, and it shows a large concentrated heat mass. We believe that is the hostages," Clara said.

"Have you seen new hostages being brought in to the area?" Phantom asked.

Javier sighed and shook his head. "All has been quiet since we set up on Saturday. That was when we first received confirmation of their location. Through the infrared we've been able to track the movements of the traffickers inside the building, but nothing further than that. We believe they intend to move the hostages within the next couple of days. More than likely they will transport them by box trailers to San Antonio."

"How are they going to be able to get through Border Patrol like that?" Santo asked.

"There are holes in our system, and we're well aware of them," Arturo said solemnly. "We believe that, whoever the leader of this ring is, he's made arrangements with Border Patrol to get them to look the other way when the time comes. He must be a very wealthy and influential man."

"We'll set up a stakeout tonight. We'll keep watch of the facility to confirm all five of the traffickers are there when we finally strike," Phantom said, and everyone in the room nodded.

"We already have three men set up on the rooftop across the street from the shopping center," Clara said. "Taking them down at night will keep civilian interference to a minimum."

"Once we confirm the traffickers' locations within

the building, as well as any security they may have with them, we'll move in." Stryker stared out the window as he spoke, still keeping an eye out for any enemies.

Phantom nodded. "Let's pack up and get ready. Tonight is going to be here before we know it."

Chapter 19

Phantom sheathed his KA-BAR knife at his ankle, then did a final check of his equipment to make sure nothing was loose, that nothing would make a sound. Stealth was their ultimate weapon. And he was ready to get the mission over with and get back home to Elena.

Just the thought of her brought a sense of peace about him. She loved him. He had never been loved by a woman before, and the feeling stole any words he could think of to describe it. His last night with her had been incredible. They had only gotten a few hours of sleep, but he had never felt more refreshed.

He hated having to hide his true purpose from her. He wondered how she was going to respond when he broke the news to her when he returned home. She valued trust deeply. Would she feel he had betrayed her?

"We've got movement." Javier's whispered comment jerked Phantom's mind back into the mission, and he focused on the infrared scanner. One of the traffickers had gone to the front door of the place and stepped outside. A flash of light and then a glow near his face let them know he had lit a cigarette.

"We make our move once he goes back inside," Phantom said, making eye contact with his team. They were all heavily armed and prepared to go up against the five traffickers and the three other tangos they had picked up coming and going throughout the day.

Phantom had to admit, using the empty retail shop had been a great plan by the traffickers' leader. No one questioned the covered windows, since a sign advertised that a new shop would be opening soon and the site was under renovation. The location also got them close to the major highway that would take them through Border Patrol and into Hidalgo, making transportation easy.

The team was focused and ready. They hovered on the rooftop across the street, watching the infrared sensor and keeping an eye on things through their night-vision optics. The man took one final drag on his cigarette before heading back into the building. It was go time.

Phantom's team moved within the shadows across the street, using everything large on the ground for cover as they crept along. They arrived at the doors and Santo quickly applied ECT, explosive cutting tape, to the hinges. After everyone stepped back several feet, Phantom nodded to him. The explosive went off and they moved into the room rapidly. They knew from the infrared where each trafficker and guard stood or sat, and moved rapidly to take them down.

The silence that filled the room after the gunfire told Phantom something had gone horribly wrong. A low humming sound filled the air, and he turned in the direction where they thought all the hostages were being kept. Instead, there were several heaters set up in a way that would read as a large heat signature to them.

"What the fuck?" Santo growled.

"They knew we were coming. Not only that, they knew we were watching," Stryker said, his voice tense.

Phantom turned to Javier. "How did you find out about this place? Who gave you the info?"

Javier shook his head. "Clara handled all the intel. She brought it to me."

"Base, do you copy?" Phantom spoke into his com.

"Copy," Buzz's voice came through. "Alpha Team Two, what is your status?"

"Still on the rooftop." Clara's voice greeted them. "My informant claimed to have escaped this place and gave me the details on the men. When we checked it out and everything seemed to add up, we contacted Admiral Haslett to put a team in place."

Phantom turned from the group and studied the location. Something about the room didn't feel right. It hadn't felt right from the moment they breached the door. There were five dead traffickers on the ground—the shots had been clean. Clear evidence showed that, at some point recently, a large group of people had been there, based on the markings on the dust-covered floor and the overwhelming aroma of body odor.

No, something about the space just didn't feel right. He had studied the schematics and layout of the facility in great detail, and the room seemed far smaller than it should have been. He paced out the space, and a warning slithered down his spine.

He held his fist up sharply, and all talking in the room immediately ceased. All of the men trained their weapons beyond Phantom's position and began to advance slowly, ready to provide cover fire. Phantom stopped, holding his fist up again, and the men stopped behind him. It seemed as if the wall in front of him was... breathing. It rippled and moved, shifted and shivered.

Phantom drew his KA-BAR from its ankle sheath, stepped to the wall, then sliced downward rapidly.

The fabric that had been designed to look like the rear of the building rent and tore beneath his sharp blade. Two sharp pops followed instantly on the heels of his movement—one from Stryker's gun and the other from Santo's. Two men hiding on the other side of the fabric fell lifelessly to the floor.

"What the hell…?" Javier whispered as they stepped through the fabric and stopped to look at what had been hidden behind it.

Phantom sighed heavily.

"They built a motherfuckin' tunnel."

They were too late.

Elena pulled a bandanna from her back pocket and wiped the sweat from her face and neck. The temperatures were creeping into the nineties already. By all signs, they faced the probability of an incredibly long, hot summer. The only thing that brought her a little hope of relief hovered far off on the horizon in the form of dark storm clouds. A good, heavy rain would weaken the oppressive humidity that lay upon them like a wet blanket and help them heading into the harsher days of summer.

She shifted slightly in the saddle, and the horse beneath her responded to the cues of her body, quickly switching its lead leg as it loped through a figure-eight pattern. She kept herself light in the saddle, pressing her feet down in the stirrups, preparing for the next cue.

She worked the horse through the steps three more times, working a different, more difficult pattern each time. By the time she decided to call it a day, the sweat on Sherman looked almost like white lather, and the sun beat down on them mercilessly.

An American Quarter Horse Association competition in a few weeks in Brenham, a city roughly five hours away, presented the perfect opportunity to show off Sherman's talent. Jonas would be thrilled to see his horse take the top prize. Jonas loved winning, as evidenced by the shrine he had built for all the ribbons and trophies. He had delighted in placing the newest winnings from the Edinburg show in the case.

Just remembering that show brought a smile to Elena's face. It had been the first quarter horse show Phantom ever experienced, and it had been successful enough for her to win him back as a client. Much to her surprise, she'd ended up winning the man as well.

She hosed down the horse, then bent over and let the water run over her head and down her back, shuddering slightly as some of the water slid down the front of her shirt and sluiced over her breasts. She ached in a way that only Phantom could satisfy, and she wished he could be with her at that very moment, his quiet strength comforting and arousing her at the same time.

Shaking her hair out, she unclipped the tired gelding and led him to his stall, giving him an extra serving of oats for all his exertion. Thoughts of Phantom ran through Elena's mind as she carried the saddle and bridle into the tack room. Then she stopped, frowning. She had ordered two new saddles for Jonas nearly a month ago, long enough for them to have been delivered already, yet they were nowhere to be seen.

She went through the tack room once more, until she

was certain the saddles weren't there. She gnawed on her inner cheek as she debated what to do. She wanted to avoid Jonas at whatever the cost. Her last encounter with him had left her more shaken than usual. For him to design his newest barn and training facility with her in mind took his level of interest in her from uncomfortable to creepy. His knowledge about her passion for puzzles continued to disturb her, and she couldn't imagine how he'd used puzzles to enhance the design.

If she didn't ask Jonas directly about the saddles, though, she would have to go into the small barn office by herself and log on to his computer to find the invoice. Even though he had shown her the log-on, it felt like snooping into the man's personal affairs. She didn't know how much digging around she would have to do to find the invoice.

Weighing the good with the bad, Elena decided she would prefer the office. The door creaked as she shouldered it open, and she reminded herself to grab the WD-40 out of her truck to smooth the hinges before she left for the day.

She sat at the desk and powered on the docked laptop. As she waited for it to boot up, she gazed around the small office, noticing several photos of Jonas with the Hebbronville sheriff. She shook her head. Of course Jonas was friends with the sheriff. Jonas probably owned half of Hebbronville.

Within several seconds the log-on screen appeared, and she frowned in confusion. The puzzle had changed. Her eyes scanned the miscellaneous words and pictures that made up the logic puzzle until she knew the answer, and she typed it in quickly. She wondered if he had changed it because she had been able to figure out the answer to the last puzzle so quickly.

The home screen opened up, and she began to move the mouse around to scroll over the different folders when, unexpectedly, another window opened. A streaming video filled the screen. Uneasy seeing whatever he had been watching, she moved to close the window. Her hand froze with the mouse hovering over the X on the screen.

"All are accounted for," a man's voice said as the camera panned over two box trailers. Her stomach churned violently. The trailers were packed full of women, children, and men who were filthy and in various state of undress. "We made it through the tunnels without a problem. We're on the road now and will arrive soon. I'll keep you posted on our progress."

Surely this couldn't be real. Surely this had to be some attempt at a prank. She clicked the box closed with a trembling hand, and her eyes were drawn to a folder labeled "work." Maybe she could find the invoice in there and be through with the nightmare.

The file was full of photos. Staring back at her were the haunted eyes of young men and boys, bound and gagged, stuffed into storage containers or animal cages. Then there were the images of the girls and the women, most of them nude. But they didn't stare back at her. No, their eyes were covered with blindfolds, and they too were bound and gagged.

Another set of pictures almost made her gag and choke right there. The images showed bodies this time, dead and mutilated.

In one of the photos, Jonas smiled into the camera,

his semiautomatic weapon pointed at a crowd of terrified men.

There were documents in the folder as well. Surely they would prove that it was all a joke. She clicked open the documents and fought the tremors that consumed her as she read the papers. They provided detailed plans of how the traffickers were going to bring in the next shipment of slaves through a tunnel system near Reynosa. The document even outlined a slave auction to be held in San Antonio the upcoming weekend.

Sex slaves. The prisoners in the photos were going to be auctioned off as sex slaves.

Elena couldn't breathe. Bile burned at the back of her throat. Jonas was a smuggler, the worst kind possible. He traded human bodies for cash. Her stomach twisted so hard that she looked around frantically for a trash can to catch her vomit.

"Elena?"

Jonas's voice sounded in the distance, and panic raced through her veins. Swallowing her bile, she quickly closed the folder that held the damning evidence and frantically searched for the invoice. A folder labeled expenses looked to be the most promising, and she clicked it open. The PDF file of the invoice was the first document, and she clicked it open.

"Elena? Where are you, my dear?"

She swallowed hard as she heard his footsteps drawing closer to the office. She had nowhere to hide. She picked up the phone and pressed it to her ear.

"Yes, I'm looking at the invoice right now. I placed this order nearly five weeks ago, and we still haven't received the saddles." She paused, standing and placing one hand on her hip as she stared down at the phone, handset pressed to her ear, the dial tone making a low hum. "Yes, yes, I understand there was heavy silver-work trim, but you've never taken this long before." Again she paused, then jerked her head up in feigned surprise when she heard a noise at the office door. Jonas stood there, his arms folded over his chest, a pleased smile on his thin lips.

Elena forced a smile, then mouthed the words, "I'm sorry," and pointed to the handset. He shook his head and his smile broadened. Elena pulled her eyes off him and frowned into the mouthpiece. "Look," she said, her voice far firmer than she felt, "we have a show coming up in just a few weeks, and I need to break them in prop-erly. How soon will you have them to me?"

She nodded silently, then drew a deep breath, doing everything possible to put on a show for Jonas. "Fine. One week. If we don't have them by then, we won't be able to continue doing business with you. You're already two weeks past your promised delivery date." She nodded again, then sighed into the phone. "Buen. Gracias."

Jonas stepped into the small office as she placed the handset back in the receiver, his smile even broader than before. "I should have you come work for me full-time. I've never heard you so adamant."

Elena forced a smile to her lips and tried not to show her nerves as he drew closer. "It was a problem that needed to be taken care of."

He stopped mere inches from her, and she felt the usual unease she faced with him, coupled with stark fear after what she had just discovered about him. The man fit her definition of monster, and she wanted to get as far away from him as she could as quickly as possible.

She hadn't imagined the photos she had seen, or the picture of Jonas with his gun. And she wasn't imagining the intent in his eyes as they roved over her body, pausing on her wet shirt clinging to her breasts.

"Today has been incredibly hot," he murmured. "Did you enjoy the cool water while you bathed the horse?"

The intimate question made her skin crawl. Desire flickered in his eyes as he licked his lips and moved even closer to her. She forced a trembling smile to her lips and sidestepped him, but she wasn't fast enough. His arm snaked around her waist, and she gasped when he pulled her toward him. "Why do you always run from me, Elena? Do you have any idea of the pleasure I could bring you? That we could bring to each other?"

"Jonas…"

She pushed against his chest, frightened by the thick wall of muscle she met in resistance. "Jonas…I've told you before… We aren't compatible. I'm not interested. The only reason you're interested in me is because I've told you no, and you're used to getting whatever you want."

He raised an eyebrow at her. "Or maybe I could open an entirely new world of ecstasy to both of us. Why do you continue to fight me, dear Elena? I can feel how rapid your heart is beating. I know that you feel the stirrings of desire when you are around me."

"I will not get involved with you, Jonas," Elena said firmly, even though she could feel her body beginning to tremble violently. If he didn't release her soon, she would be sick all over him.

A muscle jumped in his jaw as he slowly released her, and she took a large step away from him, then another until she stood at the entrance to the office. "One day, you will see the foolishness of your thinking. But I am a patient man. I am willing to wait until your passion will no longer be denied. And then I will teach you things you never thought possible."

"Please, Jonas… Please respect my wishes." She swallowed the acid that burned the back of her throat and threatened to make her eyes water. "I've told you no many times now."

His bushy eyebrows lifted in surprise, and he pursed his lips as his gaze slowly ran up and down the length of her body. "Give it time, sweet Elena. Give it time. And then you will no longer be able to deny how you feel for me."

"I have to get going. I'll see you again next week." She nodded firmly to him, trying to make it obvious that their conversation had ended.

He chuckled as she turned and began to walk away. "I will have you, Elena. Mark my word, one day you will be mine."

Phantom stared at the tracks in the muddy ground and cursed under his breath. "We've found the exit to one of the tunnels, and it's practically in the Rio Grande."

"We knew the possibility of them building a tunnel running as far as Hidalgo would be next to impossible," Stryker said over the coms. "We're approaching the exit for the second tunnel now."

As soon as they had discovered the tunnel, they had

sent a drone inside to find the exit point. They were shocked when the tunnel split in two, delaying them even further as they sent a second drone to track the other exit. Phantom and Santo had taken Clara with them to the first exit point discovered, and Stryker, Javier, and Arturo had quickly followed the direction of the second drone.

"Look for deep tracks when you get there," Phantom said. "We've just come across a set about fifty feet from the exit of the tunnel. It obviously belonged to a large rig."

"You think they loaded the hostages onto box trailers at this point and they're through Border Patrol by now?" Santo asked, his face reflecting the grim feelings churning in Phantom's gut.

"That's exactly what I'm thinking. Clara, do you have any connections within Border Patrol that can pull up images of any box trailers that passed through within the last twenty-four hours?"

"You think they could have that much of a lead on us?" Santo asked.

"It's hard to say. Given the freshness of these tracks, I'd say it hasn't been too long."

"Sí. I have someone I trust within the Border Patrol. I will do my best." She already had a cell phone pressed to one ear, communicating their findings back to her supervisor, and she gestured to one of her people for their cell phone, placing the call.

"We're here," Stryker said. "We're probably about ten klicks south of you. These bastards really have things planned out."

"The plan has to fall apart somewhere. That's how

we'll be able to stop them," Phantom said, his tone harsh. He wanted to bring down the trafficking ring with a passion that burned inside him. Knowing there were at least thirty women and over a dozen children crammed into box trailers as if they were worth nothing more than livestock sickened him.

"My contact said they lost power at the checkpoint a few hours ago." Clara approached them, her face pale. "They have no records of any box trailers moving through there during that time period."

"Not only did they plan well, they have powerful connections," Santo growled.

"You need to discover who this person was that came to you with this information," Phantom said to Clara. "She's where everything starts."

"I just found a set of deep tracks matching what you described, Phantom," Stryker said over coms. "It looks like we need to be on the hunt for two trailers headed into the United States."

Phantom shook his head. "They aren't headed there. They're already there. More than likely they've made arrangements for a place to keep the hostages for the next couple of days before the auction."

"What do we do from here?" Santo asked.

"We head back stateside. In the meantime, I've got to make a very unpleasant call to Admiral Haslett." Phantom turned to Clara. "We have very little time to spare. I'll be in contact with you soon about what we discover."

Clara nodded, her eyes haunted. "If I had known—"

"This group is incredibly organized and highly trained. You did what any of us would have done if presented with the same information. I trust that you and your men will be able to brief us on the investigation you conduct on your end?"

"Sí. Thank you, Phantom, for your leadership. It has been an honor working with you."

Phantom shook her hand. "It's our honor to work with you as well. Stay safe."

She nodded, watching him intently. "You and your team as well. I have a feeling the danger now lies in your backyard."

Chapter 20

HASLETT DISCONNECTED THE CALL WITH PHANTOM AND pinched the bridge of his nose. Things had turned into an absolute clusterfuck. They needed to find where the hostages were going to be held until the auction in only a few days. That would be their only window of opportunity. Now that the traffickers knew they were being watched, they would scatter, and chances of catching them would become next to impossible.

His gut told him something had gone wrong not only in Mexico, but within his own network as well. Too many things had to be coordinated correctly to pull off a haul this significant. He yanked open his office door and scanned the faces of the people who worked in his office, handling the endless amounts of paperwork required by the navy. His gaze landed on one of the newer faces in the group, and the wheels in his mind began to spin.

"Ramirez!" he barked, and the young woman jumped at her desk, then quickly stood and grabbed a notepad and pen and advanced toward him. She moved with confidence and gave no sign that she was nervous to have been singled out by the admiral. He smiled to himself.

When he had first brought Amber Ramirez within his administrative clerks, he hadn't done so because Phantom was her brother. She had great technical aptitude and had proven her intelligence during boot camp. He needed to replace a clerk that had transferred, and her background had been the perfect fit.

"Close the door behind you," he said as he returned to his desk.

She did as he asked and stood ramrod straight, waiting for his next order. He sighed. The last thing he needed was someone else who wouldn't even sneeze unless he gave them permission. "Sit, Ramirez, sit. And don't take any notes. What I'm about to talk to you about stays between us only."

Her face paled. "Does this have something to do with Phantom?"

"Yes and no. Don't worry, your brother is fine. But I need someone I can trust right now. Given that it involves the assignment your brother is currently engaged in, I believe you're that person."

Amber frowned slightly. "I'm not sure I understand, sir."

"I think we have a problem in this office. It could be something as small as a leak or, worse-case scenario, we may have a mole. Someone wants to see your brother's undercover assignment go up in flames, and the entire team with it. I need someone to handle correspondence with the team, transfer their notes to files, and manage the intel that comes through my office for them. Can I count on you to be that person?"

Amber swallowed hard. "I'd be honored to, sir. I'll do whatever is needed to ensure their safety."

"Good. I'll make arrangements for us to meet off base so I can bring you up to speed on everything they're working on. This is a serious matter, Ramirez.

You can't tell anyone you're working on it. Including your brother."

Her eyes widened slightly before she nodded. "Yes, sir. You can count on me."

—◊◊◊—

Elena tried not to speed as she drove away from Jonas's ranch. The reality of what she had discovered still played over and over in her mind, to the point that she had to yank her truck over on the side of the road and threw open the door and retch. She hadn't had much to eat all afternoon, so what she spit from her lips was mostly burning bile.

She needed to get help. She needed to notify the authorities immediately of what she had discovered so action could be taken. She grabbed her cell and punched in 9-1-1, but her finger hovered over the speak button. The pictures cluttering Jonas's desk of him fishing with the sheriff, hunting with him... The two men were friends. For all she knew, the sheriff could be part of the entire operation.

Her mind raced with other possibilities. She latched on to her next big hope. Evie's cheerful voice came through as she answered at her desk at the courthouse. "Evie, it's Elena. I need your help."

"Elena? You sound awful. Are you all right?"

"Yes, I mean no... I mean... Shit, Evie, things are really messed up."

"Are you hurt? Where are you? I'll get there as fast as I can."

"No, no. It's probably best you stay far away from me right now. I just came across something horrible—worse than horrible. Jonas Franklin is a human trafficker."

"*What*? Elena, how do you know this?"

"It's a long story. But I found proof on his computer in the barn office. He's smuggling two entire trailers full of people into the United States within the next couple of days, and he's going to auction them off in San Antonio. What do I do, Evie? I can't think straight."

"Okay, first, take a deep breath. You sound like you're about to hyperventilate. You need to call the sheriff. He's going to have to get a search warrant, but I'm sure Judge O'Connor can push one through for him quickly."

"No, no. I've already thought about that. Jonas is friends with the sheriff. How do I know he won't be on Jonas's side? How do we know he isn't partners with Jonas on this whole thing?"

"Sheriff Verduzco never struck me as a corrupt man, Elena. How do you know they're friends?"

"They… Jonas has pictures of the two of them all over his office. Of them hunting and fishing and drinking beer together. Trust me, Evie, they're friends."

"Shit. Let me ask Judge O'Connor what to do—"

"Didn't you say Jonas comes by to see her all the time? Hell, Evie, what if she's been compromised too?"

"No. She's a stand-up woman, and I'd vouch for her with my life. There's just no chance—"

"We can't afford to make any mistakes with this. I can't afford to take any chances, no matter how slim they may be. Is there someone over the sheriff that I can go to? Someone higher than Judge O'Connor?"

"You can try to contact the FBI. Surely someone there will be able to direct you to the correct department. There's bound to be an agency that handles human trafficking. I can look up the information and get back to you."

"Yes. Please, Evie. Do that. Call me as soon as you know anything. And please make sure no one is around you where they can hear your conversation. I think we've all underestimated the power and influence Jonas has in this town."

"I'll be careful. What about you? What are you going to do?"

"I-I…" Elena faltered, wondering exactly what she should do. It was late Wednesday afternoon. Phantom had just left the day before, but for some reason she felt she could trust him, and he would know what to do. "I'm going to call Phantom."

"Elena, he's just a rancher. How can he possibly help you?"

"I don't know. I just need to hear his voice."

"Is he back from his trip yet?" Elena had shared with Evie that Phantom had left town but would be back as soon as possible.

"I don't know. He said he would come find me as soon as he got back, but maybe he didn't want to interrupt me at work."

"If he's back, go to him. I don't like the idea of you being all alone with all this going down."

Elena swallowed hard. "Neither do I. Keep in touch. Call me as soon as you know anything." She ended her call with Evie and quickly dialed Phantom. She cursed when it went to voicemail. "Hi, Phantom, it's Elena. I-I need your help. Something very strange has happened, and I just don't know what to do. Please call me as soon as you get this message. I-I need you."

Jonas sighed heavily as he sat down at the desk in the small office in the barn. In his mind, Elena already belonged to him. She just didn't know it yet. He stared at the phone for several moments, smiling as he recalled her end of the conversation he had caught. He had always known her to be a driven and intense woman, but he had never seen her as worked up as she had been during that phone call.

He glanced over at his computer and suddenly realized she had solved another one of his logic puzzles to log on and find the invoice. She had remarkable talent when it came to puzzles. When he finally won her over, and he would, he knew she would greatly appreciate the puzzles he had designed into the new facility that had been completed that very morning.

The construction had barely finished in time. He expected delivery of his merchandise in a few hours, and he couldn't have any complications. Smiling, he aimed the mouse toward the icon for the live streaming video so he could see the new shipment as they made their way down the highway.

He frowned as he clicked on the window and noticed the time stamp. It indicated the window had been open less than fifteen minutes earlier. He hadn't looked at the feed in a couple of hours. Fifteen minutes ago would have been—

A sickening feeling churned in his stomach. Using skills he had been taught by their master computer programmer, he did a search on all recent activities. His hand clenched into a fist as he saw the folder that had been opened, as well as the documents within the folder.

The snoopy little woman had discovered his dirty secret. "Damn it!" he roared, slamming his fist down on the desk, and the horses in the nearby stalls jumped and pranced, letting out startled whinnies.

No wonder Elena had been trying so hard to get away from him. But she had certainly played her haughty-bitch role well.

He pulled out his cell phone and hit a speed-dial number. The phone was answered on the third ring. "Your call is coming far sooner than I expected," a smug voice said on the other end of the line.

Jonas spoke through clenched teeth. "We have a problem."

Elena couldn't stay in Hebbronville. She knew she could be in great danger. She had to get away, and she had to do so quickly. She debated whether to leave her truck running or not as she pulled up outside her apartment. Shaking her head at herself, she pulled the keys from the ignition and bounded up the stairs two at a time.

She locked the door behind her, fastening the dead bolt and the latch, even though she knew neither would do enough if a man as large as Jonas decided to charge through her door. There was no way for her to know if he had discovered what she had seen on the computer, but she couldn't take any chances.

She scanned her small apartment, and a pang of loss struck her. It wasn't much, but it had been her home for years, her pictures and shadow boxes on the walls, her homely, yet coordinated furniture. Now she had to leave all of it behind.

She fished underneath her bed and pulled out a duffel bag that she had only used a couple of times in her entire life. Moving quickly, she began to grab clothes from her dresser and stuff them into the duffel. She didn't own much, so it didn't take long. Then she went to the small nightstand next to her bed and yanked open the drawer. Nestled in a soft purple cloth was her SIG Sauer P320 handgun. She quickly checked the magazine, then rammed it home. She grabbed two more full magazines and tossed them into her duffel.

She had bought the gun for self-protection when she had moved away from home to live on her own and frequently visited the firing range to stay comfortable with the weapon. Already she felt more secure, knowing it was primed and ready nearby.

A knock sounded at her door, and Elena almost screamed. Her heart slammed against her chest in a combination of fear and hope. Had Phantom returned? Had he decided to come to her directly?

Why hadn't he called her first? If he had returned, why hadn't he answered her phone call? She shook her head in frustration. Her paranoia needed to be kept in check. If Phantom had decided to surprise her by showing up at her door, she could only be grateful. Still, something churned in her gut, telling her to be cautious.

"Just a minute," she called out, making her voice sound cheerful as she tried to gather herself together. When no answer came from the other side of the door, her unease grew even more intense. Phantom would have said something. He wouldn't have remained silent.

"Who is it?" she called, trying desperately to breathe evenly.

"Randall. You can call me Randy, I guess." There was hesitant, awkward laughter. "Sorry. I just moved in a couple houses over. We ran out of milk for the baby, and I just saw you get home. I thought you might have some you could spare?"

Did neighbors really still do that? Borrow milk or sugar? Seriously? She placed both hands on her gun and began to inch toward the door. "I'm all out of milk," she replied. "Sorry. Did you ask the Bells downstairs? They usually have those types of necessities."

"No, no I didn't. No one came to the door when I knocked."

Liar, liar, pants on fire. Mr. and Mrs. Bell left yesterday to visit their children. Okay, who are you? She kept the gun pointed at the floor as she kicked her boots off, then slowly, slowly slid across her floor in just her socks, making certain that the floorboards never creaked.

Soon enough, she stood close to the door and ventured a glance out the peephole.

She saw a man's face and didn't recognize him. Something in the way he stood made her uneasy. Then movement—and the barrel of a shotgun aimed right at her door. Sucking in a deep breath, she jumped backward, but she wasn't fast enough. Her stomach burned as the explosion knocked her backward, the door fragmenting, shooting splinters at her. It kept on splintering, the man outside kicking and punching in the door fragments.

Pain set in and Elena looked down to see her shirt torn and bloody, but she chose to ignore it. She had more pressing matters to deal with. The man kicking and beating at the door seemed determined to reach her no matter what. She gripped her gun tightly and aimed at the leg that kicked in her door, breathed evenly and used both hands to steady the weapon, combatting her nerves.

His whole upper leg burst through the wood, and she clenched her teeth together. She took aim and...

Pow!

His scream of pain echoed in her apartment. Blood welled up around the wound in his upper thigh, which she knew had to be incredibly painful. For a moment she stood frozen in disbelief while he regrouped and began to hammer his way through her door again, even though blood gushed down his leg.

She had to get away. She had to force her muscles to move. Elena raced toward her bed and grabbed her duffel bag, then ran out onto the small balcony of her garage apartment. She tossed the bag over the rail and heard it land before she launched herself over the support. She couldn't contain her cry as her stomach rubbed across the banister, but she quickly forgot her pain when she heard a roar inside and the door came crashing inward.

She knew without a doubt she had never seen the man before, and never wanted to again. His eyes were soulless, and he advanced too calmly, pulling out his own handgun as he limped his way across her apartment. Dangling from the balcony, she couldn't think straight anymore. Fear served as her guide.

She dropped from the balcony and landed hard on the hood of her truck, the air forced from her lungs. Gasping, fighting for breath, she grabbed the duffel bag and raced for the driver-side door. A soft sound, like popcorn popping, echoed from above her, and dirt and rocks kicked up at her feet.

She didn't bother to look up to see her would-be assassin firing on her from above. She jumped into her truck, throwing her bag into the passenger seat, then let out a startled scream as a round shattered her windshield and lodged in the steering wheel. *Damn it! He's just too fast!* She dropped her keys and ducked down to retrieve them from the floor of her truck. When she popped back up, there were three round holes in her seat where she had just been sitting.

Lowering her head again, she thrust the keys into the ignition and threw the truck into reverse. Another round whizzed through the windshield and shattered the rear as she peeled out of the short driveway. Dimly, she registered that the door Mr. Bell had lovingly installed for his wife hung from the doorjamb, obviously having been kicked in violently. She struggled to draw a deep breath. She had no doubt that Mr. and Mrs. Bell would have been killed by the madman trying to kill her if they had been home.

She felt tears rolling down her cheeks, and her stomach burned as if on fire. Sirens wailed down the street and she considered turning around and seeking safety with the sheriff, but she remembered his friendship with Jonas and knew she couldn't possibly trust him. In her state of panic, she wondered if she could trust anyone. Jonas had had plenty of time to call in a few favors while she was on the road. He certainly had the money to make things happen, especially given how corrupt the world had become, and she didn't doubt for a moment he had a powerful reach.

She couldn't sit up straight because of the pain in her stomach, and she glanced down, blinking when she saw she only had socks on her feet. Her mind couldn't quite register what she saw with all the other things demanding attention. Her world had turned on its ear, and she knew it had everything to do with what she had found on Jonas's computer. Would he try to harm or kill others if it helped him get to her?

The ringtone on her phone went off and she screamed, fumbling with the phone because her hands were slick with sweat and blood. She hadn't even remembered grabbing her cell phone before fleeing her apartment. Through her tears, she could barely read the phone number, but once she recognized it, she hastily pushed the button to answer it.

"Phantom?" She tried to keep her voice steady.

"Elena…where are you?"

"I-I…I'm not sure right now."

There was a pause on the other end of the line. "Elena, go to your apartment. I'll be there in just a few."

"No. No. I can't go back there. I can't ever go back there again."

"Elena… Okay, I'll ask you more questions later. Can you make it to the ranch safely?"

Elena tried to look up into the rearview mirror, then winced as the pain in her stomach pulled her back down to hunch over the steering wheel. "I think so. I'll be there as soon as possible."

"Santo will be following you. I'll be here for you as soon as you get here."

"How-how does Santo…?"

"Just trust me. We're here for you."

Chapter 21

TWENTY MINUTES LATER, ELENA DROVE UP THE DIRT ROAD to the ranch house. Headlights bobbed behind her, and she just accepted that they were Santo's. She pulled into the drive and parked in her usual spot, then struggled to find the energy to open her door. Her shirt had become blotched with blood, but the sheer terror and shock of everything that had happened caused her to shake.

Finally, she forced her door open and swallowed hard. What if she had brought the danger here to Phantom and his friends? What if she had brought the danger to Anya? She was about to step out of her truck when she remembered her feet. She couldn't just walk into their house with her socks on. She couldn't—

Suddenly, he was with her. She recognized his cologne, felt his warmth and strength before he even touched her. He stepped partway into the open cab of the truck, his eyes searching her face. "Elena, I got home just a little earlier today and missed your phone call. You knew I was going to be gone for a few days…"

"I'm so sorry, Phantom." *Damn these stupid tears! I am not this weak!* "I made a terrible mistake today. And I never should have come here."

"Elena! What are you talking about?" Concern and frustration made his voice rough.

"I found—I found this file…at Jonas Franklin's house. It—He-he's a slave trafficker. There were such horrible pictures. And someone's going to auction them off this weekend. All of them. So, so many innocent people. I didn't know where else to go." She reached up and touched his handsome face, then grimaced as she saw the smudge of her own blood she left on his skin. "I may have led them straight to you and your friends. And Anya. Oh please, Phantom, I'm so sorry."

"Elena...Elena! Look at me. What makes you think that they—Good grief, you're bleeding."

He began to pull away but she grabbed for his shoulder, trying to hold him close. "Is Anya safe? Can you get her somewhere safe?"

"There's no safer place for her to be than here with us. She's inside with Stryker right now. We need to focus on you. Where are you hurt? Where is this blood coming from?"

Having parked the truck, Santo appeared beside Phantom and pointed a flashlight at Elena. Her blood-splattered shirt seemed to startle both intimidating men. "I couldn't move fast enough," Elena said as a way of explanation, wincing as she tried to draw a deep breath. "He shot through the door before I could move—"

"He *shot*... Fuck!" Phantom's arms went around Elena, wrapping her in his embrace and lifting her from the truck. The world blurred as he carried her toward the house, Santo leading the way. "Where are you shot?" Phantom demanded.

Elena suddenly felt safe. Phantom had come home and held her in his arms. That was all that mattered. "It was just a shotgun," she whispered, smiling up at him. "Don't be worried. There are some pieces of wood stuck in my stomach, though, and those are a bit painful."

"Just a…" She could see his Adam's apple bob as he swallowed hard. "Where were you hit, Elena? Just answer me. That's all that's important now."

"My stomach, I think. But it's okay. It really isn't that painful. I can't stop shaking. I don't know why. Phantom?"

He looked at her face, and she could see the lines of tension around his mouth. "Just your stomach? Anywhere else?"

"Please, listen to me."

"I am, wildflower. I'm listening to you."

She heard the door to the house open and then Anya's cry of alarm, but it all sounded very distant. "Phantom." His eyes locked on hers. "I really don't think my injuries are that bad. I think I'm in shock, though. Is it normal to faint when you're in shock?"

"Yes, that will happen sometimes, but just hang tight with me, Elena. We're going to take care of you."

"Phantom?"

"Yes, wildflower?"

"I love you." Finally, she allowed herself to relax and gave in to the peaceful darkness that surrounded her.

⁓

A string of curses flew out of Phantom's mouth as Elena went limp in his arms. "For the love of Pete…where is my medical bag?" he demanded, his voice strained as his eyes scanned the stunned faces around him.

"Here." Santo spoke up softly at his elbow. "Let's get her to one of the rooms. Anya, we may need your help. We don't know how badly she's been shot."

"Shot!" Anya exclaimed. "Who would shoot Elena?"

"She said something about Jonas Franklin," Phantom said tightly.

Anya seemed to lose all color in her face but nodded solemnly. Phantom didn't wait for anyone to open one of the spare bedrooms. He carried Elena directly to his room and didn't hesitate before setting her down gently on his bed. His hands went to her blouse, but the blood had spread and he couldn't undo the small buttons. They just kept slipping through his fingers.

He was cursing again when Santo shoved a pair of scissors in his hands. "Cut everything off. We need to know every place she could have been hit."

Phantom grabbed the scissors, and for a moment it seemed as if he wouldn't be able to hold his hand steady enough to cut off her clothes. Then he drew a deep breath and focused on his objective.

Keep it simple, stupid. KISS. It had been pounded into his head during Hell Week. When it came to Elena, though, nothing could ever be simple.

His quick and efficient slices with the scissors had her clothes falling to the side, and a combination of relief and anger surged through him. She had avoided the main impact of the gun, and only a few pellets had grazed her skin. The main source of the bleeding came from the slivers of wood that protruded from her like porcupine quills. He had seen far worse in the field. But this was *his* Elena, and someone had just tried to kill her.

Anya nudged Phantom to move, and he turned on her with a growl in his throat. She had a better chance of moving hell than moving him away from Elena. *Mine*.

"Fine. Stay there. But if you're going to be in my way, then at least be useful." She handed Phantom a basin of warm water and a warm, damp cloth. Santo held the same and was already beginning to clean the blood away so they could see the full extent of Elena's injuries.

Phantom had to pull back and assess her clinically. He wasn't helping her by struggling with his anger. That would come later. "She's going to need a few stitches, but it shouldn't be that bad. We just need to get all this garbage out and make sure we keep infection at bay." He was grabbing a pair of needle-nose forceps and reaching toward Elena's stomach when Anya's hand clamped down over his wrist.

"Isn't that going to hurt her?"

"She's not feeling a thing right now, Anya. Let me do my job. When she wakes up, I'll give her something to numb the pain."

"We've got your back, brother," Santo said tensely, watching with concern.

Phantom nodded. "I appreciate it. I've got to get these pellets and wood out of her. The damage appears to be minimal, and I think she passed out from shock, just like she said. I need to work quickly before she wakes up."

Anya nodded absently and released Phantom's wrist, then took a step back to give him room. Within moments, the sound of the round pellets and pieces of wood falling into a metal basin echoed throughout the room. Phantom's muscles cramped as he bent over her with concentration, and every time he thought about how close she had come to dying, his hand would begin to tremble. So he switched his mind off as best he could and focused on the task.

He was in the process of pulling out the last of the larger splinters when she drew in a sharp breath and began to struggle to sit up. "Relax, Elena. You're safe. We're almost done. Are you in any pain?" Phantom asked, leaning over her so she could see his face.

"No. Yes." Her gaze met his and she shook her head. "What happened?"

"You fainted. Probably from shock. Do you remember getting here? Do you remember the things you were saying?"

"Yes. I remember coming here. I remember... Oh! That man tried to shoot me!"

"We're very fortunate that he has poor aim. You're only going to have some minor cuts and scrapes once I'm finished. I need to finish getting all the splinters out and clean your skin properly. If you're in pain, I can numb the area so you won't feel anything."

Her brow furrowed in confusion. "How do you have access to such stuff? How do you know what to do?"

"It's a complicated story. We'll talk about it in a minute. Will you please answer my question?"

"I'm okay. It burns, but I don't want you to numb it." Her eyes drifted around the room and landed on her friend. "Anya! I'm so sorry I brought this mess to you. I didn't know where else to go."

"You did the right thing coming here," Anya said softly, her eyes shimmering with unshed tears. "I just hate that you're going through this."

Phantom bent over Elena and concentrated on the last few tiny splinters. She winced several times, but didn't try to stop him. Her strength and resilience amazed him. He wanted to wrap her in his arms and protect her from ever being hurt again.

He ran his hand across her stomach lightly, checking

for any remaining pieces of wood and frowned at the blood that smeared under his fingers. She wasn't bleeding heavily, and he knew with some simple bandages she would be fine. She wouldn't need stitches after all. He just hated seeing blood on her beautiful skin.

Several minutes later, he and Anya had finished cleaning the area and had placed bandages over the shallow cuts. Elena had watched their faces as they worked, her gaze bouncing between him and Anya. He knew she had a thousand questions, and so did he.

She glanced down when they were finished and gasped. "Why am I naked?" She wrapped her arms around her chest, attempting to conceal her breasts. At that moment Santo stepped through the door, but kept his eyes averted.

"I have the bag you had in your truck. I thought you could use some clothes."

Anya hurried to him and grabbed the bag. "Thank you, Santo. She's going to be fine. Phantom was able to take care of everything."

Santo sighed. "That's a relief. I'll be out in the main living room with the rest of the guys when you're all ready to come out."

Anya nodded and turned to Phantom, handing him the bag. "I think I'll join the guys. You need some time with Elena before you come out with us."

"Thank you." Phantom took the bag from Anya and waited for her to close the door behind her as she left his room. He drew a deep breath as he turned to face Elena. She had pulled the blanket on the bed over her torso and watched him closely.

He fished in her bag and pulled out a T-shirt. "This should be comfortable and won't irritate your wounds."

She grabbed the shirt and quickly pulled it on over her head. "Phantom, I have to talk to you. It's really important. I didn't know where else to go."

"You said something about Jonas Franklin being a human trafficker. What happened? What made you think he's involved in such a thing?"

She ran a trembling hand through her hair. "I-I came across information on his computer. It was by accident, and I thought it was a joke at first, but the more I saw, the more I realized it wasn't."

"And what happened? How did you get shot?"

"I was terrified. I knew I had to leave. I thought Jonas might discover what I had seen on his computer. I couldn't take a chance. So I went home and was starting to pack a bag when someone knocked on my door. I don't know what made me suspicious, but I took my boots off so he couldn't hear me approach the door." She glanced down to the bottom of the bed and saw her feet still in socks. "He said his name was Randy, and I looked through the peephole and saw the shotgun. I was able to jump almost completely out of the way before he shot. Obviously not far enough."

Phantom sat on the edge of the bed and pressed a kiss to her forehead. "You did wonderful, Elena. You were brilliant."

Her eyes filled with tears. "I shot him, Phantom. I shot him as he tried to kick his way through the door."

Phantom rubbed his fingers across her cheeks, swiping away the tears that trickled down her face. "I saw the inside of your truck. The man tried to kill you. Why didn't you go to the sheriff as soon as you left Jonas's ranch?"

Elena shook her head frantically. "We can't trust the sheriff. Jonas has pictures of them together all over his office. They're clearly friends. For all I know, he could be partners with Jonas."

"He's not. The sheriff is a good man. We've worked with him before on a delicate situation. What made you think you had to run?"

"I didn't know for sure. Jonas is good with computers. If he looked around enough at what I had been doing on the computer, he would see what I had found. I couldn't take any chances. Now I know for sure that he found out."

"He's good with computers? How good? Do you think he knows how to write code?"

Confusion crossed her face. "Phantom, I feel like you aren't telling me something." She bit her lower lip as her gaze swept over his face. "How did you know what needed to be done for my gunshot wound? And why do you have medicine to use on someone who has been hurt? What aren't you telling me?"

Phantom ran a hand down his face, trying to think of the best way to approach the conversation with her. He had planned to tell her the true nature of his work when he returned from Mexico. He just hadn't planned on the circumstances being anything like this.

"Elena, you're right, there's something I need to tell you. Just hear me out before you jump to any conclusions. Please understand that everything between us has been real. I've just kept one detail from you."

"What? You're starting to scare me. What have you not told me?"

"I'm here on a special undercover assignment. I'm a Navy SEAL."

———

Elena struggled to pull in a deep breath. A SEAL? He couldn't be serious. He had told her everything about his life. He had told her about being a consultant, and... Her mind began to race. Had he been lying to her this entire time?

"I don't understand. What... How can this be an undercover assignment? You've shared everything with me, haven't you? You obviously know a lot about horses, so I know you didn't fake that with me. You-you..." She searched his face, desperate for answers. His serious expression told her he wasn't trying to keep any secrets from her. He was finally telling her the entire truth.

"You've been lying to me this entire time, haven't you? The story about being a consultant was just a load of bullshit. Tell me all your lies, Phantom. I want to know!" Her world was caving in. From the horror of what she had discovered on Jonas's computer, to the terror of being shot, to Phantom's lies, everything was falling apart.

"No! No, that's what I need you to understand. I haven't been lying to you. But I couldn't tell you about our undercover role here. Not until I had clearance to do so. It not only puts you in jeopardy, but it puts the entire team at risk."

"The *team*? Are you telling me that all these men are SEALs? Does Anya know too?" She needed to focus on her breathing because she felt as though she could start hyperventilating at any moment.

"Yes. All the men are SEALs. Anya knows, but she doesn't know the details about the missions we run. She knows the risks and dangers we face, and she's prepared to be here for Stryker whenever he gets home from a mission. We were sent here on an assignment to work with the community and network to identify any threats from Mexico and Central and South America. That's exactly what we've been doing."

Elena thought she might be sick. Even her best friend had kept things secret from her. "Am I part of your cover story? That's it, isn't it? How could I be so blind?" She pushed herself away from him, stood, and began to pace the room. "You've been using me for your cover. I thought what we had was special. Hell, I fell in love with you. Or at least I fell in love with the man I thought you were. Do I really know you at all?"

Phantom shoved himself to his feet and rounded the bed to face her, gripping her shoulders. "You know me better than anyone else in this world. Everything between us has been real. Yes, I needed you to help me network and connect with the community, but that is as far as your involvement goes in this operation."

Elena pushed his hands off her shoulders, sidestepping him. "I *trusted* you. Do you know how hard that was for me? I should have known better. I should have stayed as far away from you as possible."

"Don't push me away, Elena, please. Don't discard what we have together."

She whirled to face him. "What exactly do we have together, Phantom? A few laughs and some great sex? I fell in love with an illusion."

He raked his hair back with both hands. "This is my nightmare come true. I've never felt about a woman the way I feel about you. I knew I was going to tell you the truth when we got back from our mission. And I was terrified this was exactly how you would react."

"Your mission? Is that where you've been? Is that why you couldn't tell me anything?"

"Yes. But you seem to have stumbled right into the heart of it."

"What are you talking about?"

"Our mission was to bring down a human trafficking ring operating out of Reynosa, Mexico. The mission failed, and somehow the traffickers managed to get the hostages to the United States. We didn't know who the main point person was on this side of things, but it seems you found him for us."

"Jonas." Her trembles increased and she felt slightly light-headed. "He's the one running things here in the United States."

"Yes. And we need your help to bring him down. Will you just come out to the living room and talk to the team? We need to know all the details so we can stop him before it is too late."

"Too late for what? The slave auction is still a few days away."

"Yes, but if Jonas thinks his cover is blown, he might kill every last one of their hostages."

Elena shuddered. "Yes. I'll talk to the team. But we are far from finished with our discussion. I have a lot of questions."

Chapter 22

"Elena, I know this is going to be incredibly hard on you, and I know you need your rest after everything you've been through. But we must act quickly in order to save these lives." Stryker watched her intently from where he sat on one of the plush couches across from her.

She wrung her hands together nervously, then forced herself to stop, clasping her fingers together in her lap. "I need to know who you all are. Who you *really* are."

"That's a fair request. I'm the team leader. Several months ago our commanding officer asked me to take on this assignment and select the men who would be a part of this team. Phantom is one of our strategic and tactical experts, and is one of the first men I asked to join."

Elena glanced over at Phantom who sat next to her, though she had made sure they weren't touching. Her emotions and feelings were so convoluted she didn't know how she would respond to his touch. "So you weren't completely lying to me when you said you went into consulting for placement and strategy."

A muscle in Phantom's jaw twitched, but he didn't say anything. He continued to stare at her with an intensity that was unnerving, though. Stryker cleared his throat. "I doubt Phantom truly lied to you about anything. He's one of the most honest men I've ever worked with. But it is our duty to uphold our assignments above anything else. He couldn't tell you who he really is until he had clearance from the admiral."

Elena's eyes widened and she looked back at Phantom. He had said something about clearance earlier, but she'd been so caught up in everything else she hadn't latched onto the words. "Do you have clearance from your admiral? Or are we breaking all types of rules here?"

"I asked the admiral for permission on our drive back from Reynosa. I let him know how important you are to me, and that I wanted to open my life to you."

She swallowed hard. She knew very little about the military, but enough to understand that it must have been a very serious conversation to convince the admiral to allow him to break their code of silence. Could it be that he felt things for her after all?

"Santo is our sniper, and Brusco works closely with Santo to identify targets and gather other information that happens fast when you're on the ground in hostile territory. Snap is also a tactical leader. We rely heavily on him to map out extractions and plan infiltrations. Buzz is our communications and technology expert. He runs our satellite systems, computer databases—anything technical goes through Buzz. Lobo, as you know, is new to our group. He's got a wide variety of expertise, especially in breaching enemies' strongholds."

"You aren't really able to tell me much more than that, are you?" she asked softly, squeezing her hands together so tightly her knuckles began to turn white.

"It's not only for our safety; it's for yours as well," Santo said solemnly. Elena wondered if they were all taught to say that since it so closely echoed what

Phantom had said minutes earlier. "We don't want to put you in any unnecessary danger."

"Can you tell us more about Jonas Franklin?" Phantom asked.

She nodded, unable to look at him directly. She was afraid if she did, she would start to cry. She didn't know what to believe about their past several weeks together. She didn't want to believe it had all been a lie, and her heart fiercely refused to think it could be. Her mind, on the other hand, warned her she was in grave danger of having her heart shattered into a million pieces that she'd never be able to pick up.

"Jonas has been a client of mine for several years. I took him on not long after I moved to Hebbronville after graduation. He's always made me uncomfortable—always tried to invade my personal space and made unwelcomed advances. Today, after I had finished working his horse, I needed to find an invoice stored somewhere on his computer in the barn."

"How did you know how to log on?" Buzz asked.

"He-he somehow knows about my love of puzzles. A few days ago, he showed me the logic puzzle he had created for the log-on, and I solved it quickly. He changed it—possibly so I wouldn't find what I did today—but I figured out the answer and was able to get into his computer that way."

"How does he know about your love of puzzles?" Phantom asked tensely.

"He claims there are people in town who will talk about my hobby from time to time. That's all he would say. I think the man might be slightly obsessed with me."

"Once you logged on, what did you find? Be as specific as possible if you can," Santo encouraged her.

"A-a window popped up right away. It was a streaming video of women, children, and men, all stuffed into
these two box trailers."

Santo leaned forward. "Are you certain it was two?
Could you see the license plate or any other information
like that?"

Elena shook her head. "No, the camera never shifted
that far. It stayed focused on those poor people. But I
know for certain there were two trailers." She frowned
as a memory tickled at the back of her mind, then sat
up straighter as it came to her. "There appeared to be a
logo stamped on the sides, but it had faded over time. I'd
know it if I saw it again."

"Could you tell how many people there were?"
Phantom asked.

"No. The trailers were crowded, though. The people
looked filthy and abused. Most of them lacked any
clothing at all, and the rest wore tattered cloth. There
was a man speaking on the video. He had a thick
accent—he must have been from Mexico or further
south. He said they were about to cross the border and
would arrive soon."

"How long ago was this video shot? Could you tell?"
Buzz had also leaned forward, resting his large forearms
on his thighs.

"The time stamp indicated it was in the early hours
this morning. If they were headed for Jonas's, they
would be here already."

"What else did you discover?" Stryker asked.

"I closed the window and opened a folder, hoping

to find the invoice and get out of the office as quickly as possible. The folder was labeled 'work,' and inside were so many pictures of people who were obviously intended to be slaves. They were kept in animal cages, and most were bound and gagged. Then there were these-these photos of people who had been killed. Jonas was in one of the photos, aiming his gun at a group of terrified young men and women. The next photo showed them all shot and dead." She grabbed the bottle of water on the table next to her and drank heavily, trying to swallow down the bile that continued to rise in her throat every time she thought about what she had seen.

"Was that all you found?" Phantom asked.

"No. There were notes about some type of auction being held this weekend. I wasn't able to read much before Jonas came into the barn."

"Is that when you ran?" Brusco asked, joining the discussion.

"No. I knew I had to close down everything so it wouldn't be obvious what I had been looking at. I was able to find the invoice, but not in enough time to dial the number before Jonas came in the office. I just picked up the phone and pretended to be on a call. He seemed to believe it."

"And you left? If you closed all the windows you had open, what made you think he would come after you? Is it possible the man who shot at you doesn't have any ties whatsoever to Franklin and what you found?" Snap asked.

Elena shook her head. "No, no. It isn't a coincidence. Jonas is good with computers. I already told Phantom that. All he had to do was backtrack to see what I had been doing on the computer." She ran a hand through her hair. "I just had this terrible feeling, and I couldn't shake it. He, well, he tried to make a pass at me again before I left. He tries almost every time I see him, so it didn't strike me as that unusual. It's just that, well, this time he said that eventually I would be his. He said it was just a matter of time."

Stryker exchanged looks with Phantom. Elena didn't know what they were trying to communicate to each other and wasn't certain she wanted to know. Phantom returned his gaze to her and raised his hand toward her as if to comfort and encourage her, but stopped halfway in reach and dropped his hand back to his side.

Elena yanked her gaze away from him and stared down at her clasped hands. "I called Evie right away to see if she knew what we could do, and she wanted to go to Judge O'Connor, but I don't know who we can trust. The man has many connections."

Santo frowned "I know Judge O'Connor. Who is Evie, and how do you know her?"

"Evie is one of my closest friends. She, Anya, and I all went to A&M together. She serves as the assistant to Judge O'Connor."

"And you don't feel you can trust Judge O'Connor?" Santo raised an eyebrow.

Elena shook her head. "No. No. Evie told me that Jonas comes to Judge O'Connor's office frequently, and she isn't sure what their discussions are about. We just can't take any chances." She glanced down at her clenched hands, then looked up at Stryker. "What little I was able to read in that one document said that the so-called 'shipment' was coming from Reynosa. Phantom told me that is where you've been the last couple of days—in Reynosa to stop the human traffickers. They must be headed to Jonas's ranch. The video I saw said that's where they were going."

"Did the man on the video specifically say they were headed to Jonas's ranch?" Stryker asked.

Elena closed her eyes, her memory drifting back to the horrific video she had watched in dismay. Her eyes snapped open. "No. No, he just said he would reach him soon."

"It's possible there could be a specific location closer to San Antonio where they plan to meet and hold the hostages," Lobo suggested.

"We need to bring the admiral up to speed on all this. I think we need to get with the sheriff and take down Jonas's ranch." Phantom looked around the room at the team. "Any other thoughts?"

"The sooner the better. He tried to have Elena killed. He's probably in the process of destroying all evidence, if he hasn't already. And if he does have the hostages, we may be too late." Stryker sighed heavily.

"Elena, Anya is in the dining room. She's anxious to see you. We'll handle things from here." Phantom stood, and the other men in the room joined him.

Elena folded her arms over her chest. "You're dismissing me? I want to see this through to the end. I'm just as much invested in this as any of you."

"You've done an amazing job getting this information to us. It's our job to clean things up. It's what we do." Phantom held out his hand to help her stand. She stared at it for a few moments, struggling with her warring emotions. Finally, she slid her hand into his and felt the familiar warmth and excitement she always felt when touching him.

He pulled her to her feet and she stood close to him, breathing in his scent. "Thank you, wildflower. Promise me we'll talk again soon. Promise me this isn't the end of us."

Her heart and mind raced. Could she trust him? Should she? "I promise."

"I agree with your assessment, Phantom. Get the sheriff engaged immediately and search Franklin's ranch," Admiral Haslett said over the speakerphone in the conference room. "You know how hostile the situation can be if he does have the hostages and tries to use them as bargaining chips. I'm headed your way. I want to be there when you take this bastard down."

"Buzz is pulling up any information he can on Jonas Franklin. He's also trying to find any dark web communication about the Puppet Master that may point to Jonas as the leader," Santo said. "I intend to reach out to Judge O'Connor in the morning. Knowing Jonas has visited her frequently doesn't sit well with me."

"It seems pretty fucking peculiar if you ask me. You've already talked to her about what you're investigating. She's holding back on you, Santo. Something needs to be done about that."

"Yes, sir."

They ended the call and Phantom dialed the sheriff. Sheriff Verduzco answered his cell phone on the second ring, his voice tense and tired. Phantom quickly told him what they knew and that they needed to move on Jonas's place immediately.

"Jonas? Jonas Franklin? Is this some type of joke? I've known the guy for at least ten years. Hell, we go fishing and hunting together all the time. Are you trying to tell me this all ties back to the mess we found at the Bells' home? Their door is smashed to hell, neighbors are reporting multiple gunshots, and there's blood all over the apartment Elena rents from them. I've got a lot of people asking a lot of questions. And you think Jonas is behind all this? It doesn't make any sense."

"Are you with us or not, Sheriff? We're going to be at his door in thirty minutes, with or without you." Phantom's tone indicated he would brook no arguments.

"Son of a bitch. Yes. I'll be there. Give me a little more time, though. I need to get a warrant from the judge."

"Let me call her," Santo said. "You'll have your warrant ready by the time you get to his gate."

"We need to know the layout of his place so we don't get taken by surprise. He could have armed guards for all we know." Stryker frowned.

Phantom didn't want to put Elena through any further questioning. He knew, though, that she was critical to the success of their mission. He nodded. "I'll go get her."

Anya and Elena were silent as they sat close together in the dining room. Anya held Elena's hand clasped tightly on top of the table, and they sipped slowly on steaming cups of coffee. Both looked exhausted and numb. Phantom wished he could take away all the hurt Elena had gone through.

"Elena?" She jumped at the sound of his voice as if coming out of a stupor.

She turned her head toward him, her expressive eyes giving away her emotions. He expected her to be sad or upset, but she looked more frustrated and irritated than anything. "I thought you would have already left by now."

"We're about to. But we need your help. We need to map out Jonas's location so we don't go in there blind. Will you help us with that? Buzz is pulling up satellite imaging of the place right now."

She stood slowly. "Why don't you just take me with you? I can tell you where everything is as we go."

Phantom shook his head. "Not going to happen. I won't put you at risk for this. Will you help us or not?"

"I'll do whatever I can to help bring this madness to an end. He's evil—absolute evil—and he must be stopped."

Phantom nodded. "Good. Join us up in the conference room? You can mark out the details of his location based on the images Buzz pulls up. We need to move quickly."

She nodded firmly. He placed his hand at the small of her back and guided her toward the stairs. She didn't try to pull away from him, which he took as a good sign. "Elena, I need you to know I didn't lie to you. This is the only thing I kept from you."

"It's a pretty big thing to keep secret."

"You understand why I had to, don't you? You understand the need for me to keep it a secret, right?" Phantom stared at her and slowly reached up, hooking an unruly lock of hair behind her ear. "Elena, I've wanted you for a very long time. You know that. But I was afraid of keeping this secret from you. I was afraid that—if the time ever came—you wouldn't be able to forgive me. Tell me that I'm wrong. Tell me that none of this matters. Because it sure as hell doesn't matter to me."

Her eyes glossed with tears, and he saw her lower lip tremble.

"Don't cry, Elena. Please…I need you, however I can have you. But…I can understand if you can't forgive me for this."

"F-forgive you? I might have led Jonas directly to you by coming here tonight. Not only did I put your cover in jeopardy, but I've put you and your entire team at risk by my actions."

She sighed heavily, then much to his surprise, she ran her hand through his hair and laid her palm against his face. "I'm not angry at you for not telling me about your real job. I'm angry that you made me part of your cover. That I became this-this piece of your fitting in. I'm *in love* with you, Phantom. And I know you aren't in love with me, and I never expected you to be. But to know that the whole thing was fake—"

His breath rushed out of him. She still loved him. He wanted to shout to the world with joy. He didn't know what had transpired in her mind to convince her to still love him, but he was grateful for it. He pulled her into a tight embrace, burying his face against her neck. "I'll never get tired of hearing you say that. I wish we had some time alone so we could talk some more," he murmured, slowly pulling back from her. "But we have to go after Jonas."

She gave him a weak smile. "I know. It's what you do."

Chapter 23

"HOW COULD YOU LET THIS HAPPEN?" THE CONGRESSMAN could feel his blood pressure beginning to climb dangerously high.

"It seemed like we had an ironclad plan. We knew they were watching us for the last few days, but we thought the tunnels were a stroke of genius and would throw them off track, at least temporarily." Jonas sighed heavily.

"Obviously, your plan failed. They couldn't have known about your involvement while in Mexico, though. How did they discover it was you on our side of the border?" The Congressman took a long swig of his Texas Hill Country moonshine. Residing in Washington, DC, he liked to be reminded of his home state in every way possible.

"A woman, sir. She gained access to my computer, and unfortunately, I hadn't wiped out the video sent to me by Barbados and had saved some of the pictures and documentation in a folder she went through. I never expected her to be a liability."

"How the hell did she gain access to your computer?"

"It-it was my fault. I showed her the new design I had created, and—"

"I trusted you. I thought you would be discreet about this entire thing, that you would take care of all the details. Obviously, I placed my trust in the wrong man."

"I don't know if she's gone to the authorities. Everything I've done has been precautionary. I sent a man after her and he claims he wounded her, but she shot him, so I don't know how severe her injuries are. I doubt she'll attempt to go to the law, though. My man should have shaken her up enough to know better. I have guards stationed at the house, the barn, and the holding facility. If she tries to bring in the law, we're ready."

"It's not a matter of if, but when. You never should have let her get away! Can you move the hostages out tonight? I can make arrangements for a place to keep them in San Antonio." The Congressman drummed his fingers on the desk in front of him. This entire operation had turned into one colossal clusterfuck. He needed to salvage everything he could. Regardless, the trafficking ring was destroyed. His second string of illegal money taken out in less than three months. His business lines in Mexico and Central and South America were bleeding out, hemorrhaging with the loss of funds, and he had to stop it immediately.

"I'll contact the transporter. It will be difficult, but it isn't impossible."

"Nothing is impossible with the right amount of money. Make it happen. This sale *must* happen in San Antonio this weekend. I already have buyers lined up and ready."

"I'll make it happen," Jonas said confidently.

"See that you do. Once this is all over, we'll discuss where you fit in the structure of things going forward."

"Sir, I hope you understand this is all sheer luck on their part. They never would have known—"

"You fucked up, Jonas. You need to own the mistakes

that you made. Take care of the situation tonight, and we'll discuss things further after this weekend is over."

"Yes, sir," Jonas replied, gripping the phone tightly, attempting to control his temper. He knew he had made a mistake with Elena. But he never would have guessed the team in Mexico would have been so prepared to track their tunnels and search for them like hounds chasing a scent.

"Jonas?"

"Yes, sir?"

"Don't disappoint me again."

Sheriff Verduzco met them a mile from Jonas's ranch, after their evaluation of the layout indicated the high probability he had security cameras in place. As promised, Santo had the warrant from Judge O'Connor. The sheriff didn't ask how they'd achieved the warrant so quickly and with only Elena's testimony to go on.

Benicio Davila, the drug lord, had come to Hebbronville a couple of months ago to seek revenge against the people who had taken down his drug cartel. Anya had been pulled into the fray, and ultimately, Admiral Haslett had determined that having Sheriff Verduzco aware of their undercover role would prove helpful.

The sheriff, a former marine, had taken the responsibility seriously. He promised he would do anything and everything he could to help the team, especially keeping their true purpose in Hebbronville a secret. He'd helped them clean up the incident with Benicio and supported them with any information that came across his desk and lifted any red flags.

"I know you wouldn't bring me this information without good reason. I'm just struggling with the idea that I've been friends with such a horrific criminal for so many years," Sheriff Verduzco said with a heavy sigh.

"He's been building his business strategically for years," Phantom said. "Buzz dug into his background. He came to Texas about thirty years ago, buying up large amounts of land quickly. Soon he became known in town as a prominent new figure and started leasing out portions of his land for hunters. It's all been a cover as he developed his human trafficking ring in Mexico."

"You mean to tell me he's been doing this for thirty years?"

"Actively for the last twenty. The first ten he spent building his network. Unfortunately, his connections are not only here in Texas, but elsewhere within the United States. We're still trying to pinpoint where." Buzz seemed frustrated not to have more information than he already had.

"I'm here to support you however possible." The sheriff looked over the team, all in full tactical gear, and scratched his forehead. "I'm not sure I'm as prepared as you are, though."

Stryker grinned and clapped a hand on Verduzco's shoulder. "We need you to lie low for us on this one. If you can, keep guard at the gate to identify any vehicles that might get away from us, though we don't expect that to happen."

"Do you think the hostages are here?"

"We didn't have enough time to backtrack the satellite images to see if the trailers came here." Phantom looked up the road in the direction of Jonas's ranch. "If they aren't here, we're hoping we'll find evidence of where they've been taken. We need to move quickly."

Verduzco nodded. "I'll keep watch at the gate."

Santo stepped forward and handed him one of the wireless communication devices they used when engaged on a mission. "You'll be able to listen in as we take the place. We can hear you, too, so if you see anyone heading our way, we'd appreciate an alert."

Verduzco took the device and placed it in his ear. "You don't need someone to show you the layout of his place?"

"Elena told us everything." Phantom began to turn away, but Verduzco grabbed him by the arm.

"Is she okay? There was a lot of blood at her place."

"She's shaken up, but her injuries are minor. She's at our place, so she's safe no matter what happens here." Phantom extended his hand to the sheriff, and he shook it. "Thank you for asking. I appreciate you looking out for her."

"She's one of the good ones. I've known her ever since she first arrived here, and she's made this town a better place just by being here."

Phantom swallowed hard and nodded. "She is one of the good ones." He pushed Elena from his mind for the time being, needing to concentrate entirely on what lay ahead. "We're going into the ranch on foot from here. Too much of a chance of security cameras and being sighted."

Verduzco nodded solemnly, and the SEALs turned as a unit and began jogging toward the ranch. They paused several hundred feet from the gate and crouched in the high grass, each of them searching their surroundings.

Using their night-vision optics, they scanned for any cameras.

"Directly over the south corner post," Brusco said.

"Buzz, what are our options?" Phantom saw the small camera affixed to the top of the corner post and continued to scan the surrounding areas for any other threats to their breach.

"It's a high-powered camera, but it won't be able to see us beyond a certain radius. We need to give a fifty-foot cut to avoid it, and we should be clear to move forward from there. If we had more time I could disable it, but we can't disrupt the feed without risking discovery."

"I don't see any other cameras. No sign of security guards either," Santo said.

"Santo, Brusco, and Lobo, join me on the left flank. Stryker, Snap, and Buzz, take the right." Phantom nodded to each man as he spoke their name.

The team split apart, blending into the night in their dark attire and gear. They moved silently, quickly cutting the fence far out of view from the camera and moved onto Jonas's ranch. The ranch house was the first structure they would encounter, based on the information Elena had provided them, and they grouped back together as they approached the home.

"Two guards. One at the front door and another at the window on the right side of the home. Both armed with semiautomatics," Snap relayed to the team.

"We need to take them alive if possible. Santo, you with me?" Phantom looked at his friend.

"Always. I'll take the guy at the front door."

Phantom and Santo advanced as the team kept watch, their guns trained on the two guards, prepared to take them down if anything went wrong. Phantom crept to the side of the house, moving like the apparition that had earned him his moniker. The guard stood poised with his semiautomatic, slowly turning his head from side to side as he scanned the area for activity. Phantom waited until the guard's head had turned away from him and slid up behind him. The man's soft grunt of surprise was the only sound as Phantom disarmed him and knocked him unconscious.

Santo came from around the corner of the house just as Phantom eased the guard's body to the ground and secured his hands and feet with zip ties. "Move in," Phantom said softly over the coms, and the team advanced as planned, half heading for the rear of the home and the others for the front.

The hinges for the front door were on the exterior, making it perfect for Snap to attach explosive cutting tape. Lobo spoke over the coms from the rear of the house, informing them that they had set ECT on the hinges of the back door. The fuses were set and they all stepped back a handful of feet. "Engage." As on all missions, Phantom's senses were on high alert. He knew that breaching an enemy's location could be the most dangerous point.

The explosives went off and the door flew off its hinges. Still using their night-vision optics, the team advanced into the house, forming a semicircle with their backs to each other to cover every possible scenario. At the front of the home, Santo stayed on the porch, watching the surrounding area to make sure no one approached after the sound of the explosions, and Brusco did the same at the rear.

"Clear," Snap said after sweeping the kitchen and dining room.

"Clear," Buzz said after sweeping the living room.

Phantom gestured to the team coming in from the rear of the house to take the hallway to their left while he, Snap, and Buzz advanced down the hallway to the right. Snap checked the first room they came to, a simple bedroom, and cleared it quickly. Two more small bedrooms later, they only had the room at the end of the hall to face.

Phantom led the way and shouldered the door open, his team behind him prepared to take down anyone within. The largest bedroom so far, it had to be Jonas's room. The drawers hanging open, clothes strewn across the floor, and broken closet door indicated the last person in the room had been in a hurry. "Clear on our side," Phantom said into the com.

"Clear here," Stryker said. "The place has been trashed, though."

"Same in here. There's a safe built into the wall that's open and cleaned out." Snap pulled the picture that hung loosely away from the wall, further revealing the open safe. "Hold on…there's something in here."

Phantom stepped further into the room as Snap pulled a small, lumpy item from a dark corner of the safe. "It looks like raw gold," Snap said, turning the object over to Phantom. "I've been investigating the illegal mining in Colombia to see if there's a connection to activities we've been seeing here. This could be a solid lead for us."

"Illegally mined gold has become one of the biggest exports of Colombia in the last few years, bigger even than cocaine. It's one of the things I've been discussing with Judge O'Connor. She's been following the activities in Colombia for a while now, Snap. She may be able to help you with your investigation." Santo frowned at the small lump Phantom held in the palm of his hand.

After looking at it for only a few moments, Phantom tossed the gold to Snap. "I'll hand this over to you to do what's needed."

"They must have been moving fast to miss something as valuable as a lump of raw gold," Stryker said. "His office is a disaster zone. It's obvious he's on the run."

"We need to clear the barn next. Stryker, Snap, Lobo, Buzz, and Brusco, go clear the barn. Santo and I are going to search the office for any information we can find." Phantom looked over at Santo, and they nodded at each other. They had worked so many missions together that they knew how to think in sync and find critical information as quickly as possible.

The rest of the men headed out toward the barn while Santo and Phantom moved to the office on the other side of the house. As Stryker had said, it was a complete disaster. Papers were strewn across the floor. The docking station lacked its laptop, and file cabinets had the drawers hanging open and still holding a few folders.

Not knowing if there were tangos out on the land just waiting for a light to come on inside the house so they could take an easy shot, Phantom and Santo kept the room dark and used their night-vision optics to view everything. "I know we want to catch this bastard, but I doubt he left anything that will tell us where he's run." Santo shook his head as he sifted through the papers on the desk. "He probably kept everything stored on his computers. Hell, it's what I would do."

"I know. But when you're racing to get out, you make mistakes. He already made a mistake by letting Elena have access to his computer to find what she did. It's obvious he hasn't thought clearly through all his actions."

"You realize the man is more than likely obsessed with her, right? He probably thought he could even bring her over to his way of thinking. His statement that he would have her in a matter of time speaks volumes about the way he sees her." Santo didn't look up from the papers he was rifling through to see Phantom's pained expression.

Knowing Elena had been put in such a horrible position infuriated him. He had no doubt Jonas knew about her brutal attack a few years ago, given that the man had practically been stalking her. Jonas had pushed himself on Elena, trying to force her into a relationship she didn't want. The more he learned about Jonas, the more Phantom despised the man. The fact that he operated as a human trafficker sickened him.

He pushed his fury to the side and focused on the knowledge that at least thirty women, and quite possibly as many children, were being stored somewhere and were about to be either auctioned off or executed depending on how paranoid Jonas had become. Phantom didn't want to find their bodies. He wanted to find them alive, and he wanted to see Jonas pay for his heinous crimes.

"Three more guards at the barn. All three have been secured." Stryker's voice came over the coms. "The first two should be coming around any moment. We'll set them up for questioning."

"Phantom, you need to see this." Santo's voice was urgent.

Phantom turned to the large table at the back of the office and frowned at the blueprints. "This must be the facility Elena mentioned. I didn't expect it to be this big. Do you have any idea where it could be located? Elena said Jonas wanted to show her personally, but never did."

"There was a large area of foliage and trees on the south side of the ranch. I thought it might be the area around the watering tank. But if the facility is really large, larger than the barn we just saw, the area I saw on satellite could be where it's located,." Buzz chimed in over the coms.

"We're looking at blueprints now, and it's easily much larger than the barn. Like Elena said, on the surface it appears to be just another barn, but the schematics are wrong. There are storage rooms locked away from the rest of the area. And then…shit. Phantom, look. It has compartments built underneath the main barn. It's a holding facility." Santo tilted his head from side to side, popping his tense muscles.

Phantom flipped through the blueprints and shook his head. "This is more than just a holding facility. He built this specifically to hide hostages for as long as necessary. He has all sorts of hidden compartments and passageways. This place is a damned fortress."

Chapter 24

Santo looked at Phantom, his face grim. "Do you think the hostages are still there?"

"We need to get to this site and evaluate it thoroughly. We can't get our hopes up that we're going to find them that easily. Team, reassemble at the back of the house. We'll question the guards and make our move." Phantom looked at the blueprints one more time, memorizing the layout, before heading to the rear of the house with Santo.

Both guards were slowly coming out of their stupor, and cursed loudly in both Spanish and English at the team. Phantom stepped forward and pressed the muzzle of his handgun under the chin of one of the guards. "Tell us where Jonas is."

"Go to hell."

Phantom pulled back the hammer on the gun. "I really don't want to kill you. But I will to get the answers I need."

"You can't kill me. I haven't done anything wrong. You'll be a murderer." The guard sneered at him, and his fellow guard grinned, his mouth slightly bloody from the hard punch Santo had delivered to bring him down.

Phantom shrugged. "Have it your way." His handgun had a silencer on it, so there was only a soft pop as he shot the man in the leg. The man howled in pain and Phantom shoved a piece of cloth into his mouth, silencing his screams. He squatted down to eye level with the man and pulled back the hammer on his gun again. "Do we need to go through this process again?"

The man screamed behind the rag, trying to get Phantom to understand him. The rest of the team stood around them, their eyes scanning the entire area surrounding them for any movement. Phantom glanced up at Santo who nodded to him. The team supported him and any efforts it took to get answers and get to the hostages.

"Are you going to answer my questions, or just scream? I'll remove the rag if you answer my questions. But if you scream, I'll shove the rag back in and shoot your other leg. Depending on where I shoot you, there's a strong chance you'll have difficulty walking again. Regardless, your career as a mercenary is over."

The guard moaned around the fabric and nodded. Slowly, Phantom took the gag out of the man's mouth. "You fucking coward! You shot me! You'll never get away with any of this. The Puppet Master will see to the end of all of you."

Buzz, instantly engaged, kneeled down next to Phantom. "Have you met the Puppet Master?"

The guard's eyes widened slightly, and he began to laugh, a harsh sound in the silence of the night. "You don't even know what you've gotten yourselves into. You're all walking dead men. Once you're found, you'll be painfully destroyed."

"Found by whom? Tell us more and I won't have to shoot you again."

"You asked about Jonas. He's just the tip of the iceberg. The Puppet Master is everywhere and is involved in everything. You will never be safe again."

"Is the Puppet Master a person or a group of people?" Buzz demanded.

The guard chuckled and shook his head. "You really are clueless."

"Where is Jonas?" Phantom asked, realizing they weren't going to get far with the guard. Not at the moment, at least. Once they had the chance to spend more time questioning him, they could get more answers.

"He's gone. You won't get any answers from him. He's outlived his usefulness to the Puppet Master."

Phantom's temper flared, but he knew how to control his expressions so no one would know what ran through his mind at the guard's comment. "Where is he hiding? We know what a coward he is. It makes sense he would go into hiding."

"I don't know. He told us to guard the house and the barn, and to kill any intruders. I suppose I need to go into hiding now too." The guard's grin slipped, and his eyes darted between Phantom and Buzz. "If I give you information, will you be able to provide me with protection?"

"Shut up, you fucking moron!" the other guard growled. "You'll be found, no matter how much protection they give you! If you say anything more, they'll destroy you and anyone you care about."

They. Phantom filed the word away to come back to later. Obviously, they were dealing with a group of individuals who could cause harm to a lot of different people. They held power over these guards and, more than likely, over Jonas as well.

"I'll ask you one last time. Where is Jonas?"

"We don't know," the other guard said. "He gave

us specific instructions to guard the house and the barn. That's it. He had already vanished by the time we arrived."

—⁓—

Elena couldn't sleep. Knowing that Phantom and the team were in the process of trying to bring down Jonas's operation had her imagination in overdrive. What if Phantom got hurt? What if she hadn't given them the best information for them to attack the ranch?

Phantom had insisted that his room was her room and had told her that when he came home from Jonas's ranch, nothing would make him happier than to find her asleep in his bed. Around one in the morning, she and Anya had decided to try to get some sleep. Lying in his bed, his scent surrounded her, and it only made her miss him that much more.

Tossing and turning in bed for over an hour, she finally got up and stood at the window, looking out at the ranch and wondering how soon the team would get back. She pictured how Phantom had looked in his full tactical gear as he had given her a kiss before he left. She refused to believe it would be the last time they ever kissed. She gnawed nervously on her thumbnail. She refused to believe it, but she trembled with fear and anxiety.

She began to pace his room, thinking about every detail she had shared with the team about the layout of Jonas's ranch. Had she remembered everything? Had she given them the necessary information for them to be successful? Or had she forgotten an important detail that could have put them all in harm's way?

Feeling like a caged animal, she slid out of his room and padded barefoot across the hardwood floors toward the front of the house. She wandered down the long hallway, her mind spinning. She had grown accustomed to the sound of the men's voices whenever she visited the ranch home, and the silence surrounding her seemed unnatural.

She ran her hands along the smooth granite counter of the island in the kitchen, looking over the area that usually flourished with food and hummed with the men's laughter and good-natured ribbing. She craved the feeling of Phantom's arms around her, holding her, reassuring her, bringing her a strength she'd never thought she would long for from a man. She walked slowly toward the dining room, fighting the tears that burned the backs of her eyes. She couldn't wait to see the table full of the people she had grown close to over the last couple of months.

Somehow when it's right, you just know.

Anya's words entered her mind and she wrapped her arms around herself, standing in the dining room, leaning against the chair where Phantom usually sat. Anya's logic hadn't made sense to her a couple of months ago. The idea of falling in love with a man so completely and so quickly seemed unrealistic. Or, so she had thought until she had kissed Phantom.

Their wild race to the back forty acres seemed to have been ages ago. Her fingers lightly traced her lips as she remembered the spontaneous kiss. She had known then that a relationship with Phantom would be unlike anything she had ever imagined. Now, the idea of not having him in her life seemed unfathomable.

"I couldn't sleep either." Anya spoke softly from the direction of the living room, and Elena jumped. "I'm sorry. I didn't mean to scare you." Anya's eyes were large in her pale face, and Elena knew Anya had to be just as terrified as she was.

She walked over to her best friend and wrapped her arms around her. Anya buried her face at Elena's shoulder. "This is what they do, you know? They're the best of the best. I still can't help but feel lost when he's gone. I can't help but feel anxious, and nervous, and…" Anya choked back a sob.

Elena ran a hand through Anya's smooth hair. "I know. I know. But it's like you said. They are the best of the best. If anyone can go into this situation and bring down the bad guys, it's our men."

Anya pulled back slightly and looked at Elena closely. "You love him, don't you? You've fallen in love with Phantom."

Elena fought back her own sob. "Yes. More than I ever thought possible. It's just like you described it. And I'm so incredibly proud of him. Do you realize we're in love with two incredible men? Who would have ever thought?"

Anya chuckled lightly, sniffing. "Just wait until Evie finds out. She's going to think we've both lost our minds."

Elena smiled and wiped at a tear that had escaped and trickled down her cheek. "I didn't think they would be gone this long. What do you think is happening?"

Anya shook her head. "I have no idea. Stryker doesn't fill me in on mission details. He just tells me he's got an assignment, and then he's gone. We'd both have to be cleared at a much higher level to know exactly what is going on."

"Phantom asked me to give him a complete overview of Jonas's ranch. I know they are hoping to save the hostages, but other than that, I don't know what else they have planned."

"It all depends on what they walk into. A part of me hopes that Jonas has fled and they'll find the ranch quiet. Another part of me hopes they catch Jonas and all the other traffickers and destroy them." The expression on Anya's face had become fierce.

"There's just so much we don't know. I had no idea Jonas was involved in something so terrible, and coming across it..." Elena's voice trailed off and her eyes squinted as she looked out the dining room window. "Did you see headlights?"

Anya turned, her hand clutching Elena's. They stared out the window for several long moments before it became obvious that there *were* headlights bobbing along the rough dirt road leading up to the ranch. "They're back!" Anya said, her excitement bubbling to the surface.

Elena's hand tightened on her friend's before she could race to the front door. "How do we know it's them?"

Anya turned to look at her with wide eyes. "Who else could it be? They would have to know the gate code to get access in here."

Elena shook her head. "I won't trust anyone until I see one of our guys standing in the foyer, alive and safe. I'm not willing to take any chances. We'll watch them as they approach the house. We should be able to tell who it is since we have the lights on outside waiting for the guys."

Anya swallowed hard and nodded. "You're right. We have to think like they would, and they certainly wouldn't blindly trust anyone coming up to the house. Come with me."

Racing through the house, Anya pulled Elena over to the foyer and faced the large gun rack. "If they aren't here for the right reason, we need to be armed. I know it's been a while since you've used a rifle…"

Elena grabbed a rifle off the gun rack and a handful of bullets she stuffed into the pockets of her pajama pants. "It's like riding a bike. I'll remember quickly."

Anya nodded and grabbed another rifle, flipping off the safety. "I'll stand at the stairs. Whoever tries to come in won't see me from there and I'll have a clear shot."

Elena also flipped off the safety on the rifle she held. "I'll stand just inside the dining room facing the foyer. Between the two of us, whoever it is won't get far." She hesitated, then rushed forward and embraced Anya. "I love you. We're going to be fine."

"I love you too," Anya whispered.

They crouched together at the dining room window, staring at the person walking up to the house. Just like one of their men, he was dressed in full black military gear, but he kept looking away from the house, so they couldn't get a clear view of his face. They had to be prepared for anyone.

They moved into position and waited. Elena's mind raced with possible scenarios of who could be coming through the door any moment. Only one set of headlights had come into view, which meant it couldn't be the entire team, because they had taken three trucks out to Jonas's ranch.

Hope blossomed in Elena's chest as she heard a key being inserted into the dead bolt. She didn't want to think about the possibility that Jonas could have taken the keys off one of their men. She had to be prepared for any scenario, though, and leveled the rifle, aiming toward the foyer.

The door closed quietly. Whoever had entered the house was trying to maintain silence, something that made Elena's heart hammer and her palms slicken with nervous sweat. A shadowy figure advanced through the foyer, and Elena and Anya moved at the same time. "Stop right there," Elena said, her voice strong and steady despite the fact she struggled to draw a deep breath. They kept a safe distance from the figure so that whoever stood there couldn't grab the guns from them and put them at the disadvantage.

"Elena? Anya? What the hell are you doing?" Phantom's shocked voice greeted her ears, and she had to restrain her cry of joy.

"Phantom! You're okay! We've been worried sick. Where is the rest of the team? Why did you come here by yourself?" She had a thousand questions to ask him.

"It would be easier for me to tell you everything if there weren't two rifles aimed at my head."

"Oh!" Anya and Elena exclaimed at the same time, quickly flipping the safety back on the guns. Elena passed her rifle to Anya so she could throw herself into Phantom's arms. She wrapped her arms around his waist and buried her face in his chest, struggling not to shed tears of joy.

"Is everyone safe?" Anya asked, her voice wavering with emotion.

Phantom's arms wrapped around Elena, stroking her long, curly hair. "Yes. Everyone is safe. But we aren't finished yet."

Elena pulled back and looked at Phantom intently. "What do you mean? What's happened?"

Phantom pressed a kiss to her forehead, then sighed heavily. "We found the barn you mentioned. It looks like Jonas finished it, and it's far more than just a barn."

Elena's stomach did a somersault. "What is it? He showed me the blueprints about a week ago, but I didn't look at them closely. I just wanted to get away from him. Are-are the rest of the men trapped there or something?"

"No, no." He shook his head and looked over at Anya, who looked like she could pass out depending on what he said next. "Stryker is with the rest of the team standing guard over the building. There's a chance the hostages are being held there."

"W-why don't you already know? Aren't you able to get a good look inside?" Anya asked.

"The building is a complex structure, and even that is an understatement. There are passageways and rooms we can't gain access to because they're all locked with—"

"Puzzles," Elena finished for him, remembering the conversation she had with Jonas.

"That's right." Phantom watched her closely. "How did you know?"

"He said I was his inspiration for the design. He said he used puzzles throughout the barn but I thought he meant merely as decorations. Now it makes more sense.

He must have wanted a creative way to hide his secret, and now we know what it is."

"There's no guarantee the hostages are there. We checked the entire barn area and found a few guards, who we captured, but other than that, the place is silent. We don't even know if Jonas is there. But we can't take any chances. We have to explore the entire facility, even the areas that are closed off."

"Why did you come back here, Phantom? Is there more you aren't telling us?" Anya asked, having moved to stand by Elena.

Phantom fished in one of the numerous pockets of his utility pants and pulled out a piece of paper. "We found this when we arrived at the barn."

Elena took the paper with trembling hands and read the scribbled handwriting.

The entire place is set to explode if you make one false move. Each puzzle has only a few steps to make in order to be solved. Exceed that number, and it will all be over. Elena is the key to unlocking these puzzles. Bring her here, and you may win my game. Ignore the rules, and we all lose.

Elena's gaze clashed with Phantom's. "The way this is written it sounds like he's there. We may be able to still catch him!"

Phantom cupped her face in his hands. "I don't want you to do it, Elena, but it seems we have no choice. If there was any way around it…"

"I told you I wanted to be a part of this to the end. This is my chance to help you take down Jonas. Please don't deny me this opportunity." She gripped his wrists and turned her head in his hands, kissing one palm and then the other.

She could see him swallow hard before nodding. "All right. Come with me. We need to move fast."

Chapter 25

SECURITY HAD FAILED HIM. JONAS HAD TRIED CHECKING with his guards around the area three times already and hadn't received a response. His security cameras showed nothing out of the ordinary, but, in his gut, he knew something had gone horribly wrong.

He looked above him and listened carefully. If anyone walked within the new barn, their footsteps were silent. He wasn't comforted by the thought. He had built the structure so that noise couldn't penetrate. For all he knew, there could be an entire group of people combing the area for him.

Jonas had less than an hour before the two transport trailers arrived to take the hostages to San Antonio. He had to find a way to get out without being noticed by anyone. He needed to know what he faced. He checked the cameras again, but nothing moved. He needed to take action, and quickly.

He climbed up several steps to a spot he had designed specifically for looking out into the barn area. Peering through the narrow crack, he saw none of his guards, but he didn't see anyone else either. Something didn't add up.

Frowning deeply, he scanned the area once again, and his heart began to pound heavy in his chest. Elena. They had found his note and brought Elena. Without her, they wouldn't be able to open the various areas of the facility. Eventually, if he let her get far enough, they would find him and destroy everything he had worked so hard to accomplish.

Little did they know he had already worked out the possibility of Elena solving all the puzzles. He needed her. He needed to use her as leverage against whoever had brought her. All he had seen were a couple of men in military tactical gear. He didn't know how many more there were. Where had they come from? Did Sheriff Verduzco have connections he didn't know about?

He smiled to himself. He knew exactly what he could do to not only escape with his own life, but, if everything worked according to his plans, take the hostages as well. The men were as good as dead.

———

Elena shivered as a chill slipped down her spine upon entering the new barn. She gave a half-hearted smile when she saw the rest of the team, even though she struggled to make out who was who in their night-vision optics. Phantom pulled on his own set and handed a set to her.

He helped her slide it on and gave her the thumbs up sign to signal, asking silently if she could see. She nodded and he smiled at her. Drawing a deep breath, she began to walk through the barn, moving lightly on her feet as Phantom had instructed her. They couldn't afford to make any noise, especially if Jonas hid somewhere within.

Her eyes scanned the walls and crevices, searching for the puzzles. Gradually she found a few, but she knew, based on the letter, that they had to be solved in a specific order. The puzzles began to jump out at her as if they were glowing, separate from the rest of the wood and metal in the barn. Her heart pounded in her ears. She had to get the sequence right, or it could mean the end for all of them.

Gradually, a pattern began to emerge to her, and she recognized it as a formula equation. "I need a pencil and paper," she whispered to Phantom. He reached into one of his pockets and pulled out a small notepad with an equally small pencil. She began to jot down the formula quickly, working it as fast as she could. Within moments she knew the order in which she had to solve the puzzles.

The other men were stationed in strategic positions all around the building, watching for any potential threats that could come their way, while Santo and Phantom guarded her inside, keeping a close eye on her movements. She went to the far entrance to the barn and kneeled down where a math puzzle had been carved ornately into the wood.

Using the notepad and pencil Phantom had provided, she worked the puzzle as fast as possible until she came to the right answer. Beneath the puzzle lay a cylinder with a dial full of numbers. The correct answer had to be clicked into place using the dial. Holding her breath, she began to turn the dial.

When the last digit slid in place, a loud clanging sound made her jump and Phantom wrapped an arm around her waist, hauling her back and placing her behind him. He held his gun ready, and she realized she stood between Santo and Phantom—Phantom guarding her from the front and Santo guarding her from the back.

She couldn't see what happened as she heard the sound of gears and levers working before once more everything fell silent.

"If he's here, that certainly got his attention," Santo muttered. Elena leaned to peer around Phantom and realized a ramp had opened up, leading down partway to the lower level.

"Snap, Buzz, I need you in here to check out this new section Elena just opened for us," Phantom said softly.

Snap and Buzz moved into the barn silently and descended the short ramp, sweeping from side to side, pressing on the walls and examining the floor. "Clear," Buzz said, and he and Snap returned to their posts guarding the exterior of the barn.

"May I see it now?" Elena asked, whispering the same as the men.

Phantom grabbed her hand and hooked it onto his belt. "We'll walk into the area together. If you see something, yank on my belt so I know to stop. Don't ever let go of me. This is how I'm able to protect you."

Elena hated being reminded that their lives were at risk, but she knew there wasn't anyone she could be safer with than Phantom. She gripped his belt tightly and nodded to him. They moved into the small section, and, the same as before, the puzzle seemed to glow at her from within the wood and metal. She pulled on Phantom's belt, stopping him, and pointed to the puzzle.

"Is this the one you're supposed to solve next?"

"No." She shook her head. "I think it is meant as a trap. It doesn't follow the pattern of the others. I need to stick to the other ones in order to open this area up properly."

Phantom nodded, and they returned to the main area of the building. She moved to the second puzzle and within minutes had solved it. She concentrated intently on her work, sweat trickling down her forehead from stress and the heat of the hot summer night.

With each puzzle she solved successfully, more sections opened up. She didn't share with Phantom how disturbing the puzzles were. Most of the answers were number combinations that matched up to important dates in her life—her birthday, her high school graduation date, her college graduation date—all of them special times for her. It made her even more certain that Jonas had been stalking her.

When she had solved all the puzzles in the main area of the barn, she took her time to explore each stall, each storage room that wasn't locked by a puzzle, and every common area that could potentially hold additional puzzles. There were none to be found. She drew a deep breath and looked at Phantom. "It's time I start solving the puzzles in the newly opened areas. The pattern doesn't match what I've already found up here, so it's going to take me a little while to figure out the correct sequence."

"You're doing wonderfully," he said softly, caressing her cheek just below her night-vision optics. "We're here to support you with anything you need."

She wanted to kiss him. She wanted him to hold her. She wanted desperately for it all to be over so she could be in his arms again and she didn't have to worry that their lives literally rested in her ability to correctly solve a madman's puzzles.

She pulled in a fortifying breath and headed for the

exposed passageways that had opened as she had solved the puzzles. All of them led to a dead end, but she knew that only meant there was another puzzle to solve. Her eyes scanned the areas, taking in the shapes of the puzzles, the design, the type, and she finally figured out the pattern and the correct sequence.

The first puzzle was Sudoku. She had to slow herself down and concentrate because it was far more difficult than any of the other puzzles she had encountered so far. She worked it out on the notepad, afraid to move any of the pieces and use up too many of the "moves" she could safely make. She scribbled out the second attempt and flipped the page in the notebook to attempt her third.

She sat cross-legged on the concrete floor, focused intently on the puzzle—so intently she was startled when a warm hand settled on her shoulder. She looked up and recognized the lower half of Santo's face below his optics. "We have all the confidence in the world in you. This is your element. Forget about everything else that is going on. Treat this as you would a regular puzzle you were playing for fun."

"I just can't stop thinking about that note. If I make a mistake, Santo, I could very well kill all of us."

"That's exactly why he sent that note. It was meant to rattle you. Don't let it. Don't let him get to you. Take a deep breath and pretend it's a lazy Sunday afternoon and you're just teaching Phantom how to do this puzzle. Let it come naturally."

She smiled at him and leaned forward, pressing a soft kiss to his cheek. "Thank you, Santo. I needed that."

He grinned and stood again, leaving her to the puzzle. She closed her eyes and concentrated on breathing evenly. Santo was right. The letter had been intended to upset her, and it had been successful. She had to set it aside and concentrate on what she knew she could do.

Ten minutes later, she had solved the puzzle. She slid the pieces into place and gasped as she felt the floor move beneath her. Again, Phantom was instantly there, pulling her back away from the moving part of the barn.

The section she had been in had dropped lower, and she swallowed hard. They were getting closer to finding whatever Jonas wanted to hide in his creative facility. She had to focus on making it through the remainder of the puzzles.

The next puzzle was a sliding one, where she had to move the pieces around in a block until they formed the correct image. She knew she had to do it in as few moves possible. She stared at the image, running through the moves she needed to make. Drawing a deep breath, she began to slide the pieces, and a loud clang sounded when she slid the final block in place. The floor beneath her didn't move, but the floors in other areas of the barn did.

"How many more puzzles are there?" Phantom asked softly.

"At least four. There may be more that opened up in the other sections."

"Where's the next one?" Santo asked.

"It's located down the corridor that opened at the far end of the barn." She looked down at the puzzle she had just solved. "Have you checked all the secure rooms? Have they opened up yet?"

Phantom nodded. "Two of them have. The others remain locked."

Elena stood and rubbed at her sore back. "So many puzzles…so much effort to keep everything secure. Was there anything important in those secure rooms?"

"Nothing that will help you with what you're doing. Only files and information Jonas probably intended to destroy." Phantom eyed her closely. "Do you need a break? You've been at this for nearly an hour now."

Elena's gaze slammed into his. "When the hostages are safe, I'll take a break. I can't rest until then."

Phantom nodded and guided her to the corridor at the other end of the barn. As in multiple places throughout the barn, the concrete flooring tilted down, leading to a lower level beneath the main portion of the stalls. So far the areas didn't connect, but she hoped with only another puzzle or two the panels would open and they would know why Jonas had gone to so much trouble.

She moved quickly through the next puzzle and grinned as it clicked into place. The sound of gears and levers clamored once more, and she scrambled to her feet. Phantom pulled her behind him once again, but they couldn't see the changes taking place. They could hear them, though, around the corner where the panels had yet to connect.

"Stay here," Phantom said. "Santo, cover the corner and keep an eye on Elena. I'm going to investigate the area that's opened up."

"Be careful," Elena murmured as he moved past her, and he flashed her a reassuring smile.

She wrapped her arms around herself as Santo and Phantom advanced to the corner. Phantom peered around it with a mirror before stepping into the newly opened corridor. She held her breath as he disappeared, watching Santo keep his semiautomatic angled into the hallway, ready to take aim if needed.

Her heart hammered in her chest. Everything still seemed surreal. She had just learned that Phantom was a Navy SEAL, and she had her experiences with him to tell her that he was cautious and carried himself with confidence that spoke volumes about his skills. Still, she didn't know enough about his abilities, and she couldn't help the anxiety that caused her hands to shake.

She frowned when a new sound greeted her ears. A faint click, followed by a scraping noise unlike anything she had heard so far seemed incredibly close. Santo must have heard it, too, because he pivoted sharply on his feet, swinging his weapon around with him. "Elena!"

His shout echoed off the walls as strong arms wrapped around her, yanking her backward. "Hello, Elena. I'm glad you got the invitation."

The blood in Elena's veins turned to ice at the sound of Jonas's voice. She kicked backward and connected with his shin and he grunted in frustration, but it wasn't enough to dissuade him. His arm tightened on her waist, making it hard to catch her breath.

"Go ahead and take a shot," Jonas taunted Santo. "You can kill me with one shot. You'll probably kill her, too, but that shouldn't matter to a military man like you."

"Jonas, you need to release her. Let her come with us, and we can try to work out something," Santo said, his gun leveled evenly at them.

"No. I don't trust the military—or the government for that matter. You're all corrupt. Elena is coming with me. You'll meet my demands, and then I'll let her go."

Frantically Elena scratched at his hands, trying to gain her freedom. Jonas cursed under his breath and moved further backward. She suddenly realized the noise she had heard was a door opening in the wall. It had been hidden so perfectly none of them had seen it. "Shoot him, Santo! Shoot him! I don't care if you hit me. Shoot him!"

Jonas yanked her backward one last time and slammed the door shut. For a moment she couldn't see anything, since the area he had pulled her into had all the lights on and her night-vision optics responded poorly. She struggled to pull them off her face so she could see again.

Jonas slid a large metal bolt across the door and whirled her around, pressing her against the concrete wall. "We don't have much time," he said. "The transporters will be here soon. You'll do exactly as I say and I won't kill any of your friends. I have spots all over this place where I can take aim and destroy each one of them."

"Then why haven't you?" Elena demanded, glaring at him.

Jonas smiled at her. "Always thinking, aren't you? I know when one goes down, another one will appear, and there isn't a way to stop them from coming. So it's in my best interest to get them to do what I ask of them."

"They'll never do what you want," Elena growled. "Your plans, whatever they are, end here. I will never help you."

Jonas shifted to the side, a bemused expression on his face, and Elena swallowed hard. "If you won't help me, then at least help them. Because if you fail me, I'll kill each and every one of them in front of you and make you watch."

Staring back at her were the haunted faces of the hostages. Elena began to tremble. These people were meant to be sold as slaves, to be treated worse than animals. From the pictures she had seen of Jonas, she knew he had it in him to murder each of them in front of her without any qualms.

Jonas smiled broadly at her. "I can see you understand the gravity of the situation. You'll do everything I tell you to do, and without hesitation. Do you understand me?"

"You'll never get away with this, Jonas. Never. They know all about you. Your entire operation will be shut down."

"I'll get away with this because of you, my dear. I knew if things got to this point, the only way for me to escape required leverage. And you are the perfect leverage." He shoved her in front of him, guiding her within the interior corridor closed off from the hall that had opened up outside.

"You've lost your mind, Jonas. They won't let you get away. Even if it means I have to die."

"That's where you're wrong. I saw the look in that man's eyes. He cares about you. I've been watching you as you've worked the puzzles, and the other man with you obviously cares for you as well. Who are they, Elena? How do you know them?"

"As if I would tell scum like you! You don't deserve to be in the same room with those men. They are better than you in every possible way." She gasped as he yanked her to a stop, his grip punishing around her upper arm. He pushed her against the wall again, thrusting his face into hers.

"You're going to break. You are weak. If only you had accepted my advances. You could have been a part of this entire empire I'm building. I have connections you could never imagine. I'm going places, and you could have been a part of all of it."

"You're going to hell. That's exactly where you're going, Jonas. And I certainly have no desire to take that trip with you."

He sneered at her, then forced her to turn again and walk along the narrow corridor. He brought her to an abrupt stop in an area where a narrow crack appeared in the concrete. "I want you to tell them there are two transporter trucks arriving any minute. Tell them to let them through, or I'll begin killing the slaves."

"They aren't slaves yet. They're hostages. These people deserve to be free. You have no right to sell them, to treat them like animals, to—"

"You need to learn to watch what you say to me. I might kill one just for the hell of it because you piss me off. Now speak. Directly into that hole. It will be amplified through the barn for all of them to hear."

Elena turned and faced the crack in the concrete again, trying to control her trembles. She closed her eyes and mouthed a silent prayer. The lives of the hostages and the team now rested in her hands. She needed all the strength she could get.

Chapter 26

"WHAT THE HELL HAPPENED?" PHANTOM STRUGGLED maintain his composure. He had barely finished checking the newly opened section of halls when he heard Santo yell Elena's name. He rushed back in time to see a door close seamlessly into another hidden area of the facility, Elena nowhere in sight.

"By the time I heard the door opening, he had already grabbed her," Santo said, his hands, just like Phantom's, running along the wall in search of any give in the passage. "The bastard stayed crouched behind her the entire time. I couldn't get off a single clean shot."

"He intended for us to bring her here all along. We played right into his hands." Phantom cursed under his breath. There wasn't a crack to be found in the concrete. The man had obviously designed the facility exactly as he had originally thought—it was a fortress.

"We had no way of knowing he was still here. And we never would have been able to crack the puzzles without her. The whole setup is a nightmare."

"Ph-Phantom?"

His gaze slammed into Santo's, and they both lifted their weapons and looked around the hall for the source of her voice. "Elena? Where are you? Are you hurt?"

"No. I'm fine. The-the hostages…they're all here, Phantom. They're being kept in cages like animals, and—" Her voice suddenly broke off and Phantom's gut clenched. For all he knew, Jonas could be hurting her, torturing her to say what he wanted.

"Elena? Talk to me!" Phantom called out, moving slowly through the passageway, his eyes searching every corner, every seam.

"I'm-I'm supposed to give you a message. There are two transport trucks that should be arriving any minute. You need to let them through. If you don't, Jonas will begin to shoot the hostages."

Phantom wanted to scream his frustration. They didn't negotiate with terrorists. They never had, and they never would. But if they could get a little extra time, possibly find a way to bring Jonas out of hiding and take him down... "We'll allow them through. But Jonas has to show us a gesture of goodwill so that we know he isn't going to hurt anyone. He has to release you."

"He-he says no. Phantom, he says that you need to do what he asks, and there will be no further discussion."

Phantom ran a hand through his hair. "We'll allow them through."

Santo stared at him as if he had lost his mind. "We can't allow this to happen. He's going to try to walk out of here with all the hostages!"

"He won't make it. We'll find a way to take him down, one way or another." Phantom kept his voice hushed. Elena's voice traveled so clearly through the halls that he didn't know how easily they could hear him. "Go to Stryker and communicate to Verduzco. We need to let those trucks through."

With a grim face, Santo nodded. He turned and moved quickly and silently through the halls out of the barn and to the rest of the team standing guard on the perimeter. "We've communicated to Verduzco," Santo said over the coms. "What's your plan, Phantom?"

Phantom noticed a small crack in the concrete halfway through the longest portion of the hallway. "I'll let you know when I have one."

Fifteen minutes later, two large trucks pulled up outside the large barn facility. The team faded into the shadows, as they had told Verduzco to do, so that the delivery drivers would be none the wiser. The trucks were backed up to the main entrance to the barn and then sat in silence.

"He must be communicating to them from within the hidden area," Stryker said. "There's no movement by either driver in their cabs, other than over their radios."

"Buzz, can you dial into their frequency?" Phantom asked.

"I don't have the right equipment here. If I go back to the ranch—"

"Do it. Drive like a man possessed. We need to hear their conversation—every bit of it."

Santo came back into the barn and rejoined Phantom. Phantom held his finger to his lips and pointed to the crack he had found in the concrete. "Elena? Say something so I know you're all right," he called out loudly.

"I'm fine, Phantom. It's just getting a little hot down here. Jonas is getting anxious to be on his way."

"Transportation just arrived. We're getting things into place now." Phantom's eyes were suddenly drawn to something that looked unusual at the base of one of the large wooden beams surrounded by steel that held up the main rafters of the barn. He squinted his eyes and moved closer to it.

"Santo—we need to find a way to stall them. We need to put a glitch in their plans, and fast." Phantom's blood pulsed with adrenaline.

"Why? What have you found?"

"I think I may have just found our way to bring this whole thing to a finish."

—◆—

Elena wiped at the sweat on her brow. She hadn't been making light talk when she told Phantom it was getting hot. With Jonas's elaborate planning, he obviously hadn't considered the need for good air flow in an area that didn't have good ventilation to begin with. Add a group of over fifty humans trapped in cages and the sweltering heat of summer, and it made the atmosphere practically dense.

"What are you going to do from here, Jonas? Do you really think they are going to let you walk out of here with all these people? It isn't possible!"

"It's exactly what I expect, and it's exactly what will happen. You've always been so naive. So completely unable to see the things around you. I've always been a planner. I've always been prepared for any scenario. Do you think it is a coincidence that I built this barn with you in mind?"

"I don't know what goes on in that sick, twisted mind of yours." She shook her head at him. "You always repulsed me. I knew there was something wrong with you all along. Now I know it is because you're a depraved human being who gets pleasure at the abuse of others."

Jonas looked over at the hostages in their cages. He

chuckled and pulled her farther down the corridor and into one of the small rooms that sat under one of the larger secure rooms above. The air was slightly cooler and she drew a steadying breath, unsure of what his next move could be.

She had to find a way to stop him. The thought pulsed through her brain. There had to be a way to bring him down. She glanced around the room that had been set up like an office and grimaced when he shoved her into one of the chairs. He moved around the desk and pulled out a decanter of alcohol and two tumblers. He poured heavily into each and handed her one.

"A toast, my dear. Surely you've figured out by now that you're coming with me. After all this time, you will be mine. You may fight me at first, but eventually you'll come around and see things my way."

Her hand clenched around her glass as he tossed back his drink. He had just lowered his arm when she hurled her glass at him as hard as she could, not pausing long enough to see what happened. She heard him grunt and the glass shatter, but she was already racing down the corridor toward the door he had used to pull her inside.

"Phantom!" she yelled at the top of her voice. "He intends to take me with him as part of his escape plan. You can't let him succeed. I don't care what it takes! All these people—oh!" She cried out as Jonas's body slammed into hers, throwing her to the floor. His weight heavy on top of her, he prevented her from any attempt to escape.

"That was very foolish of you. I told you it will take time. Trust me, Elena. Just give in to the inevitable."

"I will fight you with all my strength until I can't fight you anymore!"

"Don't make me kill you, Elena. I don't want to be forced to do such a thing. I like you. I like the passion that burns in you. We'll make a good pair in many ways."

He pulled her to her feet and leaned down, forcing her to make eye contact with him by holding her chin firmly with one hand. "Don't fight me anymore tonight, Elena. There are too many things that still must be done."

"Elena? Elena, talk to me." Phantom's voice drifted through the walls to them, and she fought back the burn of the tears in her eyes. She needed to stay strong for the team to be able to do their job.

"I'm fine, Phantom. Do what you do best, please. Do what you do best."

Jonas growled and pulled her back toward the office, once again tossing her into one of the chairs. "Who are they? How many of them are out there? You need to answer my questions, Elena. If you refuse to answer me or lie to me, you will pay dearly."

"I'm already paying. Just being in your presence is painful enough."

Jonas lifted his hand abruptly as if to strike her, then slowly lowered it. "No. I will not let you provoke me like this. It's what you want. You don't want me to think clearly tonight. I won't let you do that."

"I won't give you what you want." She glared at him.

"You'll give me the answers I need. Who are they? How do you know them?"

"They're simple ranchers. I work with them on one of the ranches I call upon."

"Simple ranchers don't have these kinds of skills. Do you know how many guards I had stationed around this ranch tonight? Do you even know if they're still alive? Answer me, Elena. Do you? What makes you think these men you are with are any better than me? They've probably killed several men tonight already, and I haven't killed anyone."

Elena brushed her hair back from her face with trembling hands. She knew that killing came with the work of a SEAL. She knew Phantom would have only killed someone if there wasn't any other choice. He was a good man. She would do everything she could to make sure his mission was successful.

She lifted her head to stare blankly up at Jonas. "I don't know the answers to your questions."

Jonas glared at her, then turned to the desk and pulled out a radio. "Both of you stay in the trucks. I don't know how many men surround the area right now. Have you seen any movement since you arrived?"

"No sir." A voice with a heavy Texas accent came over the radio. "I haven't seen anyone. It's been smooth the entire way."

"They're out there. I'll have the cargo open the doors to the trailers when the time is right."

"Listen to yourself!" Elena exclaimed. "You're referring to human beings as cargo!"

"Don't be a fool. They'll have better lives in the United States than they ever did where they're from. The world isn't as pretty and simple as you are delusional enough to believe."

"You're the one saying foolish things! What kind of life do you think a sex slave has? She's going to be tortured and raped and probably kept heavily drugged. They talk about it on the news all the time. It's a horrible, horrible crime!"

"We're going to walk out of here, and no one will stop us. Just as they can multiply, my resources can too. Go ahead and stay silent for as long as you like. I don't need your help."

There was a crackle on the radio. "I have a problem," another voice spoke, and Elena assumed it was the other driver.

"What's the problem?" Jonas barked.

"One of my tires has a slow leak. I must have picked up some old fencing wire or a nail on the drive up to the ranch. I won't be able to make it out of here without repairing it."

"Son of a bitch," Jonas fumed. He stood and paced back and forth behind the desk for several moments. Finally, he spoke into the radio again. "Get out and fix it. Take your handgun with you. Be ready to shoot at anything that moves."

"Copy." The man's voice came over the radio once more, then the room fell silent.

Elena watched Jonas pace back and for and wondered if he was close to cracking. His plans were starting to fall apart. How would he react? Would he kill her and all the hostages as revenge? She couldn't let that happen. At the very least, she had to save the hostages. She just didn't know how.

"Time for a new message," Jonas said, grabbing her arm and hauling her to her feet. She yanked her arm free of his grasp.

"There's no reason to treat me like one of your

hostages. If you want me to ever look at you with anything less than contempt, you'll treat me with dignity and respect."

"Respect is something you have to earn. And you've done nothing so far to gain my respect. Now move." He shoved her forward toward the same crack in the concrete he'd used to project her voice, and she stumbled over her own feet deliberately, trying to stall.

She knew Phantom had to be behind the leak in the truck tire. He had to have a plan of some sort, and she needed to do everything in her power to help him. Her heart squeezed painfully. She wondered if she would ever be held in his arms again. She had already made her decision to stop Jonas, even if it meant her own death.

"Tell them to help the driver. Tell them to move quickly."

"Phantom?"

Silence responded, and anxiety coursed through her. He wouldn't leave, would he? Had they decided not to receive any more of Jonas's demands? Or did they simply wait for him to make his next move in the shadows with intentions of taking him by surprise?

"I'm here, Elena." His voice warmed her and made her heart jump with hope. What if the plan he had would save her while still taking down Jonas? She couldn't give up. She had to have faith in Phantom.

"One of the trailers has a problem with a tire. Jonas is asking you to help the driver replace it as quickly as possible."

"We'll do what we can. Are you all right? Has he hurt you?"

"No. I'm okay. Jonas is going to tell his driver to

allow someone to help with the tire. Don't worry about me, Phantom. Just—be careful, please."

"Always. Jonas, we will do as you ask. You don't need to continue using Elena. Send her out."

Jonas chuckled. "He'd like that, wouldn't he? What kind of fool does he think I am? You're staying with me from here on."

Elena turned, about to speak into the crack, and he pulled her back roughly. "You'll only speak when I tell you to. I don't want to have to treat you like one of the hostages and bind and gag you and put you in one of the cages, but I will if I must."

Elena tried to conceal her shudder, but Jonas saw it and laughed. She straightened her spine and faced him squarely. "You are nothing but a bully and a coward, Jonas. You can try to scare me as much as you want, but I know you'll never succeed. No matter what you try to do or how you try to use me."

He shook his head, leering at her. "You just don't get it. I'm the one in the power position here. They have no leverage. As soon as that tire is fixed, the hostages are going on the trailers, and you'll escort me to one of the trucks. My friend has already made the arrangements for us to disappear as soon as we arrive in San Antonio. They can try to follow us. Hell, they can even put tracking devices on the trucks. None of it will work, though. I told you before I have connections. My friend has made it so that I'll get every demand I ask for."

"Who is your friend, Jonas?"

Jonas rolled his eyes. "Do you really think I would tell you such a thing?"

"You've told me practically everything else. Why not

something as simple as a name? You're so confident I'll be with you anyway... What does it matter?" Elena's hands trembled. If she survived, she could gather important information for Phantom and the team.

Jonas smiled. "I'm not telling you any real information. I won't take that kind of chance. I know they are planning to try to stop me, but they will fail. Or we'll both die. Are they the type of men to sacrifice you to achieve their goals?"

Elena didn't answer. She had no idea how to answer. She was certain, though, that they wouldn't let Jonas get away. Especially with the hostages. Maybe they'd let him attempt to escape, but they would stop him at some point.

His confidence in his friend's plan once he reached San Antonio made her nervous, though. What if Phantom and the team couldn't stop him? What if Jonas's friend *had* put together a full-proof plan that they couldn't stop?

She drew a deep breath. She had faith in Phantom and the entire team. She said a silent prayer to give her strength and strength to the team. She needed to be ready to take action when the time came.

Chapter 27

"WHAT THE HELL ARE YOU DOING?" SANTO ASKED, squatting down next to Phantom.

For several moments, Phantom didn't answer, his eyes fixed on the spot at the base of the beam supporting one of the barn rafters. He drew a steadying breath as he lifted the odd square panel and grinned when he saw the box held within. He looked over at Santo. "I know this puzzle. Elena taught me—it's the Rubik's Cube."

"Yeah, we all know what a Rubik's Cube looks like. Do you mean to say she taught you how to solve it?"

"Yes. I can solve this puzzle, Santo."

"How do you know it is in the right sequence? If it's out of order, we could be blown to bits."

"Think carefully. Have you seen any wiring anywhere connected to these puzzles that make you think there is a bomb?"

"I've seen plenty of wires. That's how all these panels keep opening up." Santo hesitated, studying the wires connected to the Rubik's Cube. "But you're right, none of them look like what I'd expect for a bomb."

"Do you think Jonas would really put his life in danger like that? Look at everything we know about the man. He's selfish and greedy. He wouldn't take a chance that he could be blown up if his plan fell through. He's been bluffing all along."

"What do you think solving this puzzle will accomplish?"

"I don't know. But it's worth a shot. It could open up another area so we could take him by surprise. Right now he has the advantage. We need to take it away from him."

"I'm at the ranch. I've locked onto their frequency." Buzz's urgent voice came to them through their coms.

"Any chatter?" Stryker asked from his position outside the barn, watching over the two box trailers and the drivers. Brusco and Snap were helping the one driver with his tire. They had approached the truck cautiously with their hands up to show they weren't armed. The driver never knew that Stryker kept his gun trained on him. Fortunately, Jonas had done as Elena said he would and had notified the driver he would get help. Brusco and Snap were doing everything in their power to delay the process and make it more difficult.

"None. What's happening there?" Buzz asked.

"We were able to puncture one of the tires to delay the driver," Lobo said from where he stood at the other end of the facility. "As you know, Jonas ordered for us to help the driver with the tire, but we're taking our sweet time. We can only stall for so long, though. Once that truck is ready to go, I suspect Jonas is going to move the hostages."

"Phantom, what are you planning to do?" Stryker asked.

"I'm working on that right now. Regardless, those trucks aren't leaving, and neither is Jonas." Phantom's mind flashed to Elena and he closed his eyes briefly. He couldn't let her get hurt. He couldn't lose her.

He realized he should have told her before he left for Mexico that he had fallen in love with her. He had been afraid, though, afraid she would reject him once she knew that he had kept his role as a SEAL secret from her. So he had held on to his profession of love, deciding it would be best to wait for her reaction to the news. His heart clenched painfully. Now he might not ever get to tell her. He couldn't let that happen.

He studied the cube closely, remembering Elena's fingers on his, guiding him as he rotated each part. They had laughed and shared kisses between each move, until he had finally solved the puzzle on his own. The one he looked at in Jonas's barn didn't have the colors that a usual Rubik's cube had. Instead it consisted of wood, brushed nickel, gold, polished steel, simple gray metal, and copper.

He drew a deep breath and reached for the block, only to have Santo's hand grab his. "Are you sure about this? Are you sure you know what you're doing? What if this closes us in here? What if the panel goes up and we're flattened like pancakes?"

Phantom turned his eyes to his best friend and gave him a reassuring smile. "I learned from the best. You and I have always lived life on the edge. Why stop now?"

Santo slowly smiled. "You realize you owe me a steak dinner in Laredo."

"You're going to gloat about that now? Yes, you were right. I love her, Santo. I can't let anything happen to her."

Santo nodded. "I've got your back. Solve the damned puzzle so we can take down that bastard."

Phantom turned back to the cube and squeezed his

hands into fists before reaching for it. Elena had taught him how to solve it with just a few moves. He had to do it perfectly, or everything Santo feared could happen. He had no idea how Jonas had the system rigged.

He moved the first two sections quickly. With each move he heard a click behind the wall. His hands began to sweat. He knew once he completed the puzzle, something would happen, and he had no way of knowing whether it would be good or bad.

Twelve steps. Elena had shown him how to complete the puzzle in twelve moves. He could almost hear her voice in his ear, gently coaching him through each step. He moved a couple more sections, and there were more clicks in the wall.

"Phantom, the tire is almost repaired," Stryker spoke.

Sweat trickled down his temple and he moved two more sections. "Can you delay them any longer?"

"Not with the tire. It will be finished soon, and there isn't anything else we can do," Stryker answered.

"Admiral Haslett just arrived," Lobo said tensely.

Phantom squeezed his eyes shut. He had no idea Haslett would arrive so quickly and hadn't anticipated this additional complication to their situation. He had no idea what Haslett thought he could accomplish by coming into the situation. He became an extra person they had to protect and keep safe.

"Looks like he brought an entire team with him," Stryker said.

"Please tell me the drivers haven't seen them. Please tell me some good news here. I sure could use a little." Phantom wiped at the sweat hastily before returning his focus to the cube.

"They came in the same way we did," Stryker said. "I don't think the drivers saw them. There's no indication they have, at least."

Phantom slowly moved the pieces two more times. The colors were beginning to align. Half of the puzzle was complete. Only a few more moves to make—

"They're using their radios," Buzz said over the coms, his voice urgent.

Phantom hesitated in his movements for a moment as he waited for Buzz's next report. It didn't take long.

"The driver of the second truck just notified Jonas that the truck has been repaired and they are ready to receive the cargo. The chatty driver told Jonas they were wearing military tactical gear. He now knows there are at least four of us out there." Buzz sighed heavily.

"How many men did Haslett bring with him?" Santo asked, scanning their surroundings as the clicks continued in the walls.

"At least ten—maybe fifteen soldiers. They're approaching now." Stryker's com went silent for several moments as he talked to Haslett. Phantom concentrated on the cube. He only had two more moves to make.

"Haslett says these trucks don't leave here. We take Jonas down before he even exits this barn."

"And what about Elena? How do we ensure her safety?" Phantom clenched his jaw tightly. He already knew the answer.

"If she's collateral damage, we have to take the shot. We have no other choice."

"Then I'll *make* another choice."

"Phantom, I know you care about Elena. Hell, we

all do. We can't let Jonas leave." Snap sounded as frustrated as the rest of them.

"Phantom?" Elena's sweet voice floated through the walls to him, and his heart pounded harder in his chest. Jonas must be ready to make the move. Which meant he needed the team to be ready to make theirs.

"Stryker," he said softly so Jonas couldn't hear him, "get two of the men Haslett brought to replace the drivers in the trucks. Keep the drivers in their trucks and have them respond to any messages from Jonas, but with our guns on them so they don't reveal what we've done."

"What are you thinking, Phantom?" Snap asked.

"We're going to let Jonas think the hostages are being loaded onto the truck, but we're going to move them a safe distance away from the building."

"Phantom?" Elena called to him again.

"I'm here, Elena."

"Jonas wants the hostages loaded onto the trucks. They're going to come out the door he took me through."

"We'll be ready for them," Phantom answered. He spoke softly again so only the team could hear him. "Team, come into the barn. Take up positions at the openings to both of the halls that unsealed earlier. We're going to take Jonas down."

"On our way," Brusco said.

"Jonas just told the drivers to report to him as the hostages are loaded," Buzz said.

"Stryker, are Haslett's men in place?" Phantom asked.

"Yes. They have their orders to keep the drivers talking."

"The first driver just responded," Buzz said. "He

asked Jonas if he wanted them to open the back of the
trailers or have the hostages do it. Jonas is answering…"
Buzz paused for a moment as he listened to the discussion. "Shit. Jonas ordered the drivers to get out and open
the doors for the hostages, load them, and get back on
the radio as soon as the trailers are secure."

"Brusco, Snap—escort the drivers to the back of
the trucks. Keep them there until we have the hostages
safe." Phantom drew a deep breath. Everything had to
play out just right for him to save Elena.

Phantom and Santo stood at the corner of the hall,
their guns trained on the spot where Elena had vanished
several minutes earlier. The door slowly swung out, and
two naked Hispanic women timidly stepped forward.
Their hands were bound in front of them by coarse rope,
and black bandannas were wrapped tightly around their
heads, gagging them. Their eyes widened when they
saw Phantom and Santo.

Phantom nodded his head toward the other direction,
and the women slowly walked out toward Snap who
stood point at the end of the hall. The hostages continued to file out of the room, and Phantom felt queasy at
the sight of the children. Jonas would pay for his crimes.
But not until he had Elena safe.

There seemed to be no end to the hostages. The line
of them continued to file out until suddenly the door
slammed shut. Phantom looked over at Santo. "It's time
to make our move."

Santo watched him closely as he rushed back to the
Rubik's Cube and turned the next to the last piece. "The
drivers just radioed Jonas that the hostages have been
loaded and secured," Buzz said, his tone urgent.

Phantom looked over at Santo as he turned the last piece. The clicks within the walls increased in intensity and they both turned together, facing the area where Jonas hid behind the interior wall with Elena. A creak and a groan sounded, and a panel in the wall in front of them lowered, exposing the area.

Phantom's heart pounded even harder. Elena and Jonas had to be within the area somewhere. He prayed Jonas hadn't heard the noise and they were going to catch them by surprise. "Stryker and Lobo, we've opened up the interior where Jonas is. We could use some backup. Snap and Brusco, stay at the entrances in case he gets past us."

Phantom and Santo stepped into the area and saw the cages that had held the hostages only minutes earlier. Phantom clenched his jaw tight. Jonas deserved to be locked in one of those cages and treated just as poorly as he had allowed the innocent women, children, and men to be.

"Get ready to move. I'm coming out with one final hostage. I want us headed out as soon as I'm in the truck." Jonas's voice drifted down the hall, and Phantom and Santo exchanged glances. Turning together, Phantom took the lead heading down the hall. Their steps slowed as they neared a corner. Jonas wasn't talking any longer.

Suddenly Elena emerged from around the corner and Phantom's eyes quickly searched her for injuries. She appeared to be unharmed, but the expression on her face made him pause. She moved slowly around the corner, and he saw the black muzzle of a handgun pressed to her temple and wanted to curse out loud.

"Did you really think I didn't see this coming?" Jonas

asked harshly. He came out from around the corner, though he kept himself behind Elena. "I've been several steps ahead of you this entire time. Now, I'm going to leave with Elena. You're going to let me, or she's going to die, and it will be all your fault."

"Don't let him, Phantom. I don't care what you have to do. You can't let him do this." Elena watched him intently. The same as with the other hostages, her hands had been bound in front of her with rope.

"Shut up!" Jonas yelled, shaking her with the arm that held her shoulder. He glared at Phantom. "Who are you, anyway? How many of you are out there?"

Phantom smirked at him. "Do you really think I'm going to answer any of your questions?"

Jonas smiled at him. "You have no idea what you've gotten yourself into. You can't stop me. Not unless you're willing to sacrifice her. And I can tell by the way you're looking at her that you can't do it. Even if you do take me down, the drivers know to leave within the next five minutes with or without me and not to stop for anyone or anything. They'll plow down anyone you have out there."

"He says he has a friend—a powerful friend who is—" Elena's words ended in a gasp as he pressed the gun tighter against her temple.

"Who's your friend, Jonas? Who do you work for?" Phantom asked.

"I don't work for anyone!" Jonas growled. "I have connections. Good connections. They'll make your lives miserable once I tell them about you. They'll be able to track you even if you don't tell me who you are. They have tools and skills beyond your wildest imagination.

They'll find you. And they'll destroy you. Each and every one of you."

"You're talking about the Puppet Master, aren't you?" Santo said softly from where he stood at Phantom's shoulder.

A muscle ticked in Jonas's face. "How do you know anything about the Puppet Master?"

Phantom knew they had hit a nerve. Things were beginning to turn in the right direction. "How do you know this isn't part of the Puppet Master's plan? We've got the hostages. The auction will take place with or without you. You aren't necessary any longer."

Jonas's face paled. "I don't believe you. I've been a valuable part of the operation for years. My knowledge and experience alone will help ensure our success with the plan. There's no way I'd be cut out of it now."

"Whatever you need to tell yourself, Jonas," Santo taunted.

Jonas shook his head. "No. You're lying to me. You heard about the Puppet Master somewhere, and you just think you know what's going on. I would have heard about you. I'm too important to the plan!"

"You're done," Phantom said. "Your usefulness is no longer relevant."

"Then there won't be any hurt feelings if I kill Elena, will there?" Jonas sneered.

"Phantom, do your job. You know what needs to be done." Elena made eye contact with him, and Phantom's gut clenched. She was going to do something, and it terrified him. One false move, and Jonas would shoot her dead on the spot.

He wanted to shake his head at her, to tell her to

forget about whatever she planned to do, but he couldn't give anything away to Jonas. He held his breath, watching her and searching for any open spot where he could shoot Jonas, but the man cowered behind Elena, using her as a shield. Jonas cocked the gun and time seemed to stand still.

Elena flung her head back hard, obviously aware that Jonas hid behind her, and the back of her head cracked into his nose and forehead with a crunch. Jonas roared in pain as Elena threw her body forward and down, breaking free of Jonas's hold as his hand flew up to his bloodied nose. Instantly, Phantom fired a round into the man's shoulder.

Jonas seemed unfazed by the shot, and Phantom knew the man had to be pumped full of adrenaline-powered strength as he lifted his arm, his handgun pointed directly at Elena. Phantom fired at the same time as Jonas, striking him directly in the heart, and he fell backward, landing hard on the concrete floor.

Santo advanced rapidly toward Jonas, while Phantom fell to his knees and pulled Elena into his arms as she began to push herself up from the floor. "Do you realize the risk you just took? He was going to kill you!"

She trembled in his arms and stared at him with tears in her eyes. "Will you please just hush and kiss me already?"

Emotions tightened his throat as he captured her face in his hands, pressing his lips to hers tenderly. "I thought I was going to lose you," he murmured against her lips. He kissed her more intensely, overjoyed to have her in his arms again.

"I couldn't let him succeed," she whispered when he

finally pulled back from her. "I knew there was a good chance I would die, but I couldn't let him get away with his crimes. And I was so afraid that after he shot me, he would try to shoot you and Santo."

Phantom shook his head at her, his thumbs wiping the tears that had slipped down her cheeks. "I knew we could stop him. One way or another. I just hadn't expected you to be the one to take matters into your own hands."

She gave him a wobbly smile. "Being with you has given me courage to do things I never thought possible."

Phantom glanced over at Santo, who stood nearby. His eyes dropped to where Jonas lay unmoving, and Santo shook his head. Jonas was dead. Elena began to turn to look, but Phantom turned her face back to him. She'd been through enough trauma already. She didn't need to see Jonas's body on top of it all.

"Looks like we missed the party," Stryker said from behind them. "Elena, are you all right?"

Elena nodded. "I am now. The hostages… Are they okay?"

"They're being tended to right now," Lobo said. "The admiral coordinated with a local shelter before he got here. They've got blankets and are being assessed by a couple of medics who came with him. Buzz is already coordinating transport for them to a facility where they'll receive the care they need."

Elena smiled at them. "You all did it. You saved them."

Phantom couldn't take his eyes off her as he brushed her curly locks away from her face. A deep red against her pale-blue shirt caught his attention, and he sucked in a deep breath. "You've been shot." His hands shook as he lifted the sleeve, and she winced slightly.

"I think the bullet just grazed me. It burns, but it doesn't hurt."

Phantom examined it closely and realized she had indeed only been grazed by the round. "We'll have one of the medics clean it and bandage it for you. Do you have any idea how lucky you are?"

Her gaze swept over his face and she smiled at him. "Yes."

As a group, they exited the barn and Brusco and Snap rushed over to them, tenderly embracing Elena with relief. Phantom hovered over the medic as he tended to her arm and only took his eyes off her when he heard someone approach. Admiral Haslett nodded to him. "You did one hell of a job, Phantom. I knew I could count on you to see this through."

"The team made it possible, sir. Thank you for trusting me."

"I heard everything you said to Jonas about the Puppet Master. It's obvious that name means something within this criminal community, and we need to find out more."

Santo, who had been standing nearby, stepped forward. "I agree. I think Judge O'Connor may know more than she's told me so far."

Haslett raised his eyebrows. "So you agree with me that she's keeping secrets from us?"

"Possibly. I don't know what her reasons would be. I want to press her harder about this Puppet Master and see what kind of reaction I get."

Haslett nodded. "Good. Run with it. Make it happen.

We need answers as soon as possible. If there really is anything to this terrorist theory, we need to get ahead of it now."

Phantom turned back to Elena, who had been conversing with the medic while he, Santo, and Haslett had spoken. "Elena, I'd like you to meet Admiral Frank Haslett. He's my commanding officer."

Elena smiled at him and extended her hand. "It's a pleasure to meet you, sir, though I wish it could be under different circumstances."

Haslett smiled at her as well. "I've heard great things about you, and you've certainly impressed me with your actions tonight. I'm glad you and Phantom found each other. He's a good man."

Elena's eyes drifted over to Phantom and her smile broadened. "Yes, sir. Yes, he is."

"Are you all patched up and ready to go home?" Phantom asked.

She glanced down at her arm. "Well, yes, I'm all patched up, but...I don't have a home to go to. Jonas made certain of that, and I don't know if the Bells will even want me to be their tenant any longer. My apartment is a crime scene. I don't know if I'll ever go back there."

"Walk with me? I need to get away from this chaos for a moment."

Elena nodded and slid her hand into his. Phantom nodded to Haslett and Santo before turning away from them and slowly walking away from the large building and the chaos around it. "I've been on some incredibly difficult missions and seen some frightening things. But I've never been more afraid than tonight when Jonas had you. The thought of not having you…" He paused and turned to face her, holding both her hands in his.

Elena looked up at him, her beautiful brown eyes shining in the moonlight. "I knew you were going to do everything in your power to save me. I never lost faith in you."

He shook his head. "I don't know what I did to deserve you, but I'm grateful every day that you are in my life." He leaned down and kissed her gently, then pulled back slowly, searching her face. "What I'm trying to say is I can't bear the thought of not having you in my life. Every day. For the rest of my life. I love you, Elena. I love everything about you. I want to help you achieve your dreams, and I want to be able to always come home to you."

Elena's eyes became moist with tears. "Oh, Phantom, I love you too. You know that. I love you more than anything."

"Will you do it, then? Will you join our crazy family of SEALs and live with us at the ranch with Anya and be mine forever?"

"Yes. Forever, Phantom. I'm yours."

About the Author

Holly Castillo grew up spending many lazy summer days racing her horses bareback in the Texas sun. But whenever she wasn't riding her horses or competing in horse shows, she was found with pen and paper in hand, writing out romantic love stories about Texas heroes.

Today, Holly lives in a small community just south of San Antonio with her husband and two children. On the family's ranch, surrounded by cattle during the day and hearing the howl of coyotes by night, Holly has endless inspiration for her writing. Her current romantic suspense series about heroic Navy SEALs is set in her own backyard of south Texas.

Also by Holly Castillo

TEXAS NAVY SEALS

A SEAL Never Quits

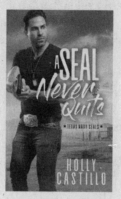

HELL ON WHEELS

From *New York Times* and *USA Today* bestselling author Julie Ann Walker, the men of Black Knights Inc. will ignite all your hottest fantasies...

Behind the facade of their tricked-out motorcycle shop on the North Side of Chicago is the headquarters for the world's most elite covert operatives. Deadly, dangerous, and determined, they'll steal your breath and your heart.

"Edgy, alpha, and downright HOT."

—Catherine Mann, *USA Today* bestselling author

For more info about Sourcebooks's
books and authors, visit:

sourcebooks.com

THE COST OF HONOR

The sizzling, action-packed Black Ops Confidential series from award-winning author Diana Muñoz Stewart will keep you on the edge of your seat!

When an attempt to protect one of Tony Parish's vigilante sisters went horribly wrong, he had to fake his own death to escape his fanatical family. As "Lazarus," he disappeared to Dominica—only to awaken face to face with the woman of his dreams...

When Honor Silva plunged into stormy waters to rescue a drowning kiteboarder, she had no idea resuscitating the sexy stranger would bring life-changing love—and life-threatening danger—crashing into her world.

"Poignant in places, nail-biting in others, there's plenty of sizzle and emotional clout. An electrifying ride."

—Steve Berry, *New York Times* bestselling author, for *The Price of Grace*

For more info about Sourcebooks's books and authors, visit:

sourcebooks.com

RISK IT ALL

Meet a band of bounty hunter sisters...and the men who steal away with their hearts, from author Katie Ruggle

Cara Pax never wanted to be a bounty hunter—she's happy to leave chasing criminals to her more adventurous sisters. But if she wants her dream of escaping the family business to come true, she's got one last job to finish. Too bad she doesn't think her latest bounty is actually guilty...

"Sexy and suspenseful, I couldn't turn the pages fast enough."

—Julie Ann Walker, *New York Times* and *USA Today* bestselling author, for *Hold Your Breath*

For more info about Sourcebooks's books and authors, visit:

sourcebooks.com